Death in Advertising

a whodunit by

Stephen Hawley Martin

RICHMOND, VIRGINIA

FIRST EDITION
First Printing, 1997

Death in Advertising, Copyright © 1997 by Stephen Hawley Martin. All rights reserved. Printed in the United States of America. No part of this book may be used or reproduced in any manner whatsoever without written permission except in the case of brief quotations embodied in critical articles and reviews. For information address The Oaklea Press, P. O. Box 29334, Richmond, Virginia 23242-0334.

ISBN 0-9646601-1-3

"The author lifts the mystery about what goes on inside an ad agency. His characters are real ad people, talking the talk, while murder is added to their list of anxieties."

David Martin, Founder,
The Martin Agency

"An authentic inside look at the advertising business. And an exciting murder mystery. Your friends will thank you if you recommend it to them."

Marvin Chernoff, Chairman,
Chernoff/Silver & Associates

"An engrossing murder mystery wrapped around the inner intrigue of the agency business."

Jim Osterman, Editor, ADWEEK

"... enough twists and turns to keep you guessing to the very end.... Martin weaves interesting characters together, keeps the plot moving and gives the reader a fun read."

Richard E. Klein, Principal,
Fogarty Klein & Partners

"Stephen Hawley Martin knows the ad business well, but we already knew that. Now we know that he can also write a taut, compelling thriller that keeps the reader guessing from the opening page."

O. Burtch Drake, President & CEO,
American Association of Advertising Agencies

"A great murder mystery that keeps the reader on the edge of his or her seat, so to speak, until the very end. Finally, a novel about the advertising business that portrays it as it really is. A great read!"

Ed Eskandarian, Chairman & CEO,
Arnold Communications

"Well done!"

Joseph J. Cronin, President & CEO,
Saatchi & Saatchi

Also by the author

Out of Body, Into Mind

Soul Survivor

DEDICATION

For my good friends in advertising.
Enjoy.

"Without advertising, nothing happens."
--Anonymous

1

Now that I look back, it does seem odd that the alarm was set. The lights were out, too. That didn't make sense. But I shrugged and punched in the code. Through the glass I could see the blue letters on the clear plexiglass rectangle that spelled out the name of my newly-adopted place of business, The Durston Negus Agency. The sign seemed suspended in the air above a huge marble desk with a mirrored front and chrome legs. I remember shaking my head. It wouldn't be long. Once I got my hands on the reins I'd get rid of that white elephant. That's what I thought at that moment. How quickly things can change.

I pushed open the door and headed between the big ficus trees in the well between the double staircases. Not one, but three big skylights had been cut through the roof two floors above. During the day this space was as bright as a Saturday morning in May in Central Park. Still, the way the area had been decorated left a lot to be desired. Whoever had designed it must have just come off a job dreaming up the set for a bathroom in a movie about a Beverly Hills brothel.

At least the big Heriz had dignity. Too bad about the

black marble floor with white swirls. Muted brick and blue tones, the handwoven texture. A hundred years old if it was a day. And smack dab in the middle of a high-traffic area.

Why had Uncle Rod turned off the lights?

I flipped the switches--spots flashed on--and walked briskly along the oriental runner that formed an inch-high hump on the dark planked flooring of the hallway. Oil paintings were here and there by well-known local artists. An original Matisse. The northeast corner of the building was the only area of the agency I would describe as formal. In this inner sanctum, visitors--even staff--spoke in hushed tones. And rightly so. This was where my uncle, Rod Durston, and his founding partner, Larry Negus, had their offices. Where they took multimillion dollar clients to ink multimillion dollar deals. Where they took ineffectual mid-level executives for execution by pink slip. Figuratively, of course. The way to do a guy in was to look him in the eye and tell him he was through.

What the heck was I doing here at this time of the evening? What could Uncle Rod possibly want that couldn't wait until morning?

What an inconsiderate S.O.B.

Right. So what else was new?

Ah, but he'd agreed to give me stock in the agency. A big hunk. Make me his heir so to speak. I'd be CEO of a company with more than eleven million in revenue before the age of thirty-five. Not bad. Not Erie, Pennsylvania, either. I was a lot of things but not an ingrate. I ought to be willing to jump through a few hoops.

Jump, Brian.

How high, Unc? This enough?

What? You want the ol' nose up the--

Odd that his door was shut.

I tapped. Waited. But no answer.

I tapped again . . .

I took hold of the knob. He'd asked me to come so I doubted he was in there casting some young lovely on the couch. Slowly I opened the door, looked in the direction of Uncle Rod's desk, and--

My initial reaction was that my eyes must be playing tricks. They had to be. I blinked, moved forward for a closer look. Felt dizzy. I blinked again. Sweat broke out. Cold, slimy sweat. I realized I wasn't breathing and forced myself to inhale.

It was still there.

Or was I seeing things?

Salty saliva gushed into my mouth. My gut wrenched.

It was there.

I brought my hand to my mouth to hold back bile that surged from way down in my gut straight up to the back of my teeth. I turned away, the horrific scene seared on my brain: Uncle Rod's body crumpled over his desk. His head and the mop of salt and pepper gray swimming in a pool of blood. Pink flesh and splotches of red against the wall. A revolver in his hand. The smell of burnt gunpowder.

Now, with my back turned, I thought I must have been hallucinating. Maybe it was the chicken enchiladas in verde sauce I'd had for dinner. If I turned around I'd see an empty chair. A desk clean.

What if I turned and saw something else? Suppose I saw Uncle Rod sitting up, bleeding?

I whipped around.

It seemed that lights were flashing. My mind was underwater, a strange ringing in my ears. I rotated my hand to cup my palm over my mouth and ran down the hall, around the corner, everything I passed a blur: the carpet, the magazine articles in frames, potted plants, more ficus trees, advertising awards, the huge blow up of the startled man and his dog in front of a TV with the caption, "By gosh, that commercial is aimed directly at us!" All of it was scrambled and askew. A nightmare. It had to be. Why couldn't I wake up?

I didn't make it.

After the first heave I was able to reach the bathroom. I

stumbled into the stall, knees unsteady. My stomach heaved--ejected more enchiladas and verde sauce. Some Spanish rice, too. A few ounces of Corona. I knew it was no dream.

I heaved again, pulled toilet paper from the roll and wiped my mouth. I tried to calm myself, to breathe deeply. I rubbed small blotches from the seat of the antique john, dropped the paper in the water, flushed, pulled more paper from the roll.

Uncle Rod was dead . . . half his head blown off. My thoughts spun. I couldn't force them to slow down. My mind wouldn't take hold. All I could think of was that horrific scene, and that Uncle Rod was gone . . . gone forever.

He may not have been the nicest person in the world. The truth was, sometimes he could be a lowdown S.O.B. To some he was precisely that one hundred percent of the time. But he'd treated me like one of his own ever since my father had died. Now I'd never see him again, never talk to him, never even have the opportunity to say thanks for taking me under your wing.

Who would have done it? Why? You don't shoot someone just because they're an S.O.B.

Or do you?

Or, maybe *he* realized he was an S.O.B.

But suicide?

No, no. We'd just talked on the phone no longer ago than half an hour. He sounded as grumpy and rotten as ever.

Was it murder?

An employee? An intruder? But how had they gotten in?

I flushed the toilet again, went to the pedestal sink and turned on the water.

Then it hit me that whoever did it might still be in the building. I looked in the mirror half expecting to see someone behind me. Nothing--except my own mug, ashen with a tinge of yellow. Verde sauce trickled from the corner of my mouth. Cold sweat oozed. That tingly sensation returned.

No, no. Whoever had done it would be long gone by now. The alarm was set.

How could the alarm be set?

I swished water back and forth through my teeth, gargled, and spit it out.

The first thing to do was call the police.

An hour later I was bent forward, resting my forearms on my thighs, studying the Heriz. Oriental carpets had fascinated me ever since I'd been old enough to be aware of them. Some are supposed to be magic, of course, but I guess it was the time and effort they took to make that had earned my respect. Every strand from a single hand-tied knot. This one definitely was old because there was very little symmetry in it. The designs, the little animals, flowers and trees, were different at each end. Shades of the colors were, too. Especially the tones of blue and brick. The yarn had come from separate batches, died with vegetables and berries at different times. When a Persian rug maker ran out of blue he simply crushed more blueberries. Only, the yarn that came from the second batch might not fade the same. The weaver might not leave it in the dye as long.

I was trying to keep my mind off what had happened, trying to ignore the hollow feeling and to hold back tears. By staying focused on the carpet I was able to hold them off, to push away the void, the nagging emptiness.

Only seconds before I'd found Uncle Rod I'd been thinking that I didn't mind being his Steppin' Fetchit as long as he gave me what I wanted--his interest in the agency. Had his spirit been hanging around in the room, disembodied? Had he heard?

"Mr. Durston? Brian Durston?"

I looked up. A mustached man in a rumpled summer-weight blue suit looked down at me, a clipboard in his hand.

"You're Brian Durston, the victim's nephew?"

"That's right."

"I'm Lieutenant Ryan, Mr. Durston." He flashed a badge and I.D. "Sorry about your uncle, sir, but I'm afraid I need to ask some questions. Mind if I sit down?"

"No problem," I said. The lieutenant took a seat in the chair across from me. A thought flicked that this guy didn't look much like a cop. Not like Peter Faulk, either. Too pudgy.

"Let's see if what I've got so far is accurate," he said. "You arrived for a meeting with the deceased and the building was locked. The alarm was set, correct?"

"Uh-huh."

"And that didn't surprise you?"

"Maybe a little. But there's another keypad in my uncle's office. I figured he'd set the alarm because he was here alone. Maybe it made him feel safer."

The lieutenant scribbled on his pad, looked up. "Why did he ask you to meet him? Late, wasn't it?"

"It was about 7:30 when he called, so I supposed he was still working, that's all. It's the nature of the business. Anyway, as far as why he asked me to come tonight, it could have been for a number of reasons."

"Such as?"

"It might have been about Benton Furniture. The president of the company died a few months ago and the new one has put the account in review. They notified us about it today."

Lieutenant Ryan looked over the top of his clipboard. "Mind expanding on that a bit?"

I sighed. "This agency's had the Benton account for a long time, but we're going to have to compete against some other ad agencies to keep it. We'll have to make a presentation. So will they. My uncle just heard about it this morning. I'm sure it was fresh on his mind."

Not only had it been on his mind, it had put him in a snit.

The lieutenant stopped scribbling and lowered the clipboard to his knee. "What other reasons?"

"Frankly, officer, from what he said on the phone, or at least from the way he said it, I thought he wanted to talk with me about his succession plan."

The lieutenant's brow furrowed.

"My uncle was ready to retire. Until a couple of weeks ago, I was working in New York at an ad agency there. He persuaded me to come to Richmond, to join The Durston Negus Agency, with the understanding that he would turn over a good portion of his interest to me."

The officer lifted his clipboard and began to write. "What did you mean, the *way* he said it?"

"He said something like, 'Brian, there are some things we need to talk about. How quickly can you get here?'"

The lieutenant's eyebrows lifted. "So, he was in some kind of hurry--is that it?"

"Well, he sounded irritated. But I chalked it up to the problem with Benton. Anyway, he was like that. When there was something he wanted, he wanted it right then."

"What time did your uncle call, and what time did you get here?"

"He called at 7:30 if my watch is correct, and I'd say I was here by eight o'clock--give or take five minutes."

The lieutenant stopped writing and looked at my watch, nodded and said, "Was your uncle depressed?"

"No, no. He had no reason to be depressed. I mean, Uncle Rod was a worrier. He could get worked up, that's for sure. A type-A, you know? But I don't think he was depressed."

"So you have no idea why he would want to kill himself?"

A lump formed in my throat. "Kill himself?"

The lieutenant stared at me. "You did discover the body?"

"Yes. But I didn't stand around and analyze it."

"He had the gun in his hand. We've already checked the

registration. It was his. The bullet entered his temple and appeared to exit near the top of his head."

I swallowed hard; shook my head. "But Uncle Rod wouldn't do that . . . he had no reason. Why would he? It's not like we'd lost the account. Not yet, anyway."

"No reason you know about, Mr. Durston."

"Couldn't it have been an intruder?"

"There was no sign of a struggle. You said yourself the alarm was on." The lieutenant stood. "That's all for now, Mr. Durston. I'll give you a call if anything else comes up."

A uniformed policeman approached the lieutenant and handed him a piece of paper. "Thought you'd want to see this. We found it in the output tray of the victim's desktop printer."

I stood and looked over his shoulder:

Dear Brian,

Sorry you have to find me like this,
but I'm sick of life, and I can't take
it any longer. Please tell Sally and
the kids I love them.

Love,

Uncle Rod

"No signature," Lieutenant Ryan said. "Must have left it in the tray and pulled the trigger."

"I can't believe it," I said. "He wasn't sick of life. My uncle was hard as nails. This doesn't make sense."

A male voice called my name. I turned, and Larry Negus wrapped his arms around me. "Oh Brian, this is a terrible, terrible thing. You have my deepest sympathy, you and your aunt, and . . . oh, Jesus, Brian, this is awful."

I gave Larry a couple of pats on the back and pulled away. He always seemed to project a sleaziness that made my skin crawl. It struck me that his face was more pallid than usual, too, his liver spots more pronounced. His jowls hung lower. Even his hair seemed whiter than it had only hours earlier.

"Can you believe it, Larry?" I said. "They think Rod killed himself."

Larry shook his head. "I know, I know. I don't know what to believe. I never thought . . . Jesus, I've got to call the clients, I don't want them to read about this in the paper--you know damn well it'll make the front page. And the employees. What are people going to think?" Larry started to pace, alternately pointing his finger at his temple and up into the air. "I guess I'd better call Ben Haley and Mary MacMann. And Paul Williams. Get them all in here and get them on the telephone making calls. What a time for this to happen. Oh Jesus, Brian, we've got a helluva mess on our hands."

I watched Larry pace. It was almost surreal. The old coot looked like a frayed nerve ending but I didn't detect a sense of loss emanating from him at the passing of his business partner of the past six years.

"Jesus," Larry continued, "I guess I'd better call Mavis Alfonso, too. She can make some of the calls to employees. We'll get a phone list and divide it up."

He stopped and turned to me, his expression a question mark. "But what in hell are we going to say?"

"I don't know, Larry. But I hope you won't mind if I don't stick around. I guess I'd better go and tell my aunt what happened."

Comprehension transformed Larry's liver-spotted face. "Oh, yeah, sure. You do that. Listen, I'm really sorry about all this, I mean, I guess I'm acting kind of crazy but, Jesus, I never expected anything like this . . . and now it's happened." He placed a hand on my shoulder. "I'm really sorry about your uncle, Brian. Really am. My condolences to Sally, too. If there's anything I can do for her, or for you, let me know, okay?"

"Right."

"And Brian . . . thanks for calling me. Everything here is in good hands. Don't worry about a thing."

"I'll talk to you tomorrow, Larry." I walked past him and out the door.

Electric flames flickered inside the wrought iron cages of antique street lamps. A mixture of jubilant yuppies, college students and hillbillies spilled from sidewalks into the cobbled street. Beach music wafted from an open doorway of a bar called The Bus Stop. I was reminded of my college days--of fraternity parties and good-looking coeds. Of riotous behavior. Of oceans of beer and unspeakable frivolity. Imagine. Two hours ago, before I'd discovered Uncle Rod lying in a pool of blood, I'd thought life was headed my way. I'd even found a parking place in the same block as the agency.

Minutes later, I turned the wheel of the beat up old roadster I'd bought when I landed in Richmond and headed west on Main. It was cooler now, almost too cool to have the top down. I hunched my shoulders and turned my wrist to look at my watch. Nine-thirty. An hour and a half since I'd found Uncle Rod.

It began to dawn on me that I was stunned.

The grayish-white brick structure of the Hotel Jefferson loomed ahead, lit up like the Taj Mahal. I remembered someone saying that it was built in 1895. I rolled past the Tuscan columns of the Main Street entrance and thought of horse-drawn carriages dispensing ladies in frilly ball gowns and men in top hats. Then it hit me full square that I was headed to see Uncle Rod's widow to tell her what had happened.

What was I going to say?

How was I going to say it? How did you tell someone her husband had shot himself? I didn't particularly care for her. But I couldn't just blurt out something like that.

I'd always preferred his first wife. Her name was Millie.

Millie and Uncle Rod hadn't had kids and when my father was killed in action they took on the role of godparents. I still kept in touch with her even though they had divorced when I was thirteen.

Uncle Rod had said he hadn't noticed Sally until he and Millie were separated. Yeah, right. Sally had been employed for at least a year at the agency where he'd worked. Let's see. Two plus two . . .

I drove across Belvedere and into the campus of VCU. The location was a mixed blessing. It brought culture into the city but my apartment was not far away, smack on a thoroughfare between the campus and a number of watering holes. I'd already learned I'd have to put up with turned-over flower pots on the porch and beer cans on the sidewalk. Then there was the sweet scent of pot wafting from a gathering place under the streetlight in the alley.

A Jeep in front switched lanes and I stepped on the brake. This snapped my mind back to Uncle Rod's death. The lieutenant seemed to believe that it was suicide. But that didn't make sense. Sure Uncle Rod was worried about Benton. Who wouldn't worry if his largest account was in review? But he'd been at the game of advertising a long time. This was not the first problem he'd faced.

Shoot. A recent issue of *ADWEEK* had named Durston Negus the hottest agency in the Southeast. Billings had doubled in the last year. The work coming out of the shop was sweeping the shows--two Golds and four Silvers in the New York Art Director's, eight in Communication Arts, a Gold Lion at Cannes. The buzz was that Durston was a place to make your mark. If I hadn't thought so, too, I'd never have given up a big job and the fast track in New York.

The traffic light ahead turned from yellow to red and I stepped on the brake.

My colleagues at the agency in New York had regarded me as the fair haired boy. I was 32 and pulling down a $150,000 a year. Of course, it took that to live in Manhattan.

At least to live well.

Why had I come to Richmond?

I'd come to take back control of my life.

I suppose we all do what we must in order to survive. But that doesn't mean we're proud about it. And we certainly don't want to think about it.

But that was history. I could feel a new bounce in my step. It wouldn't be long; I'd be running my show.

The light turned green. I stepped on the accelerator and my thoughts shifted.

Suicide?

Could it have been something in Uncle Rod's personal life? Something to do with Sally?

They had seemed happy enough. This go-around Uncle Rod appeared to have turned into a family man, certainly more so than when I was growing up.

Oh, yes, the girls. Let's see, Mary was 12 and Jessie was 14. They would be devastated.

I braked, turned left onto Thompson Street, drove past the Citgo Self Service Station, turned right onto Cary and came to a stop at the light on the overpass of the Powhite Expressway. Cars whizzed by underneath.

They were nice kids, too. Both top students. Mary played the piano very well, and Jessie was so good at tennis she was ranked in the Mid-Atlantic as a junior. Rod had high hopes each would excel in her chosen field, but he didn't think either would be interested in going into advertising. I guess that was why he had pinned his hopes on me. Keeping the Durston name alive in the business was why he wanted me to take over.

Maybe he had cancer--an inoperable brain tumor.

Even so, would he kill himself?

The light turned green and I started onto Cary Street Road, past Colonial style houses in red brick and white wood trim.

Wait a minute. He'd said something about suicide, and it hadn't been long ago. We had been sitting on the terrace behind his home.

The house is on a bluff above the James. We were looking down at vegetation that stretched as far as we could see, the sky that vivid blue that happens sometimes before the sun slips below the horizon--lit with streaks of orange. Clouds fanned out from the huge, glowing ball. Overhead, the puffy pink and white forms seemed close enough to touch. A mockingbird scolded us.

"A view like this makes you stop and wonder, doesn't it?" Uncle Rod had said. "About life, about God, about why we're here?"

I sipped Scotch and soda from a heavy highball glass--hefted it, inhaled the smell of whisky. I resigned myself to hearing one of his philosophical little lectures.

"I'll tell you what I think," he said. "I think we're here on earth to learn. The earth is a school where obstacles--challenges--are put in our path. We grow by facing them, and by overcoming them--by learning from them. You see, I believe in an afterlife. A before life, too, maybe many lives in the physical world. It's something you need to think about, Brian, if you haven't done it yet."

My gaze returned to the sunset. "I'm not sure it would help me get motivated if that's what I believed. For example, suppose things don't go your way? Why not check out? If what you're saying is true, you'll get another chance."

"You've missed the point," Uncle Rod had said. "If you don't like the life you have, it's because obstacles are in your way, and obstacles are what life is about. Life's a school and the problems are lessons. The more you face, obviously, the more you need to learn. That's not going to go away if you kill yourself. You'll still have the need and you'll still have the problems, too, only no way to do anything about either."

I pounded the steering wheel. Would a guy kill himself who thought that?

I put my foot on the brake. I'd passed the turn. I wheeled

the car around and stepped on the accelerator.

If Uncle Rod hadn't killed himself--then he was murdered!

But the alarm had been set, the door locked. No indication of a struggle.

Whoever did it, knew Uncle Rod. Whoever did it, knew the code.

I braked and turned onto the lane that led to his house. Huge old elms, oaks and walnuts were on either side with large homes tucked among them that looked like English cottages, country manors and Georgian plantation houses.

Who knew the code?

Only seventy-five or eighty people who worked at The Durston Negus Agency--plus who could guess how many who had left since the last time the code was changed.

And the suicide note? What about that?

Anyone could have written it. It seemed to have been done in a hurry. Why, it wasn't even signed. Whoever had typed it probably hadn't even waited for it to finish printing.

What had the note said?

"Dear Brian . . ."

Dear Brian?

They'd known I was coming.

How would he, or she, have known?

Uncle Rod had told him.

You'd better put that gun away and get out of here. Brian's on his way.

How had he finished the letter?

Love, Uncle Rod.

Love? That wasn't a word that came easily from him.

Of course, if it were suicide, he would hardly have been in his normal frame of mind.

It was dark. I strained to see ahead.

At last the stone columns came into view. The first floor lights all were on, and the outside lamps as well, including spots that lit up the front. It was a white clapboard house with a black slate roof, green shutters and mullioned windows. Massive brick chimneys arose between the main center section of it and the wings. Under normal circumstances it would have been a welcoming sight.

A sense of dread crept over me. I looked at my watch. It was 9:50. Sally probably wondered when her husband would get home.

I steered the old roadster up the right side of the circle and brought it to a stop a few feet from the door, my heart thumping. I stepped out and pushed the button. Bells chimed.

Moments later Sally opened the door, a slender, fortyish woman dressed in a sweat shirt and jeans. She held a handkerchief to her face. Her hand trembled, her eyes red and puffy, mascara smeared.

"Sally? What is it? You know? How could you?"

She pushed a strand of too blond hair from her forehead. "A reporter called for a statement just five minutes ago."

I moved through the door. "Oh, Sally--no. I came as quickly as I could--as soon as the police let me go."

"I can't believe it, I just can't," she wailed. "Oh God, they said he took his own life."

I put my arms around her. It felt awkward but I had to do something. So what if she'd been the office tart who'd stolen Uncle Rod from Millie?

"I don't believe it either, Sally. Not for a minute. I don't believe Rod would kill himself."

Sally pressed her face into my chest. "Oh Brian, Brian, I'm not prepared for this--it's so horrible, horrible. . . . The girls are already upstairs. What am I going to do?"

"Let them go to sleep. The morning is soon enough. And don't tell them Uncle Rod killed himself. I know he wouldn't. He wouldn't because of the girls, and because of you. He wouldn't because it was against what he believed."

2

I spent an hour with Sally, doing my best to comfort her, although I've never felt particularly good at giving solace. I even started to explain why I didn't think Uncle Rod would shoot himself. She agreed as far as I got, but became so distraught I decided to drop the subject.

I drove home, fed my dog and called Aunt Millie. It was bound to wake her up, but I didn't want her to find out from the newspaper about her ex-husband.

It wasn't the sort of news one could easily grasp when they first woke up and it took a while for her to collect her wits. I went over every detail including my theory about why he would not have committed suicide. We ended the conversation with her trying to decide if it would be appropriate to come to the funeral. My opinion was, why not? An individual didn't live with someone 15 years without feeling something when they passed away. The second wife should understand.

I decided to give my own mother a break and wait until morning. She lived in Connecticut so it was highly unlikely anything about Uncle Rod would be in the papers there.

With so many thoughts running through my head and the empty, nagging feelings, I couldn't sleep, so I let my dog, Soho, on the bed even though it was something I'd been trying to teach him was not allowed. I guess I needed another being in close proximity to assure me I wasn't all alone.

For most of the night, the details of that horrible scene played over and over in my mind. I'd push them away; try to figure out what really had happened. The faces of people at the agency would flash before my eyes. Who had a motive? What was it? The killer might be someone I came in contact with every day. Who was cold blooded enough to hold a gun to Uncle Rod's temple and pull the trigger?

A lot of them probably had fantasized about it. After being on the wrong side of a tongue lashing, who wouldn't? But that wasn't the same as going through with it. Squeezing the trigger and watching his brains go splat against the wall--a person would have to be crazed to do that.

One thing seemed certain. The murder had been premeditated--the way a suicide had been staged, right down to the use of Uncle Rod's own gun.

At seven-thirty I had counted 253 cracks and 98 spider webs, so I decided to get up, walk Soho, and go to the office. I was not in the mood for a leisurely jaunt around the Fan or a run through the campus of the University of Richmond. I'd have enough time to think and was ready to get on with the day. So we went for a quick one around the block. We ran west along the tree-lined street to Lombardy, turned past a hole-in-the-wall bar and a mom-and-pop grocery and then into a small park with a four-foot brick wall where Stuart Avenue peels off from Park. Several of these pie-shaped green spaces were scattered through this part of town because the streets fan out as they head west. That was how the Fan District got its name. It looks like one on a map.

Soho found his favorite bush.

When we got home I felt guilty I hadn't given him more

of a run. Fortunately, a prior tenant had made a swinging dog door that opened onto the porch and the walled garden behind my apartment. It was the right size and Soho had learned to use it. So, he could let himself out whenever he needed to.

Forty-five minutes later I arrived at the agency. I called my mom first.

"You mean he's dead? How?"

"I think the police believe it's suicide. But I'm not so sure."

"Suicide? Wha . . . what do you think it was?"

I dropped the word softly. "Murder."

"What? Did you say, murder? Brian Durston, what exactly is going on down there? Is this some sort of fantastic joke? Murder! Suicide! Has the world gone crazy?"

She burst into sobs, hysterical.

"Mom, please calm down."

I love my mother; still recall the agony of separation when she left me at preschool that first time. But now, as an adult, it had dawned on me that she never took things calmly. When I was a child she freaked every time I came home with a scrape on my knee.

"Brian, he isn't *really* dead, is he?" Her voice was small, most of the energy gone.

"Sorry, Mom, he's dead. As dead as it is possible to be."

I told her I'd be glad to put her up if she wanted to come to the funeral and didn't mind the mess--I was in the midst of painting my apartment. I'll admit I was relieved when she said she couldn't afford the trip, though her lack of financial resources made me sad. I made a mental note to send her some money--after the funeral.

I puttered around for an hour shuffling papers from my in-box, trying to focus. I stared at the pages of a report on Benton Industries and furniture marketing which had been assembled by the research department, but I'm not sure how much of it sank in. By nine-thirty I was in Larry

Negus's office with my rear pressed against a hand rubbed leather wing chair. A pale and jittery Larry sat across from me behind a polished antique walnut partner's desk. His white hair was slightly mussed. I tried to shake off the creeps.

"So far so good," Larry said. "The clients--everybody--all have been very sympathetic and understanding. They just couldn't believe Rod would do that, but I guess everyone knows someone who has been clinically depressed. It happens. Often times, and this is surely one of them, even close friends and colleagues fail to recognize the symptoms."

I wondered for a half-millisecond if I should tell Larry I didn't think it was suicide, but it already had occurred to me that he might have a reason for wanting Uncle Rod dead. Something told me it had to do with m-o-n-e-y.

"Speak to me of stock ownership, Larry. Before I agreed to leave Flint, Uncle Rod promised he was going to turn over his share of the business. There's a helluva lot that needs to be done around here, starting with Benton. How do we get it transferred?"

Larry looked at me as though I had just asked him to recite the Lord's Prayer. "Transfer his stock?"

"You know. Those pieces of paper about so big that say a person owns some of the business. I believe Uncle Rod had a bunch of them that totaled forty percent."

Larry stood--he never sat for more than thirty seconds at a stretch--and scratched the back of his head.

"Well, Brian, your uncle did own forty percent, that's true." He began to pace. "He was the largest single shareholder. But he never said anything about turning over his stock to you--or to anyone else, for that matter."

"Who owns the stock now that he's dead? Does Sally own it?"

"I'm sure his lawyer can tell you about his will. But as I recall, I don't think he could leave it to her, or to anyone. Not even to you."

Larry stopped in front of a bookshelf, removed a three-ringed binder and flipped some pages. "This is the shareholder's agreement that governs who can and can't own stock in Durston Negus. I'm certain you have to be employed here. Yes, it's in this section." Larry put on reading glasses. "The stock can be traded only among active employees of the firm. It's to be bought and sold at book."

"I'm actively employed, Larry."

He looked at me over black-rimmed half-moons. "I realize that, Brian––but there's more, I don't recall the details––this was written five or six years ago when we started the company." He flipped pages. "I believe the agency is obligated to buy back the stock in the event of a shareholder's death. Yes, it's right here. The firm will purchase, within fifteen days of the death, termination of employment, or retirement of a shareholder, the shareholder's outstanding interest in the Company. Current book value will be paid."

One of those oh-no-I-think-I've-been-screwed feelings struck me in the solar plexus. "So what does that mean, exactly?"

"There's more. Yes––I remember. Your uncle was thinking of you when he insisted we insert this clause. In the event of the death of a shareholder, a blood relative who is actively employed by the agency may purchase the shareholder's stock at book value." Larry flashed me a smile. "Your uncle always thought you would be part of the agency one day."

"So that means I can buy it?"

"Right. You've got fifteen days." Larry closed the binder and returned it to the shelf. He took a pen out of a desk set and scribbled on a pad. "I'll have Mavis make a copy of this agreement for you, but the bottom line is you can buy your uncle's stock at book value."

"How much is book value?"

"As you know, book is the agency's value if we were to

liquidate--assets minus liabilities." Larry pulled a small calculator to him. "Your uncle owned forty percent, and our most recent financial statement said our net worth was about a million-three, so . . . " He pushed buttons. "It's yours for about . . . $520,000."

"Five hundred and twenty *thousand?* Guess you haven't seen my September bank statement."

Larry did not blink.

"If Uncle Rod owned it, why do I have to *buy* the stock? He wanted me to have it."

Larry shook his head. "That's not how it works. The agency can't give away your uncle's assets to you or to anyone. To adhere to the terms of the Shareholder's Agreement, the firm will have to purchase the stock from your uncle's estate. You will have to buy it from the agency." He shrugged. "If what you say is true, though, Rod probably left you enough to buy the stock. You need to talk to his lawyer."

"I guess so."

Larry put his hands behind his head. Two seconds later his brow wrinkled. "You know, Brian, I would be doing you a disservice if I didn't warn you about something."

"What's that, Larry?"

"There aren't many around here who understand the implications of the Benton pitch--what it would mean if we were to lose the account."

"It's our largest account, right? It doesn't take a genius to see that makes it pretty important."

"It's more than *pretty* important." Larry leaned forward. "It's a $20 million account, of which the agency keeps 15 percent, which means it's a three million dollar revenue stream, plus or minus. That's roughly 25 percent of our business, Brian." His beady little eyes held mine. "This company has done well over the past few years. After big losses the first two years in business and a break-even year, we've enjoyed net profits of just under two million each year now for three years. We've paid off debt and we've built net worth, but not enough net worth to weather the storm from a loss like Benton. A three-million-dollar reduction in revenue would put us a million in the red--more than that, really, because we've been in a growth mode and operating with a growth mentality. We've been staffing as though that growth were going to continue. If our revenue shrinks by three million instead of growing, well--it will be devastating I assure you."

"How devastating?"

He stood and paced again. "I'd say we'll have to lay off about 30 people."

"Thirty?"

"You know what that means?" Larry said. "People will wonder what's wrong. It will shake them up. Clients we have will get the jitters. Potential clients will play the killer game of wait-and-see. The air will be out of our balloon. Lord help us if our clients begin to bolt." He flopped down in his chair and exhaled like the balloon he'd just spoken of, leaned forward and spoke in a soft, low voice. "Brian, if you put the loss of Benton together with the suicide of your uncle--well . . . I don't want to think about it, but I guess I have to think about it." He shook his head. "It will be the kiss of death--absolutely the kiss of death."

"We're not going to lose it. Not if you let me head up the pitch."

He stared at me over half-moons. "Your confidence is commendable, Brian, but it will not be up to me to decide that. With your uncle dead, with no CEO in charge, it will be up to the shareholders collectively to determine how we move ahead. Maybe they will want me to take the reins on an interim basis--I don't know. But whatever happens, I can assure you Paul Williams will want to head up the Benton pitch. He's already lobbying for it."

"You and I both know that would be a mistake."

"Maybe so, maybe not. You have to admit, the work coming out of his department has brought a lot of recognition to Durston Negus."

Paul Williams, our creative director, was a hot-head who in my opinion consistently demonstrated a lack of judgment. But I decided to keep my mouth shut.

Larry tapped the desk lightly with both hands and stood, which I took to mean that he considered our session to be at an end. "It goes without saying that you need to keep what I've said between us. I simply wanted to let you in on the situation before you plop down $520,000. Anyway, it's up to you. You'll have two weeks to decide."

"Thanks, Larry. That's decent of you." We shook hands. "By the way. Is Rita Maloney still coming tomorrow to give us that briefing?" Rita Maloney was the new president of Benton Industries, the one who had put the account in review.

"She is indeed. I spoke with her last night and encouraged her not to postpone. And Brian, I know the timing is rotten because of your uncle's death, but we need you to be here to take her in hand. You've been positioned as the exec who will be managing her business."

"You bet I'll be here. But Larry, if I'm heading the account, doesn't that mean I should be calling the shots?"

Larry frowned. "Theoretically, I suppose--except at Durston Negus one of the shareholders usually has the ultimate say on a particular piece of business, even though someone else might be the point man--the one visible to the outside world."

"I'm already practically a shareholder, Larry."

He pursed his lips. "Yes, I suppose. Tell you what. All the shareholders will be at the briefing. I'll ask them to stick around afterwards and you stick around, too. We'll get this question decided about who is heading the pitch."

"Fair enough."

On the way back to my office I stopped at that God-awful, gaudy reception desk in the lobby and checked my messages. Sally had called, and someone named Henry Valence. I looked up into the ficus trees. The sun shone through the skylights in bright columns and reflected off the leaves. Henry Valence? Something told me he might be Uncle Rod's lawyer.

I called Sally first, and she let me know the funeral would be the day after tomorrow at Bliley's and that in lieu of flowers, donations should be made to the Richmond Ballet--Uncle Rod's favorite non-profit. Then I called Henry Valence, who indeed turned out to be Uncle Rod's lawyer. He said he had an opening at 2:30 that afternoon and suggested I stop by so he could brief me on Uncle Rod's will and irrevocable trust. Valence said he had already spoken to Sally and she was fully aware of the details because she, Uncle Rod and he had collaborated on the documents several years prior.

I said I'd be there, then did my best to get my head into the report on Benton and to start thinking about what we needed to do to keep the account.

Valence's office was high up in one of the twin towers of Riverfront Plaza. It gave me an uneasy feeling to think that one of the agency's most fierce competitors, The Arnold Agency, was located in the same building. It was like walking into the lion's den. I kept looking over my shoulder to see if anyone I knew had seen me.

When I got to Valence's floor a young woman led me to a conference room with an impressive view of the river. Richmond is built on the falls of the James, the line that separates Tidewater from Piedmont. It was placed here in colonial times because this was as far inland as boats could come before a canal was built.

White water came toward where I stood and passed by underneath in a fury, cascading over rocks and small dams. It had rained hard a few days ago and what had fallen in the western part of the state now was reaching us. The air was clear. I could make out the Blue Ridge Mountains on the horizon far away, 80 or 90 miles across rolling terrain. Except for the immediate downtown area, the land appeared to be heavily forested, a patchwork of vibrant yellow and gold. I hoped views like this did not inspire the competition. Arnold was likely to be in the Benton pitch.

Henry Valence was short and muscular with a barrel chest. He wore a pin-striped suit, the sleeves of which probably had been lengthened. No doubt his elevator shoes were necessary so his knuckles didn't drag.

We shook hands. He took the seat and opened a folder. "The main purpose of an irrevocable trust is to avoid as much estate tax as possible. You see--each generation gets a deduction, so if you set it up right you can take full advantage." He took out a brief. "It was your uncle's intention for you to be remembered, and beyond that, for his two children to divide his estate equally, following his and Sally's deaths."

I felt my brow wrinkle. "That was nice of him, but are you saying I have to wait for Sally to die? She's only ten years older than I am."

"No, no," Valence said. "Your uncle had the trust set up primarily for his wife and children, but it was also designed to pay $500,000 to you upon his death."

A strap that had been around my chest loosened and my breath came easier. All my life I'd been short of money. Now those days were over.

"So. When do I get it?"

His face was stone. "You'll recall I said 'was designed to pay.' Unfortunately, there has been a rather major complication." He cleared his throat and folded his hands. "You see, the trust was to be funded by life insurance. Between personal policies and what he had through Durston Negus, it would have paid more than two million dollars into the trust."

"Why do you say, *would have?*"

"You see, Brian--I hope you don't mind if I call you Brian--insurance companies won't pay when a policy holder commits suicide. You might say they consider it cheating."

The strap pulled tight again.

"But he didn't commit suicide. He couldn't have--wouldn't have. I'm sure of it. We talked about suicide and he told me how he felt. He believed it didn't accomplish a thing--that it made a situation worse."

Valence stared at me. "I spent a good deal of time with the police this morning, Brian, and I'm afraid they don't share your view. There's a copy of his death certificate in this folder and suicide is listed as the cause."

"You mean they've closed the case?"

"Open and shut. His gun, in his hand, a single shot through the temple. The alarm was set. He even left a suicide note."

"But the note wasn't signed. Anyone could have written it."

"I'm sorry Brian, this is difficult, but it's bad news you needed to know."

Thoughts flashed: no inheritance meant no stock, and no stock meant I was nothing more than an employee of the agency--a drone. Would Flint have me back? I'd be better off in a big, publicly held company where I'd be on even footing with everybody else. There'd be stock options, bonus incentive plans.

Then the reality came flooding back that someone had *killed* Uncle Rod. I should be thinking of him and his family. Not only had some demented lunatic taken Rod's life, not only had the evil maniac stolen a husband and a father, he had robbed a mother and her daughters of two million dollars in insurance money.

Why, the fiend had taken $500,000 from me.

I said, "Will Sally and the kids have enough to live on?"

Valence rubbed his chin. "Most of what your uncle owned was in Sally's name as well as his. The house, another at Wintergreen. Sally will get the proceeds of his stock in Durston Negus, and what they had together in a 401(k) retirement plan, which amounts to maybe another

$500,000. But with real estate taxes on the two houses and those two kids in private schools, I'd say they'll have to sell one or both of the homes. Trim back. Way back. Otherwise they'll be cutting into principal. The taxes on the one overlooking the river are more than $15,000 a year."

"What if I were able to prove it wasn't suicide--that it was murder?"

Henry Valence pursed his lips. "You'd be doing everyone including yourself a big favor--except whomever is responsible. And the insurance companies. They'd both have to pay." He stared at me, then shook his head. "But frankly, I don't believe that's what happened. I think you'd be wasting your time, and your money--if you decided to hire an investigator. It would take an awful lot of evidence for the police to reopen the case. You'd have to have airtight evidence--maybe even a confession."

I felt like a worn out balloon with a slow leak. Had someone concocted some kind of conspiracy simply to make my life miserable?

Maybe so.

3

Before I returned to my office I stopped to see a friend from college who now was a commercial loan officer at Central Fidelity Bank. The bank was headquartered four or five blocks from the agency in a glass and chrome tower that boasted a bronze sculpture out front of three huge, practically nude men hoisting the sail of a ship. I had yet to figure out what it symbolized. With all the workers in that building slaving away, a galley with men and women pulling on oars might have been more appropriate.

It was almost five o'clock by the time I got back to my office. I sat at my desk and thought about what my friend had said.

"Bad luck, Brian, really bad. I'd like to help, but I'm afraid your application would have as much chance of passing the loan approval committee as I would of passing Doctor Crawford's organic chemistry class." He gave me a sympathetic look and shook his head. "No bank is going to lend you $500,000 to buy stock in an ad agency--especially in one with its major account in review."

I stared at the doorway to my office and wondered if I should go home. Did I want to spend the evening looking at the ceiling, counting cobwebs and cracks, and cuddling with a part golden retriever, part who knew what? Of course, I still had my living room to paint--that would keep me busy. The ladders and brushes were right where I'd left them. I could stir up the paint, loosen the brush and really work myself into a deep depression. I put my elbows on my desk and propped my head on my hands. I almost never swear, but my mouth formed a four-letter word.

"Hey, looking a little on the dark side, there."

She stood against the doorframe, a slender hand tucked into the pocket of her vest. Jet black hair, blue eyes that looked deep into me--pupils dark and wide. Her nose wrinkled. A vision flashed of Maggie the Cat.

Something stirred I hadn't felt in a long time. Twenty four hours, minimum--not since Uncle Rod had died. It was a tingly sensation beneath the skin of my shoulders and my arms. It was tingly in other places, too. Some think a feeling like that is caused by Cupid's arrows but I knew better. It had to do with the translucent white texture of her skin and the shape of firm, ripe breasts poking against a red silk blouse. The curve of her thigh figured in as well. And the creases her legs made in her skirt. I knew darn well what it was.

Testosterone.

"You okay, Brian?"

"To tell the truth, I did feel awful."

Thin red lips--the same shade as her blouse--separated to reveal a glimpse of straight white teeth. "I was on my way to the Bus Stop for a drink. Maybe I can cheer you up. Want to come?"

What was going on? I didn't even know this woman's name. All I had was a vague idea that she was a copy writer who'd just been hired.

"You know, I could use a drink. Maybe two." I stood and grabbed my blue blazer. "No, make it three. Okay, four. Five. Six--if there's enough credit left on my MasterCard."

Her name, as it turned out, was Nickie D'Agostino, Nickie being short for Nicholene. "It's N-i-c-k-i-e," she said. "And I never cap either 'i' with a Valentine heart. Not even when I was fourteen. Never have, never will."

In her book, girls who had drawn hearts no doubt had been brain dead. Instead of spending time with them she'd rather have wiled away the hours laughing at men who groveled at her feet.

She led me to the Bus Stop, a spot two blocks west of the agency frequented by a curious mixture of Main Street pinstripes and jail bait. It had a long wooden bar, exposed brick walls, a rough hewn wood beam ceiling. An old fashioned juke box belted out beach music. She climbed on a stool, wound her legs around it three times and ordered chardonnay. I leaned against the bar and told the bartender to make mine a double Dewar's on the rocks with a splash of soda--no twist. I'd have made it a double martini, shaken not stirred. The only problem was, I didn't like vermouth. Or gin.

I was now on my second and already feeling a flush.

"So what do you do at the agency, Nickie?"

The corner of her mouth curved upward. "I write a little copy, among other things."

"Such as?"

"Well, let's see. Lately I've been going down the phone list, checking out all the single guys in the office. You see, I'm unattached."

"And you've only gotten as far as Durston?"

"Just started a couple of weeks ago."

"At the agency, or on the phone list?"

"Both."

"Where were you before?"

"Boston--Hill Holliday."

I held up my drink. "Here's to a long and fruitful career in Richmond." We clicked glasses.

Was she aware of her knee pressing against my thigh?

She peered at me over the rim. "Were you referring to my career writing copy, or going down the phone list?"

"That depends on which you find most rewarding. In either case, you must be pretty good at it. I understand we don't hire just any copy writer off of the street."

"Must be a pun in there somewhere," she said.

I took another of many sips. "So tell me how you got the job."

"Oh, you know. I have a way with words."

"Uh-huh. There must be some award-winning stuff in your portfolio as well."

"That, too, I guess." She sighed. "The One Show, Clios, Cannes, Communication Arts. Nothing out of the ordinary. Paul Williams doesn't hire anyone who doesn't have several paper weights from each."

"Where I come from a list like that would be far from ordinary. So tell me, is Durston Negus a stepping stone, or are you going to stay the agency awhile?"

"Stay, of course." She cut her eyes toward me. "You wouldn't expect me to say otherwise, I'm sure."

"Why not? Because my name is Durston?"

She looked into her wine. "Actually, I was planning to take another job next week."

"Now I get it. You're never going to be able to level with me because of my name. And I thought we had a future."

She kissed away a stray drop of wine. "So, do you really like it? Advertising?"

"I suppose there are one or two other things I might be happy doing. Publishing, broadcasting, film making. But there's something exciting about using your wits to sell a product to a lot of people at once--and sex is about the only thing I know that even comes close to the thrill of winning a new business competition."

"Really? Just any old sex?"

I felt my eyebrows lift. "There's only three kinds, as far as I know--good, better, best. You know any others?"

She gave me a twisted little smile. Where'd I seen one like it before?

"I'll let you in on a secret about me that not many people know," she said. "I prefer the ads for Nescafé to the Nike spots with André Agassi."

We sipped and talked about advertising and sex. Or rather, sex in advertising. I noticed that her glass always seemed to be half full, whereas mine became empty every few minutes. After an hour I felt weak at the knees and decided I'd better eat or risk passing out. Nickie accepted my dinner invitation. We strolled out the door. Cars were bumper to bumper, creeping along Cary Street, so we weaved between them across the cobblestones and headed toward the Tobacco Company, one of the best known restaurants in Shockoe Slip. Once a tobacco warehouse and exchange, it is in an old red brick building with mullioned windows and dental molding around the roof.

A crowd had formed under the antique clock. A line from it led to the door. My stomach called out with a rumble and a gurgle. I suppressed a hiccup and suggested we press on to the Omni, where we found a quiet table for two in an elegant little place called Gallego's.

We finished off the better part of a bottle of Pouilly-Fuisée over appetizers and salad, or rather, I finished most of it. While the waiter placed grilled chicken breasts in Dijon mustard sauce over wild rice mixed with white, I ordered another.

"It's terrible about your uncle," she said. "You must have been looking forward to working with him."

"I was. He was good to me, but I hadn't spent much time with him since I went to college. It would have been a chance for us to get reacquainted."

"Well, it could be worse," she said. "At least you're going to inherit his share of the agency. Right? That's the buzz."

"No kidding?"

She gave me that twisted smile again. "Guess I'd better

watch what I say, hadn't I?"

"This Durston thing seems to be a recurring theme. Let me assure you once again, I feel confident you and I can keep our personal lives and work separated. Even if you say you hate your job, it will never go any farther. I promise."

Now her look was sullen. "Since you mention it, advertising is not a passion for me the way it is for you. Oh, it was for a while, I suppose, but now I want to move on. I'm ready to write books, novels. I've written one already, although I haven't found a publisher. It's, you know, the autobiographical first novel that all writers have to get out of their systems, but now I'm in the middle of a thriller I feel pretty good about. If it sells, Durston Negus can take my copy writing job and stuff it right up you know where."

"My, my," I said. "Such hostility. I like that in a woman."

We talked about her novel. We talked about power trips. We talked about how most people spend as much time kidding themselves as they do kidding others. We had dessert and a cordial, as if I had needed that, and I invited her for an after the after dinner drink at my apartment.

My memory is a little hazy from then on, although parts of what happened are as sharp as a sword. I don't think I even noticed Soho--maybe he was out back--or the ladder, or the paint cans and brushes and newspapers. I did have the presence of mind to clear a place on the sofa and find some candles.

I sank into the cushions as she drew her legs under her. It seemed to me we were enclosed in a bubble formed by the candles' glow.

"When do you do it?" I said softly.

"Do it?" A sparkle in her eye.

"Write your novel."

"Oh," she said. "Every morning, from six to 7:30."

"Good luck tomorrow."

She licked her lips. I inched closer.

"Tell me something," she said. "Are you really going to inherit your uncle's interest in the agency?"

I blinked. "I believe that's the second time you've asked me that."

"Pretty obvious for me to have on my mind, though, given the way this evening looks like it's headed--wouldn't you say?"

"I don't think I follow."

"If you inherit your uncle's stock, that would make you a pretty desirable catch, wouldn't it? You would have an awful lot of power and money."

"Power and money? Power and money. Let me think about that. The agency's done all right, so maybe I can see the money part. But, what power are you referring to?"

"The power to hire, fire, promote, demote, give out raises, bonuses, the good jobs, the lousy ones."

"I see your point."

"And it never occurred to you?"

"Not really."

"I don't believe it. I also can't believe I'm saying this, it's the wine talking, and I'll hate myself in the morning--but, either you've decided to string me along--use me before I use you . . . or you're terribly conceited . . . or, or you're not as smart as you seem to be."

"Brother. I don't like any of those. Isn't there another option?"

She pursed her lips. "The only one I can think of is you're not going to inherit your uncle's interest."

"That's the one I choose."

"Oh, come on."

I thought for a moment--to the extent I could think with all that alcohol in my blood. "I wasn't going to tell you any of this," I said, and proceeded to tell her the whole thing: about my theory of the faked suicide, the shareholder's agreement, the insurance money. The only thing I left out was the critical nature of the Benton pitch. No sense upsetting her with that.

She had a wry little smile on her face.

"I feel so much better now," she said.

"Better? My uncle's been murdered, his family has been cheated out of two million. I've moved from a great job in New York with one of the largest ad agencies in the world to be a drone in the third largest ad agency in *Richmond, Virginia*--and you feel *so much better?*"

"I'm sorry about your uncle."

"Thanks." I shook my head.

She put her hand on mine. "But don't you see why, Brian? You're not trying to use me because I want to use you." She squeezed. "I *can't* use you, and that means you *can't* use me. We're just people, you and me--no ulterior motives."

I looked into those dark, dilated pupils that seemed to be calling to me to do something more than simply look into them. "Yeah, you're nuts all right. I knew it the minute I saw you standing in my doorway." I leaned forward and planted a kiss on her.

She melted into me and started breathing hard almost immediately, pressing her body against mine. But I didn't realize what I had on my hands until she pushed me down on the sofa and ripped off my shirt. I mean she didn't even bother to undo the buttons, just jerked with both hands. One after the other popped off. Pop, pop, pop. Then she slid her hands under my t-shirt and pushed up over my head, ran her fingers through the hair on my chest and kissed my neck, shoulder blades, ears--breathed into them, heavy, warm, moist air with a hint of Dijon mustard sauce mingled in.

Seconds later I felt her hands on my belt, undoing it, and in an instant my waist button was undone, my fly was open and she was tugging at my trousers. It actually made me a little nervous, but what the hell. I was crocked, but certain, nonetheless, that my equipment worked.

She'd stripped me naked and hadn't shed a stitch of her own. I had my eye out for the whip. She raised upright, straddling me, a mischievous smile on her face as she slowly undid her blouse. Her lips curled in a sexy pout as her fingers took the buttons one at a time. The front was open and she let the slinky red silk slide off her shoulders, then arched her back and reached behind, unhooked her bra and shook free.

She was slim with narrow hips and full, firm, upturned breasts. I wanted to wrap my lips around them, but I watched instead as she rubbed herself until the nipples became erect. Then she slipped off her skirt and panties and leaned forward until all I saw was the top of her head.

I'd never felt anything like it before. My whole body was alive with tingling and my blood was pumping and she was in control and I was out of control and headed up, way up into the heavens, then down, swooping lower, then up again, higher, shuddering each time the direction changed and thanking heaven. If it weren't for all that alcohol in my veins I'd already have gone off like a Roman candle. I reached down and cupped her breasts, rubbed smooth firm skin, felt hard, pointed nipples against my palms. I squeezed as I felt myself plunge deeper, the pressure building, expanding to critical mass, my insides now poised on the edge, ready to rush out at any second. I realized if I didn't do something it would all be over and so I grabbed her arms and pulled her up until her face plunged into my neck. She wiggled away and magically produced a condom, which she put on in the most tantalizing way I've ever experienced. Then I planted my hands on her hips and pulled her down on me as I pushed up. Suddenly, we were soaring together, diving into deep wide valleys, flying up, upward over oceans, plains, foothills, mountains. We kept on like that, on a wild and frantic and frenetic journey, like two swallows, ducking and turning, locked together in tight formation, determined to see who would outlast the other, all the while the pressure building inside until I could no longer hold back the explosion that pushed everything inside me out--hell bent--like the contents of an airliner that loses pressure at 50,000 feet. This exodus kept on and on until I was completely drained and empty and trembling--but fulfilled, content and out of breath.

I lay for a few seconds gasping for air, then inhaled the musky scent of her, caressed her hair and felt her warm sweet breath on my neck. . . .

Next thing I remember, pale gray light was coming though the window and I was cold and naked--lying on the sofa, all alone.

4

I woke up later in a cold sweat, this time in my bed. I'd had a nightmare, something to do with me telling Uncle Rod I was only in it for the money, at which he'd turned to show me the other side of his head. I tried not to remember the details. Instead, I made an effort to turn my thoughts to the interlude with Nickie. This worked for a while, but then the pending meeting with Rita Maloney, the president of Benton Industries, started nagging for attention. The meeting was scheduled to begin at nine o'clock, only a couple of hours away. I knew I'd better start thinking about how was I going to convince her to keep her account with Durston Negus. But thinking wasn't easy. I was reminded of a guy I went to college with from Paris who told me that our English idiom, "I have a hangover," translates roughly as "My hair hurts" in French. This accurately described how I felt. Plus, Soho was jumping up and down. He was crazy to go out and refused to heed my pleas for mercy, so in the spirit of sacrifice for a fellow earthling I put on shorts and a t-shirt and took him for a run.

Each time my foot hit the pavement my brain jarred against my skull. Nevertheless, we ran north on Lombardy, over to the traffic circle with the statue of J. E. B. Stuart in the middle, looped around and headed west. I looked up as we went by and it hit me the guy was only thirty-one, a year younger than I, when he was killed in action. A hundred and thirty-odd years later the South's youngest general still faced north in defiance of the enemy, his horse locked forever in a prance.

We jogged up Monument Avenue's grass median between tall oaks decked in autumn colors, and I thought, if Stuart could do it why couldn't I? Of course, it wasn't the rank of brigadier I was after, except in a figurative sense. I wanted to lead my troops into battle and onto glory, as he had done at Chancellorsville. But things did not look promising. Maybe I, too, was fighting for a losing cause.

Another statue came into view, this one of Robert E. Lee. As we approached I looked over to what was Durston Negus's most formidable competitor, The Martin Agency. Housed in two landmark turn-of-the-century buildings just off Lee Circle--one a former men's club and the other the city's original high rise apartment building--this outfit had brought fame to Richmond's ad community. Their account wins included Saab automobiles, Remy Martin cognac, Wrangler jeans, Seiko watches among a list of other big national advertisers, which meant they had beaten a bunch of giant New York firms at their own game. If they were in the pitch for Benton as I expected they would be, we were going to have to play over our heads to win.

I was convinced it wouldn't happen with Paul Williams out front. Oh, maybe he and his group would come up with some cute or clever ads. But more would be required. The ads would have to be based on airtight marketing strategy, and I suspected Paul Williams held such things in disdain. A lot of creative directors did. Especially the prima donnas, into which category Paul Williams fell like a hunk of lead.

I tried to shake off this thought as Soho and I continued past the Confederate cannon which marked the inner line of defense of Richmond during the Civil War, past stately old homes like the 33,000 square foot Branch House, a gothic mansion built by a financier for himself, his wife and two children. It had been placed across from the monument to Jefferson Davis, the one and only president of the Confederate States of America, who stood with his arm outstretched in permanent oration, hot air emerging from his lips. The cobbled street made the going rough, but in a moment we were back on the grass. Soho dashed ahead, sniffing trees, chasing squirrels, covering three times the distance I did. We crossed North Boulevard and passed Stonewall Jackson, who had inspired the phrase, "There stands Jackson like a stone wall." The old boy had been shot dead by one of his own men when he hadn't given the password. His tragic flaw had been that he was deaf.

Finally, we ran past the cannon which marked the outer line of defense where a trench, long gone now, had encircled the entire city. I imagined what it might have been like when the enemy had charged, guns and cannon blasting body parts all over the place. That made me flash on Uncle Rod. The mayhem of war and the charge over the top had never happened, though. Not here. Even though Richmond was burned to the ground, the phrase, "like Grant took Richmond," was in error since Grant bypassed the capital. The last major battle of the War had been fought 26 miles to the south at Petersburg. Richmond had been torched by its own, by rebel zealots who wanted to ensure nothing of value was left for the Yankees.

I'd run far enough west, I decided, and turned south to Grove Avenue, then east and back to my place--a helluva run for someone as hung over as I.

Not enough, however, to fully satisfy Soho. "I know, good buddy," I said when we were back in the apartment. "You're ready for some serious exercise." I rough-housed with him. "Maybe later today we'll head out to the University of Richmond and I'll throw you some sticks. Wanna chase sticks into the lake? Yeah?"

He rolled on top of me and a big drip of slobber fell on my face. I took this as a yes.

Four Advil tablets and three cups of coffee later I was inside Larry Negus' office dressed in my most sincere blue suit discussing strategy for Rita Maloney's visit.

"So you'll take her in hand when she gets here, Brian," Larry said. "You'll turn on that boyish charm, tour the agency, and end up in the large conference room. The rest of us will be there and you'll make introductions." The phone rang and Larry picked it up. He looked at me and nodded.

When I spotted her in the lobby, it struck me that boyish charm probably would not go far. She was tall and distinguished looking--dignified is the word--dressed in a chic outfit that resembled a man's charcoal gray suit. Her salt and pepper hair was pulled back in a French twist. A firm handshake and intense eyes greeted me through tortoise shell rim glasses.

"I only saw your uncle twice," she said, "but in the short time we spent together he won my respect. He impressed me as a straight-shooter."

She seemed a straight-shooter, too. The no-nonsense sort. I wished I could keep her away from Larry and Paul, but they were waiting in the conference room.

We started on the tour, meandering first though the area inhabited by account executives, where the account supervisor on Benton was primed and waiting.

"Rita, I'd like you to meet Jill Lathermill. Jill oversees day-to-day operations on your account."

Jill was a businesslike woman a couple of years older than I, a buttoned up executive who looked the part. Maybe it was the wire rimmed glasses. It struck me she and Rita were a lot alike.

Rita took hold of Jill's hand; looked her in the eye. "I've heard your name many times. Our advertising manager, Sam Trenton, says he's come to depend on you."

Jill told her in a sincere but professional manner how much she had been looking forward to meeting the new boss. Then she led Rita to the offices of other account service staff who worked on Benton, which consisted of four account executives--one for consumer advertising, one for trade, one for events and publicity, and one for sales promotion.

Next, I led Rita to the media department. Here, too, it appeared we had simply arrived at a fortuitous time. What we saw was a well-rehearsed demonstration of our computer firepower. Our media director explained the various steps while one of our time buyers matched the audience compositions of different tv shows with the demographic and psychographic characteristics of target customers for a particular line of bedroom furniture Benton would soon be paying us to promote.

When we got to the creative department I held my breath and crossed my fingers. The creative staff at Durston Negus, like their counterparts at other agencies with a highly creative bent, were prone to antics that could easily knock the not so proverbial pants off of a straight-laced client like Rita Maloney.

We walked by Nickie's office. I peeked in and saw her at work at her computer. Maybe she could feel my presence because she looked up while I still had my eyes on her and puckered her lips. Then slowly and deliberately she circled them with her tongue. I watched every nanosecond of this excruciatingly graphic display of affection. I didn't turn and I didn't blink. No way was I going to let Rita see me my crimson blush.

Then we stopped at a large central work station with a color monitor and printer and I asked our production manager, who just happened to be there by prearrangement, to explain how our computers took a magazine or newspaper ad from concept to finished form without ever being touched by human hands.

As we headed to the large conference room, she said, "It's incredible how much computers have changed how things work, isn't it?"

"Tell me about it," I said. "Everyone here including the receptionist has one, and we're all linked by a local area network to the Web. E-mail. Even my uncle did most of his own correspondence."

"So did my predecessor at Benton," Rita said. "It's annoying, though--his computer was gone by the time I moved into his old office."

"Must have been commandeered. That's something that could easily happen here."

"I've had it replaced, of course. Too bad though. I could use the information that was on the hard drive."

We reached the conference room door where Larry Negus stood with a grin on his jowly mug, his white hair slicked back, a brand new liver spot on his forehead. He held out his hand. "Larry Negus, Rita, so good to meet you."

"Rita and I were just discussing the pitfalls of computers in the workplace," I said.

Larry kept his smile plastered in place. "I'm afraid that's one area where I've been left in the dark ages," he said. "I've got one in my office but don't know how to turn it on."

An impromptu receiving line formed to Larry's right.

"Rita, here are some people I'd like you to meet," I said. "First, Paul Williams--our creative director."

Paul had his feet together at the heels and swayed forward like a maitre d' with menus under his arm, except that he wore a silly grin above his slightly oily double chin. Rita's brow wrinkled as she took his hand. Her eyes darted from the unruly long blond locks that fell in ringlets around his face to the body hair that sprouted from the open collar of his flowered shirt. She didn't puke, though.

Next in line stood Mary MacMann, our chief administrative officer, who was the let's-cut-straight-to-the-bottom-line type I thought Rita might relate to if the vultures that surrounded her would hold their extroverted personalities in check.

Rita towered over the last in line, Ben Haley, our director of client service. His salt and chestnut beard and neatly trimmed hair made him look like a combination of Robert E. Lee and a squirrel with acorns in his cheeks. He was the quiet type whose baritone voice surprised me every time he opened his mouth.

With the introductions complete, I led Rita to the head of the polished walnut conference table, then took my seat with the others.

She rested her hands casually on the back of the chair in front of her, clearly used to being in control. "Thank you for meeting with me today," she said. "I know this is a busy group, and that your time is valuable. I also know that Benton Industries is an important account to this shop. Rod Durston told me the day after I took this job that it was the agency's first account--the one he and Larry started with--so I guess there's sentimental value, as well as monetary value." She looked squarely at each of us in turn. "Rod gave me a thorough briefing on the work you've done for Benton, and I can honestly say, I haven't any problems with it. So I know you're wondering why I've chosen to put the account into review.

"Every one of you has been in this business long enough to know that clients often change agencies when a new president or marketing executive comes on board. It's natural for the new man or woman to want her own team, a team she hired. Well, I must admit that's part of it. But it's far from the only reason. I believe it's healthy to take a hard, objective look at what you're doing every so often, to consider alternative ways of doing things and to seek new ideas from different sources. What better time than when a new chief executive comes on board? That's reason enough, I believe, for a review to be held at this time . . . but there is another, a very compelling reason from my perspective. Benton Industries will be launching an entirely new product line next year. . . . Now, let me make this clear, I'm not talking about a piddling line like coffee tables, I'm talking about an effort so big we're building a new plant to manufacture the line exclusively. For us to be successful we'll have go head-to-head with an established leader and take a healthy share of market away. So we've committed an additional ten million dollars to advertising and promotion for this new line alone."

A murmur arose among the five of us, the words "Ten million dollars" reverberating over a kind of hush. Dollar signs clicked over in Larry Negus' eyes.

"It's a gamble," she continued, "a calculated risk. And if we fail . . . well, you know what the board of directors and the stockholders are looking for, and they are who I answer to. They're looking for sales increases and they're looking for healthy, expanding profits. If instead they see flat sales and shrinking profits because of money squandered on a failed project, I can assure you that Rita Maloney will be history in less time than it takes to say, 'You're fired.'" She looked from one of us to the next. "I do not wish to fail."

"What is the new line?" Larry Negus asked.

"Hope chests," she said, and I could feel the others flinch. "Hope chests. There is only one other furniture manufacturer that turns them out in quantity because that manufacturer has the market cornered. We plan to take the corner away, to challenge their position, which is why I'm giving you and the other agencies I've asked to compete for the business the assignment to develop an advertising campaign to introduce the line. The agency with the campaign that makes the most sense to me will win the entire account.

"Let me put in right here that the campaign that will win favor with me is the one I think will sell the most hope chests--no ifs, ands, whereas, wherefores, or buts."

I was thinking, *Hope chests? Lord help me, I could have been working on the tourism promotion for a Caribbean island,* when Paul Williams raised his hand.

"Which other agencies?" he asked.

"My researchers have informed me there are a number

of excellent agencies right here in Richmond, so there's no need to go outside of the area. We've selected three. Your agency, The Martin Agency and Arnold."

At least she left out Barber Martin.

Ben Haley, our director of client services, raised his hand.

"When do you want to see our presentation?"

"Ten days from today, same time, same place."

Paul Williams hand shot up again. "Your last job was in the fashion industry. Do you think the same advertising techniques apply?"

"If they'll sell hope chests they certainly do. But I'm not setting any ground rules. I want you to tell me . . . no, I want you to *convince* me that whatever you come up with will have people lining up and breaking down doors to buy our cedar chests."

Mary MacMann was next. "Will we be reimbursed for time and out-of-pocket?"

"Up to $20,000, which I realize probably will only cover out-of-pocket, depending on how elaborate you decide to get. But remember, whichever agency wins will land a $30 million account."

The questions and answers flew back and forth for another quarter hour until Rita looked at her watch and said she was due at Arnold in ten minutes.

I escorted her to the lobby and gushed all over her about how she was going to love whatever it was we came up with, then followed my brown nose back to the conference room.

Larry was in the middle of a dissertation. "Talk about double or nothing, either we gain ten million in billings or we lose twenty. Mary, better tell the caterer to have both champagne and cyanide on hand the day we're supposed to find out."

"This is going to be a piece of cake," Paul Williams said. "She's got garment industry written all over her. I met a million like her when I was at Hubert Blatz. She's looking

Death in Advertising

for flash and she's looking for glitter. We do flash and glitter in our sleep."

Hope chests, I was thinking, *for Pete's sake.* "I wouldn't be so sure that's what she's looking for if I were you," I said. "She's going to need some good reasons why flash and glitter will sell--" I could hardly bring myself to say it, "Hope chests."

"Ah bullshit," Paul said. "I'm telling you they're all alike. The brain of everyone I ever met in the garment industry is below the belt. Trust me."

"Why couldn't it be bug repellent?" Mary said. "Paul repels bugs in his sleep."

Paul cut his eyes toward her.

"You know, Paul, your bias is showing," I said. "She seems awfully competent to me."

Mary MacMann returned Paul's glare. "Twenty thousand is not much to do a presentation." She raised a finger. "For instance, Mr. Williams here went ape shit on the FasTrack Pizza pitch and spent over a hundred grand in out-of-pocket. It hurt so bad to sign the check I didn't even calculate what the time cost us."

Paul leaned over until his nose was an inch from hers. "Listen, Little Miss Tightwad Bitch, that was a ten million dollar account. You've got to roll the dice on an account like that."

"This one's thirty million," Larry said. He turned to Ben Haley. "You've been awfully quiet, Ben. What do you think?"

Ben stroked his beard and looked meek. Then his voice boomed. "I think Brian is right. Miss Maloney is a bottom line oriented individual, but I also wonder if she hasn't made a huge mistake by betting her career on hope chests. The damn things went out with buggy whips and button shoes." He shook his head. "I wonder if they've done any research."

"You heard her," Mary said. "There's only one competitor. They know the sales volume of that competitor. That's where they plan to get theirs."

"Why are we sitting here?" Paul said. "Let's get the hell out of here and get started. Ten days to prepare a full blown presentation. Jesus."

"Wait a minute," Larry said. "We have to get organized first. There are a couple of things we need to decide. Now, normally Rod would have picked a team captain from among the shareholders." Larry explained my situation. Eyebrows went up around the room when he said I'd probably purchase Uncle Rod's stock. Larry didn't know I had no way to get the money. "Anyhow," Larry continued, "I nominate Brian as team leader. Do I hear a second?"

"Second," Ben Haley said in his baritone.

"Wait a goddamn minute," Paul Williams said. "What the hell does he know about the fashion industry?"

"This isn't the fashion industry, Paul," Ben said. "It's furniture."

"The hell it isn't fashion. The product's supposed to be pretty, isn't it? The client came out of the fashion industry, didn't she?"

Mary MacMann leaned over in Paul Williams' face this time. "I suppose all we need to win the account is some pretty fashion ads with some pretty fashion pictures in them--in which case you won't have to spend a fucking fortune this time on the fucking presentation."

"Oh, I don't know about that," Paul said.

My head was really beginning to throb when Ben Haley's deep voice boomed, "Look, with all due respect, Paul, you're not the guy to head up this pitch. You have a creative department to run and that's more than a full-time job. Lord knows, you'll be plenty involved as it is and don't need the additional hassle of keeping the damn thing organized. Plus, I've got my hands full, too, and this is out of Mary's area. So who does that leave? Either Larry, or Brian, right? I think Brian hit it off with Rita Maloney. What do you think, Brian? Did you hit it off with her?"

"I think the two of us hit it off okay," I said. "But I'll be honest. She's a tough cookie. Not the type to be swept off her feet by some ad guy."

"Amen," Mary MacMann said.

"Maybe we could import an accountant," Larry said.

"I'm telling you, we're talking high fashion here," Paul said. "Picture one of those long, bean-pole models in a filmy white gown--she's draped over the product--and there are four simple words: 'Hope Chest by Benton.'" He closed his eyes, leaned back and smiled a dreamy smile. "Damn that's good, and right off the top of my head. I'd say we've got it knocked."

"Let's vote," Ben said.

I couldn't believe it. Three in favor of me and one abstention--by Paul Williams.

A strategy session was scheduled for first thing the next morning--at which I was to have a battle plan drawn up and ready for implementation. Then the meeting dispersed.

My head felt like an over-heated pressure cooker by the time I was weaving my way among the cubicles of junior executives and administrative assistants. Their heads were on rubber necks, curious about what was up after the meeting with the client who was opening her account for review. I didn't bite; plunged ahead.

Jill Lathermill, the supervisor on Benton, sat in a chair in front of my desk. She stood as I came in, her concern palpable.

"How did it go? Are Martin, Arnold and Barber in it, too?"

"No Barber. Just Arnold and Martin." I took a seat and gestured for her to do the same. "Without Barber Martin the odds are better than I thought. But I'll tell you something, she's tough. I think she'll be fair, though. Of course, you can never be sure. Clients say one thing, mean another. She said she didn't have any particular problem with the agency, that as long as she's new in the job she wants to see what's out there, make sure she's got the best."

"She wants her own team," Jill said.

"Of course she does," I said.

"I've been doing some checking," Jill said. "As best I can tell Rita doesn't have any buddies at Martin or Arnold. No friends of friends, either. That may put all three of us in the same boat."

"That's a relief. Question is, how can we get her to be *our* buddy? Think I should call and ask her to dinner?"

Jill frowned. "She'd see through a dinner invitation from a hunk like you."

"Think so? Sometimes people know they're being sucked up to but they like it anyway. I've sucked up to hundreds. See the end of this nose?" I touched it. "Clients love this baby."

"Maybe so. But I think we'd be better off to let Martin and Arnold do the sucking up. She may go out with one of their hunks, maybe she'll even go to bed with him. I guarantee it will do more harm than good. You know the old saw about respect in the morning?"

"It would be good, though, if I found some reason to see her. Don't you think? Something that would give us a chance to get to know each other better--for her to get familiar with me, gain some confidence, and for me to try to get a better read on her."

"I'm planning to go to Benton on Tuesday to present a new series of ads for the Chelsea line of bedroom furniture, a promotion scheduled for January--buy a bedroom suite and get a mattress and box spring free. You could come along."

"Yes, good. Shows I'm interested and involved, a perfect opportunity to show her my face."

"I should warn you. We may not even see her. The old president, Arthur Fletcher, made every decision from the number of paper clips to which magazines should be on the ad schedule. Rita seems more of a delegator. We may only see Sam Trenton, the ad manager."

"It's worth the chance. What else?"

"I suggest we prove we're the best agency for her.

What's she want to see in the presentation?"

I told her about hope chests.

"I'll get the troops working on it right away," she said. "We'll have a file a foot thick by this afternoon."

We also decided that a couple of Jill's account execs would make a swing through North Carolina and Virginia to visit dealers that sell cedar chests and talk with them about product promotions and the competition--what works and what doesn't.

"Another thing," Jill said. "I have a friend in research at a brokerage firm--Wheat. They follow the furniture industry. I'll get him to give me what he's got on the competition and rundown on any industry gossip on Rita."

Jill stood, but hesitated before she turned to leave. "I'm glad you decided to come to Durston Negus, Brian. I think it improves our chances of keeping the account."

"Thanks. But, why do you say that?"

"Rita's going to feel comfortable with a pro like you on the management level. Someone she can interface with and feel is a peer. Without you, there'd be no one she could relate to."

"What about Ben?"

Jill paused. "Ben's okay, but he has his hands full. Plus, he has personal problems which have him distracted. His mother has cancer, and she's dying. Don't say anything about it. He doesn't want people to know."

"I'm sorry to hear that. Of course. I won't say anything."

"We have to keep this account, Brian. I don't want to think about the blood bath around here if we don't. My staff. Me. There's a lot of hungry mouths depending on us. My husband is between jobs. Sure as hell don't want both of us to be."

I knew Jill was married and had a young son, but I hadn't realized her husband was out of work. "I know how important the account is. A lot is riding on it--for you and for me, too. But I'm convinced we'll keep it. We'll keep it because we're the right agency for Rita. You can count on it."

The truth was that *maybe* we were the right agency and that *maybe* we'd end up keeping the account, but what the hell. Jacking this prognosis up a notch seemed to help. Jill's step was lighter when she left.

The thought of losing the account made me think of money, which caused me to remember that yesterday was payday and I'd forgotten to pick up my check. I went to accounting. A clerk told me our comptroller, Ham Sheldrake, was the man I needed to see.

He looked up from a thick computer printout, a puffy cheeked, cordial little guy with a twitch, who had been nice enough to offer his condolences about my uncle the day before.

"I understand you're the keeper of the paychecks," I said.

"No problem." He opened a drawer. "How did it go with Rita Maloney?"

"She's no pushover. Plus we're up against Martin and Arnold."

He handed me the check. "We've been up against the two of them before."

"And won?"

"We're batting .333. One win two losses."

"We'll whip them again this time," I said. "Bring our average up to .500."

I was becoming a habitual liar. But it seemed to make sense to try to build confidence among the troops.

"I guess then the talks with Transpublic will resume," Sheldrake said. "Word came down about three o'clock on Tuesday they'd been called off. At least till we find out about Benton."

Transpublic was a huge international advertising agency holding company, the shares of which were traded on the New York Stock Exchange. I hadn't heard of talks with them, so I probably hesitated longer than seemed normal.

"Don't worry, I know all about it," Sheldrake said. "Who do you think pulled together all those reams of financial data?"

"Yes, right, of course." My mind raced. Uncle Rod hadn't breathed a word. Transpublic was one of those companies that bought and sold ad agencies like a Brooklyn broker bought and sold penny stocks. They even owned my old employer, Flint Worldwide.

"No doubt about it," I said. "Once we get Benton nailed down, they'll want to talk again--for sure. What's your guess on how much they'll be willing to pay?"

Sheldrake shrugged. "The buzz says Scali paid ten times net for Martin. Why would we sell for less?"

"Guess you're right. Let's see now, what would that work out to be?"

Sheldrake put his hand on a calculator, punched in a few numbers and hit the equal button. "Net earnings have averaged a million eight the last three years. Ten times that is 18 million. Plus they'd probably add book value on top of that. I'd say a fair price would be about $19.3 million."

"Nineteen million three hundred thousand dollars," I said.

"Has a nice ring, doesn't it? It's awful about your uncle, I know, but inheriting forty percent of that--"

"Could cushion the blow?"

"I'm sorry," he said. "That was crass. I didn't mean to be."

"Forget it. How much is forty percent of nineteen three?"

He punched in the numbers. "$7,720,000."

I slipped my paycheck inside the pocket of my jacket and gave him a two-fingered salute. "When it happens, remind me to buy you a drink."

5

Back at my desk, I struggled to grasp what I'd just heard. Then the telephone rang.

"How is your headache, lover boy?"

"Okay, so maybe I could have done without the cordial at Gallego's."

"Tell me. Did you snow the lady in the gray flannel suit with your boyish charm?"

"Turned it on full blast, but all I got was an occasional flurry. Guess I didn't have much left in me after last night."

"Really? I'd have thought otherwise."

"Is it a subtle way of telling me something?"

"Sorry. Won't say. I have my enigmatic image."

I looked at my watch. "Lunch?"

"Hummm. Who's buying?"

"We'll flip for it. Matt's Pub, twelve o'clock?"

It was a fabulous fall day and normally I'd have enjoyed the walk to Matt's, which was a few blocks west and around the corner on Twelfth, across from the Omni. The restored buildings and cobblestone streets of Shockoe Slip created the feeling of being in the past, which seemed odd when one looked up and saw the glass and chrome towers a few blocks away. But I wasn't in the mood for looking at blue sky or buildings. Nor was I particularly interested in watching the working women who'd turned out in force now that it was lunchtime, nor even the stylish West End matrons who frequented quaint little shops along the way. I was preoccupied with the revelation handed to me by Ham Sheldrake.

My mind raced as I entered Matt's, a typical English pub that was lodged in an old building which abutted The Tobacco Company. A young woman led me upstairs onto a mezzanine that overlooked the plaid carpet and lunch crowd on the first floor.

Nickie made her entrance three minutes later in a deadpan but sophisticated way, picked up a menu; made a face. "Kidney pie? What a way to ruin crust. Anyway, I've heard that English beer is good."

"I think I'd better lay off."

She nodded knowingly. "Your over-indulgence will be excused this time."

"Thanks. Speaking of dirt, wait until you hear the latest."

"Don't tell me. You know who did it."

"No, but I've just learned something that has blown my mind."

She leaned forward. "Okay. Spill it."

"Talks have been going on with Transpublic International to sell the agency, although they've been halted now because of the Benton pitch."

"So?"

"That means the plot has thickened. You'll recall that because of the shareholder's agreement, stock in the agency is bought and sold at book, and if one of the shareholders leaves--or dies--the company buys back their stock at book."

"Uh-huh."

"So, if the agency is sold to Transpublic, the value of the stock will be many times book value, possibly more than

15 times, based on what rumor says The Martin Agency brought."

"So the other shareholders did it."

"Think about it. Because of Uncle Rod's death, the agency has to buy back his stock at book value. So instead of five shareholders there will now be four. The percentage of outstanding stock owned by each will jump. Uncle Rod owned forty percent." I turned over a paper place mat, pulled a pen from my pocket and started on the arithmetic.

"Someone who owned ten percent before my uncle died would suddenly own, let's see, more than 16 percent, so . . . instead of $1.9 million they would get more than *three* million from the sale. Right, $3,200,000, or there abouts."

"So what you're thinking is that the four remaining shareholders can now be placed at the head of the list of suspects."

"Precisely."

Her brow furrowed. "Which one had the most to gain?"

"Larry Negus had 30 percent." I scribbled figures on the place mat and worked the math. "His 30 is suddenly 50 percent after the stock is repurchased, and his take increases . . . from $5.8 million to--to almost *ten million dollars*. Let me finish multiplying this--"

"It's $9,650,000--to be exact," Nickie said. She shrugged. "How much champagne and caviar can one person consume? He already had almost $6 million coming to him. Would he *kill* for another four?"

"Wouldn't be the first time." My mind clicked off each of the shareholders and searched for tell-tale signs of guilt. "You know, Larry tried to talk me out of buying Uncle Rod's stock, sort of, by telling me the consequences if the agency loses Benton Industries."

"It doesn't add up, Brian. Suppose you buy your uncle's stock? None of the shareholders would gain a thing."

"*If* I had the money I could buy it, but that's a really big if."

"Larry doesn't know you don't, does he? None of them

do."

I felt the air leaking out of my balloon.

A waiter in a white apron stopped at our booth and took a pencil from behind his ear. "Something to drink?"

I was thirsty for a draft, hair of the dog and all, but I knew I needed all my wits and ordered Diet Coke. Nickie asked for iced tea.

When he left I said, "We *think* Larry doesn't know I can't afford it. Anyone could figure out there's just no way for me to come up with that kind of cash. For starters, the fact the account is in review means no bank is going to lend the money, and beyond that all he'd need to know is that the trust was to be funded by life insurance." I snapped my fingers. "The staged suicide, of course. The clever bastard. He's a whole lot smarter than I thought."

She did not look convinced. "The suicide just may have been an easy way to cover up a murder. Period."

"Know something? Maybe it's a conspiracy. Maybe all four of them are in on it together."

"Yeah, right," Nickie said. "I can see them now, meeting in the dark of night in an old abandoned house, drawing straws to see who the triggerman will be."

The waiter returned with our drinks and Nickie ordered a salad. I decided on steak, rare. Somehow, it seemed like that might help my hurting hairs.

He left and Nickie said, "I was in a staff meeting last week with all four of them, and from what I saw, I'd be surprised if they could agree on where to go to lunch much less agree to murder someone and keep it a secret."

"You can't deny that three of them have ten percent, and Larry's got thirty."

She looked pensive as she wrapped her ruby-red lips around the straw and began to sip tea. "So three of them go from under two million to over three, and Larry's haul goes from roughly six to ten. When you think about it, its more of a motive for the ten percent shareholders, don't you think? Jumps them into a category where they can tell the world to take a hike."

"You're right, especially when you consider what they'd have left after taxes. Two million after state and federal--that would only be about, oh, maybe $1.3 million. A lot of money. But not enough to put you on easy street for life. You could spend half of it on a house. Now, *three million,* two hundred thousand--after taxes . . . that would leave more than two million. Not a bad little nest egg."

"Know what I think?" Nickie said. "You need to find out where each of them was the night and the time of the murder, and if any of them had more of a reason to do it than the others--a strong need for a lot of cash, for example."

"How?"

A tuft of shiny black hair had fallen across her forehead. She pushed it back. "Sneak a peak at their appointment calendars, ask around."

"I've been thinking I should go through Uncle Rod's files. There could be clues."

"And don't forget his computer."

"Right. Want to help me, Watson?" My stomach twitched.

Her lips broke into a smile. "Is the Pope a Catholic? Tell you what, it'll be easier for me to ask people questions than it will be for you. People love to gossip, but won't open up to you because they think you're one of them."

"Good thinking."

Did I detect a hint of smugness on her face?

"Of course, you realize this will give me the Sherlock role," she said. "Hope you don't mind, Watson, old boy."

The waiter arrived with our food.

"By the way, I've been meaning to ask," I said. "How do you like Richmond?"

"Faked suicides and murder make life here quite interesting, actually."

"I mean as a city."

She chewed lettuce. "Not sure yet. In a way, it's a lot like

Boston. You know, colonial, history, handmade red brick--that sort of thing. But unlike Boston with its screaming liberals from pinko universities, Richmond has a traditional atmosphere that would have sent me packing when I was younger."

"Really? Why?"

"Let me put it to you this way. When my teachers sent recommendations to colleges they always started the same, 'Nickie D'Agostino is a top student who marches to the beat of a different drummer.'"

"A sort of non-conformist?"

"More than sort of. My parents tried to push psychoanalysis on me, but I refused. Then, when I got to college, I found there were plenty of people who were even more kooky than I. What I didn't know, of course, was it was the school I chose, but even so, it was good for me to meet others who liked Kafka and bean sprouts. I finally had human beings around I could relate to."

My fork was halfway to my mouth. I stared at the red center of a hunk of meat.

"By getting to know others like myself," she continued, "I've become more tolerant of people who are different."

"I see. How do you feel about former college football players who are partial to red meat and Southern history?"

She regarded me with sultry eyes. "Sometimes opposites attract."

Whoa.

"Besides," she added, "we bean sprout eaters can be pains in the butt. Being one is bad enough. I'm not sure I'd want to be around another all the time. Wait 'til you hear me chant 'Oooommm' at 4:30 in the morning."

"Wait 'til my upstairs neighbor hears it." I wondered if tonight were the night she was planning to sleep over.

For the rest of the meal we talked about her novel. When the time came to leave, we agreed to meet at 5:30 in Uncle Rod's office to begin our roles of Sherlock and Watson. It occurred to me later that her company was doing me a world of good--keeping my mind of my heartfelt loss of Uncle Rod, and the impending loss of my dream of independence.

I worked on Benton all afternoon. Jill brought me what she and her troops had been able to uncover and we went over it. They'd found out an amazing amount about hope chests and the company Rita Maloney had said owned the market. By 4:30 we'd gone through it completely and discussed several strategic options and ways we might proceed. We were ready for the strategy meeting the next morning.

"Want to come with me to present all this?" I asked.

She shook her head. "Most people in my position probably would, I guess--to show how much they know and how indispensable they are. But your opposition is going to come from Paul Williams. I learned long ago I'm no match for him." She looked me in the eye. "Sorry. I'm pinning my hopes on you."

Great. Now I was co-responsible for her kid's tuition and the mortgage, not to mention food on the table. As if I didn't have enough to worry my mind. Still, it felt good to have earned Jill's confidence.

After she left, I decided to go to Uncle Rod's office and get started on his files. Mavis Alfonso, the executive secretary Uncle Rod shared with Larry, sat at her desk in the hallway outside. She was a stocky woman with dark hair piled on her head in a twist.

"If you don't mind," I said, "I'm going to begin cleaning out Uncle Rod's office and files."

I saw tears welling. "It's such a terrible, terrible thing. I just can't believe it. I'll be glad to help. Want me to organize things to make it easier?"

"That's thoughtful of you, Mavis, but no. I'd rather do it myself."

The door of his office was shut. I hesitated before taking

hold of the knob. My legs felt weak. That dizziness returned. Images of him lying in blood came flooding back.

I was being irrational, I told myself. Nothing was in there.

I forced my hand to close around the cool brass knob, took a shaky breath and pushed. Spots flashed before my eyes. That salty taste returned.

But his desk had been cleaned. The computer and printer were still there. Only the leather blotter was missing.

I moved to Uncle Rod's side of the desk. This wasn't going to be easy. I felt my hands tremble. I like to kid around, even with myself, make light of serious stuff, but S.O.B. or no S.O.B., Uncle Rod was the closest thing I'd had to a father. My mind turned for an instant to Sally and the girls and what they must be going through. Maybe at this very minute Sally stood in his closet wondering what to do with his suits and his shirts and his shoes. It was such an empty, helpless feeling.

A memory came to mind from the day of my college graduation. Uncle Rod was there, as well as Sally, Millie, my mom. He came over and wrapped an arm around my shoulders. "Your dad would have been proud," he said softly. "He'd have been proud, no matter what, to have a son like you. But if he could have seen you today--"

The intensity of the moment had surprised me. Then my mother came toward us and broke the spell. Uncle Rod slapped me on the back. "Bet you and the boys are going to get trashed tonight, eh, Brian?"

I closed my fingers around the pull of a drawer and gave it a tug. Inside were files which hung on a metal frame that could be lifted out, the green kind that contain manila folders. All were askew and sticking up as though someone had been looking for something and had closed up shop in a hurry. My pulse raced. Uncle Rod never would have left them in such a mess. His most distinguishing characteristic, beyond the fact that he could be as cold and calculating as a Mafia bookkeeper, was his penchant for neatness. I wondered what someone had been looking for and whether or not he or she had found it.

I began with the file marked "personal."

Half an hour later Nickie appeared in the doorway clad in a royal blue dress and matching beret. The color matched her eyes and set off her pale skin, red lips and jet black hair. Maggie the Cat without the hot tin roof. But sultry nonetheless.

She strolled in, looked around, let her fingers caress a teak cigar box on an antique mahogany sideboard.

"Not bad," she said. "At least, I'll bet *you* could get used to it, Mr. Red Meat Avarice Double Scotch With a Splash of Soda."

"Dewars, for goodness sake. Not just any Scotch."

She sat, crossed her legs at the knees, allowed one perfectly shaped calf to swing gently in a circular motion.

"And no twist," I said, feeling a bead of sweat form on my forehead. "You're just in time. I think I'm onto something."

"Speak."

"Here's a letter, pink stationery. Listen to this, 'Dearest Rod, You probably think I'm silly, but the reason I left the agency was so we could be together. Sounds like a contradiction, doesn't it? But, I know of your reluctance to mix business with pleasure. That's the wisdom of my leaving. Now there's no longer anything standing in our way. My place, seven o'clock. Do come, Rod, darling. I promise I'll be waiting with absolutely nothing on, except Saran Wrap and a smile. Love, Lauren.'"

"Saran Wrap?" Nickie shook her head. "Saran Wrap went out the day *Fear of Flying* dropped off the best seller list. I wasn't even born yet."

I handed her the letter. "It's dated about four months ago--June 14. No envelope--he probably threw that away. My guess is it was hand-delivered. Of course, by itself this letter doesn't prove a thing."

"At least she could have thought of something more

original, like reminding him of her uncanny ability to suck a golf ball through a garden hose."

"You have such a way with words. Perhaps later this evening we can explore the deeper meaning of them. Meanwhile--" I held up an official-looking document with the light blue back some lawyers use. "Exhibit B--a prenuptial agreement between Sally and my uncle. If they were to divorce, all she would get is what she came into the marriage with, plus a lump sum payment of $50,000--adjusted for inflation."

"You think his wife did it?"

"Suppose my uncle was involved with this woman? Suppose he was planning to dump Sally? They'd been married for 17 or 18 years, the best years of Sally's life, and all she'd get is $50,000. Even adjusted for inflation, that wouldn't be more than maybe a hundred thou."

Nickie's nose wrinkled. "Speaking of avarice, what happened to the avarice of shareholders?"

"Nothing . . . it's just that I'm not ruling out anything at this point, that's all."

"The world is full of women in relationships with married men they hope will divorce their wives. How often do the scum-balls actually deliver?"

"He told me once he was glad he had a second family," I said. "On the other hand, I have a strong suspicion that he left his first wife for Sally, who at that time was the younger woman. Why wouldn't Sally think he'd do the same thing again?"

She shook her head. "Men are such creeps."

"Present company excluded?"

"One thing argues against your theory," Nickie said. "Unless of course she hadn't thought it through. Insurance companies won't pay because it's suicide, right? Don't you think she'd like to have had that $2 million bucks?"

"On the other hand, making it look like suicide would remove all suspicion, wouldn't it?"

"So would staging a break-in."

"The insurance money isn't all that was at stake. She gets to keep the house on the river and the house at Wintergreen. I'm not sure how much equity is in each but I'm willing to bet that between the two there's over a million and a half."

"Be realistic, Brian. There are only two reasons your aunt would have staged a suicide. She didn't know the insurance companies wouldn't pay, or she acted in haste to save herself."

"Even so, we need to check out this, this other woman--Lauren."

"Maybe *she's* the one who did it," Nickie said.

"You mean, maybe she and Rod were making it on the side until one day Rod decided to dump her?"

"It wouldn't be the first time a jealous lover gave the object of her affection an extra hole in the head."

"My, my. That way with words, again. I like that in a woman"

"Speaking of words, want to know what I learned today?"

"Already?"

"I was showing some copy to an account exec--the ditzy one with red hair. Wears skirts that barely cover her cute little tush? Name is Ellen. She gave me the low-down on Ben Haley."

"Nice upper thighs, as I recall. Perhaps her strongest attribute."

"You red meat eaters are insufferably aggressive."

"By the way, what *is* tofu?"

"Now, let me see. How did she put it? Ben Haley is a self-made man. Grew up in southwest Virginia in a place called Galax or Grundy. Wasn't sure. Anyway, it's one of those coal mining towns, and he was determined not to follow his father's footsteps into the mines. Ben was president of his senior class, valedictorian, came to Richmond to VCU on a full scholarship and graduated with a 3.75 GPA. Spent the first eight years of his career at

VanBlake in Baltimore. Made it to vice president before turning 30. Married, two kids, both boys. Was hired away by Larry Negus more than five years ago, a few months after Durston Negus was founded."

"You probably left out the part that he was an Eagle Scout. Any reason he'd need a lot of money?"

"Not that he would *need* it. The only thing I can figure is, a guy like that has been without money all his life--has struggled, watched his parents struggle and his friends struggle because money was scarce. It can be grim in those coal mining towns. Even worse than way out on Long Island where I come from."

"East Hampton? West Hampton? Fire Island? That's degradation, all right."

"So money would be awfully important, wouldn't it?--the reason he's worked so hard and done so well. Selling his share in the agency and suddenly becoming a millionaire would be quite appealing."

Wait a minute. I was letting my infatuation with this woman cloud my thinking. I'd grown up on the edge, never certain whether we were having baked beans or corn flakes for dinner. Even so, I couldn't imagine holding a gun to someone's temple and pulling the trigger. "No one enjoys the thought of going hungry," I said. "But would he kill to make it three million Big Macs instead of two? I don't think so."

"Can't rule him out."

"Nor can we rule out Miss Saran Wrap or Sally the Second Wife."

"They all go into the same category," Nickie said. "Further investigation required."

I put the letter and the prenuptial back in their respective folders, straightened the stack and returned it to the hanging file marked "personal."

"We have a lot of stuff here to go through," I said. "How do you want to tackle it?"

She looked around the room. "Does this place give you

the creeps? It gives me the creeps."

"Perhaps it's the teak cigar box or the solid gold desk set."

"It's not so much the symbols of opulent wealth. In a way I'm used to that. My father had a marble nude with a clock in her belly on his desk in the den. You know what? I think it may be that this is the site of a brutal murder."

"We could take everything to my place," I said. "The hanging files lift out."

"And we could download the hard drive onto discs."

"But there'd be no way to look at them. No computer at home."

She stood and looked at it. "It's the same as mine, a Macintosh Performa." She flipped the switch.

"How much trouble is it to copy what's on the hard drive?"

"Depends how much stuff is on it. Know his password?"

"Try his initials: RFD."

"Bingo." There was a burst of activity on the computer screen. "Let's see what's here." She took hold of the mouse. "A lot of stuff--that's what. Let's open this." She clicked. "Uh-huh. You don't happen to have thirty blank discs on you? And about an hour and a half to wait?"

"No wonder there are only two drawers of hard copy files. All his correspondence and reports--everything he generated himself is in there. Let's pack up the computer and the printer and take them home. We can go though all that stuff in the comfort of my apartment."

"I guess you don't mind walking out the door with several thousand dollars worth of equipment that belongs to the agency."

"They'll get over it." I stood. "Let's see if I can find some boxes for the hanging files."

"Try the production department. And bring a hand truck--unless you plan to carry it all yourself."

An hour later, we were standing in the foyer of my

apartment, a box between us with a hanging file in it. The stepladder was in the same place as the last time I'd seen it--in the middle of the living room. Newspapers were still spread all over. Paint cans, brushes, rollers. Soho sat by the ladder wagging his tail. The only clear patch of space was the sofa.

"There's a room down the hall," I said.

The apartment I'd rented encompassed the first floor of a huge old shotgun style townhouse and had two bedrooms. I'd set up the spare as a den. We walked in and came to a stop on one of my prized possessions, an old handwoven Kazak carpet with geometric patterns in red, several shades of blue, beige and brown. There also was a desk and swivel chair, a bookcase chock full of books and a sofa covered in dark chocolate-colored velvet.

Before long we had everything arranged. I changed into shorts and a t-shirt and took Soho out for a ten-minute run, then came back inside and settled myself on the sofa next to Nickie.

"At least having Soho around keeps me from turning into a complete, unadulterated blob."

"At the first sign of it, it's tofu for you for the rest of your life. But don't worry, you can break the monotony with bean sprouts."

She sure looked good and was only inches from me. Damn that tingly sensation. "By the way, you never said. What is tofu? An aphrodisiac? Is that why a person loses weight?"

She gave me the deadpan. "You ex college jocks are all alike. So darned concerned about proper diet and exercise. Too bad the kind of exercise you have in mind takes two. This half of the potential combo is not presently in the mood."

"In the mood. Yes. A song by Glen Miller, isn't it?"

She rolled her eyes. "If I were smart, I'd say, Glen who? Instead, I will compliment you on your efforts to create that which he blew his trombone about. The nicest touch is the

Bach playing softly on the CD."

I listened. All I could hear was a cat screaming in the alley. Okay, Maggie, I thought. I got up and put on the only classical music album I owned. I'd received it as a so-called free gift with some negligee I'd bought at Victoria's Secret for a former girlfriend in New York.

"All right, then, we're getting somewhere," she said. "Speaking of which, where do we begin this project?"

"Okay, okay. You know how to work the computer, so you do that--print out anything that looks interesting. I'll tackle the hanging files."

It was slow going. I was sitting on the floor only a third of the way through the first box when I realized it was almost too dark to see. I got up, stepped over the dog and turned on a lamp.

"Hungry?" I said.

She looked up. "Guess I could use a bite."

Soho yawned.

I ordered a pizza, vegetarian, fed Soho and went back to work until the delivery came. Then I got a beer and a Perrier from the frig and we sat on the sofa with the box. I waited for her to serve herself, then picked up my own slice and stared it in the face. It wasn't pepperoni and sausage but it sure looked good.

"Find anything interesting so far?" I took a bite.

She covered her mouth. "It would help if I knew what I was looking for."

"Let's ask ourselves why someone would commit a murder," I said. "What are some basic motives?"

"Greed. That's where shareholder's agreement comes in."

"So we look for anything that indicates greed, or anything that implies a need for money such as--"

"A favorite cat needs a kidney transplant," she said.

"Oh no, Don't tell me. You're a cat person."

"No, I'm not. These things just pop into my head."

"Thank God. Tell me some other motives."

"Let's see. Anger--rage."

A strand of cheese connected my mouth and the slice of pizza in my hand. I managed to deal with it and say, "No sign of a struggle. That means it must have been premeditated. Rage and anger leave broken lamps and ashtrays. Miss Saran Wrap or Sally or someone else who harbored anger would have to have thought it through, first."

"Yeah. You're probably right. Guess that also rules out love and jealousy since they fall into the violent, unpremeditated ashtray throwing category."

"You throw ashtrays?" I said.

"No. I don't know anyone who smokes. Blackmail?"

"Hummm. Don't think Uncle Rod would blackmail anyone, but I guess we need to be on the lookout for anything that might indicate it."

She took a sip of Perrier. "Ambition and rivalry are good old standbys."

"And self-defense. . . . Naw, that couldn't be. Fear maybe? Fear of being found out? Maybe Uncle Rod knew something, and the murderer wanted to shut him up."

"That would work." Nickie put down the remainder of a slice of pizza, drew her legs under her and rested against the sofa back. "Here's another. How about revenge?" She yawned. "Revenge works for Miss Saran or Sally. They might have been playing the part of cold-blooded, thwarted lover. I kind of like that image. Has the sordid tinge of romance to it."

I put down what was left of my piece of pizza and leaned back, too, my face only half a foot from hers. "Yeah. Poof, and half his head is gone. That's romantic."

"You're right. Revenge is a definite possibility. No doubt your uncle made a few enemies in his time."

"I don't want to coin a phrase here, but you know what they say. They say you can't make an omelet--" I leaned toward her, closed my eyes and pressed my lips to hers.

Our cheese and garlic breath mingled. My testosterone gland kick in.

She pulled away and took a breath. "Sorry, Brian, not tonight. I'm afraid I have the proverbial headache. You see, my mamma told me to keep them guessing. Hope you don't mind, but I always take her advice. When it suits me."

"You're kidding. Aren't you?"

"Yes."

"What is it, then?"

She took time to think, an unusual requirement for her. "How shall I put this? I hope you won't mind if I employ a somewhat tired cliché, but this train is moving just a little bit too fast."

"Really? I thought you liked fast."

"It's difficult for me to admit, especially given the cool, calm and enigmatic image I try so hard to cultivate. But sometimes speed frightens me."

"Seriously? What do you know," I said. "Anything I can do to help? Let's see." I looked around. "You're right. There aren't any seat belts on this sofa."

She took my arm and wrapped it around her. "Okay, if you insist, I'll allow you to be chivalrous this time, but only because I now realize you jocks sometimes need coaching. We'll slow down the train by keeping tonight's contact to a cuddle. Listen carefully for a subtle pointer I'm about to share. The goal is for me to begin to feel close to you, rather than like a hunk of pastrami that you're going to have for lunch." She shifted her weight. "Yes, much better. This is what we'll do for five minutes, then we'll get back to work."

#

I got up at 6:30 the next morning and put on sweats. A troubling dream had caused me to abandon sleep. The sense of loss I felt about Uncle Rod threatened to plunge me into depression if I allowed myself to dwell on it, so the best course was to leave the emptiness of bed. Anything to put my mind in another place, another frame. Anyway, I'd promised Soho a serious workout and it was well overdue. It would get the cobwebs out before the strategy session, which was to take place at nine o'clock.

I got a bag of dry bread which I kept hanging from the door of the broom closet and hooked the red leash to Soho's collar. He saw the bread and got excited; started prancing--bouncing up and down. I ran my hand across the smooth golden hair of his back and told him, "Chill out, good buddy." His coat had become so thick and shiny, it made me proud. When I'd found him he'd been a shaggy stray with mangy bald patches, hair in matted clumps. I'd named him after SoHo--South of Houston in lower Manhattan--where I'd lived before I moved. It had taken the better part of a month for him to gain enough weight for his ribs not to show. I brushed him every night and fed him a high protein diet with a few drops of oil, as the vet had recommended.

We took the my car, top down, all the way out Grove Avenue, which was a straight shot west, past the Virginia Museum of Fine Arts--one of the best in the country--over top of the Downtown Expressway, and past the Shops at Libbie and Grove, a quaint little area which appealed to the silk-stocking crowd. Then, we turned down Three Chopt Road, once an Indian trail blazed with three chops of a tomahawk. I'd always loved this area. The road meandered lazily between huge trees which were now in full autumn glory. Big old homes were nestled in the park-like setting on either side. Antebellum mansions, English manors, Dutch colonials, French country, and even one Spanish style--many went way back in time because the trolley used to run to the end of Grove and then along this road. The turnaround was near the entrance to the University. Back before the end of the nineteenth century and well into the twentieth, when not everyone and his brother had a car, this was where people came to escape the hassle and the heat of the city.

We turned down Towana, then Campus Drive, passed between brick pillars trimmed with stone. In looking at schools to attend, and later as a college football player, I had visited a number of campuses. I could only think of one or two which possessed the charm of this one--Wake Forest and The University of the South, or Sewanee, as it was called. Even Washington & Lee, my first choice when I'd been a high school senior, did not quite measure up. The buildings here were red brick collegiate Gothic with peaked archways of stone and steeply pitched slate roofs. They were nestled under tall trees on gently rolling terrain covered by manicured grass and shrubs, and they were connected by a network of walkways. As the school had grown, the trustees had remained true to the design so that it was all but impossible to tell which were recent and which were original structures.

By the time we reached the lake in the middle, which

separated Westhampton College--the original women's school--and Richmond College, the men's, Soho was beside himself to get out of the car.

Soon we jogged along briskly. I inhaled the cool autumn air and the odor of decaying leaves and algae in the shallow water near the edge. The lake was man-made and there was a little island one could reach over arched, Japanese-style wooden bridges. Soho loved that lake. He loved to bark at the ducks and geese and chase them into the water if they happened to be on the bank. He'd go in after them willy-nilly, splashing and thrashing about. There was no way to keep him dry for long, so I let him have his fun. It seemed a sure bet he had plenty of retriever in him. I even had trouble keeping him out of the shower.

After a couple of loops around the perimeter, maybe a mile and a half run, I settled on a bench on the bank with a couple of sticks and the bread. I'd worked out a system so that Soho would be too busy to bother the ducks or to shake water all over me. I'd throw one stick out. Soho would go barreling after it. Then as soon as he got back on shore I'd throw the second one. Soho would drop the first stick, dive in and swim like mad toward the other. That way I had time to toss bread to the ducks who closed in while he was gone and to spend a few moments in thought.

My mind settled into a reverie and it occurred to me that I never knew how my father had died. Maybe that explained the nightmare I'd just had of finding him in a hut slouched over a table, half his head blown off. You see, my dad was killed in action in Vietnam.

I remembered the funeral as though it were yesterday: The sound of rifles being fired. My mother flinching. A tall, graying man in uniform handing her the folded flag. I'd never seen it after that day.

Afterward, my mother had worked as a receptionist and secretary in a lawyer's office to support us. I was a latchkey kid. Her salary plus social security and Army benefits were barely enough to make ends meet. I'd even selected the college I went to because they'd given me a football scholarship--James Madison University. I'd wanted to go to Washington & Lee, ironically only an hour farther south in the Shenandoah Valley, but the football team at W & L was Division III. They didn't give scholarships.

I threw more bread and did my best to turn my mind from the dream and the memories. I tossed the stick for Soho and went over my suspects and the possibilities--who did it, why--but found I was not in the mood to keep myself focused on the crime. Suppose Sally had done it? Suppose I caught her? Her kids, my nieces, would then be out another parent.

A spray of cold water startled me. Soho was before me, happy and panting, his long tongue hanging over his jaw. He blew air from his nose with an impatient toss of his head and shook again.

I lifted my arm in self-defense, looked at my watch. Time to go. I dumped the rest of the bread into the water and the ducks returned. Soho moved toward them with his ears pricked, so I started away and called him to follow. We jogged toward the car.

The fresh air and the ducks had not helped my mood. For one thing, I couldn't stop thinking about Nickie. Things with her had started with such a bang. Now, the woman I fleetingly had thought might be the girl of my dreams seemed to be having second thoughts. She claimed the train was moving too fast, but that simply did not ring true. She was anything but the meek and mild type who hadn't been around enough to know that when trains were ready to pull out of the station, they didn't wait. I had to face it. Maybe she'd cooled off and this was her way of letting me down. If she had experienced what I had experienced that first night, if all her little nerve endings had gone berserk with heavenly rapture, would she now be holding out?

I had to conclude that I hadn't held up my end.

What I needed was to shift my attention away from satisfying my own libido and give her a series of long, intense, mind-blowing orgasms. Then I would have her groveling at my feet instead of the other way around.

We arrived at the car, and I opened the door for Soho. He jumped in and circled between the open space in back and the seats in front, water still dripping from him. I shoved him into the back, told him to sit, and in a moment was behind the wheel. We were on our way.

As I guided the car along Campus Drive, I thought back to the time just before I'd discovered Uncle Rod's body. It was difficult to believe I'd felt that things were headed my way. Now I faced the prospect of returning to a life of working for others instead of myself.

A scene from my early days at Flint flashed in my mind. The month was May. Outside the sun shone bright, but it was dark in the small, windowless office I occupied on the thirty-nineth floor. The year-to-date profit and loss statement on the Pickwick account was to my left. To my right was a desk calculator I punched in a futile attempt to make uncooperative numbers total something remotely approaching the figure I'd submitted in November.

My boss and the account supervisor on Pickwick, Les Greenhill, poked his head through my door. "Ah, Durston. I see you're working on our problem."

"You betcha, Les."

He didn't smile. "Don't let me down, Durston. Tell me the words I want to hear. Tell me we're going to catch up."

"Sorry, Les." I shrugged. "They had a budget reduction, remember? No way it's going to happen."

His eyes grew narrow. "I have three words of advice, Durston. Make it up."

"But Les. The budget reduction."

"Look, Durston. Our comptroller doesn't care about that. Our CEO doesn't care. We quoted a figure. We're expected to deliver it."

"But there's just no way--not unless I pad the production bills."

"Then pad them."

"What?"

"Pad them."

"But, Les. What if we get audited?"

A spot twitched near his eye. "You'll take the blame, of course. In the meantime, you'll keep your job, you'll continue paying rent and eating regularly, and I'll be off your back."

"That isn't fair, Les."

He gave a little shrug. "Didn't your mother tell you life isn't fair? Welcome to life, Durston."

I lowered my eyes to the printout. For the next seven or eight months I couldn't look my client in the eye. We'd become good friends, too, before that. He had to wonder what the matter was with me. Thank God he never found out. Each time I prepared the billing I added a little here and a whole lot there, and a piece of my soul went straight to hell. When the nightmare finally was over, I promised myself I'd be my own man someday, that I'd be able to tell the Les Greenhills of the world to go take a hike. Now it looked like that wasn't going to happen anytime soon. Imagine having to live with Larry Negus telling me what to do. Sleaziness oozed from his pores.

At nine o'clock I was sitting in the conference room waiting for the others to arrive when white-haired, jowly, liver-spotted Larry Negus walked in.

"Morning, Brian."

I stood, shook hands, and noted one thinning eyebrow slightly raised.

"Mavis tells me you were in your uncle's office yesterday cleaning out his files."

"That's right, except I decided it would be easier if I took them home. I took his computer and his printer, too."

"His computer and printer? That equipment belongs to the agency, and as for his files, well, I guess they are his personal files, but there may well be certain items--"

"I want to go through his stuff, Larry, and that includes

what's on his computer. If I see anything that belongs to the agency I'll turn it over to you. Once I'm finished, I'll bring back the computer and the printer."

Larry looked as though he wanted to say more, but Paul Williams and Ben Haley walked in. They were trailed by Mary MacMann. Everyone helped themselves to coffee and took seats. I walked to a flip chart I had prepared the afternoon before.

"Before I give my recommendation about moving ahead, I'd like to spend a couple of minutes reviewing the market as it now exists for hope chests, or cedar chests as they're also known."

I flipped the first page. "As Rita Maloney told us yesterday there's only one serious manufacturer and that company, which also happens to be based in Virginia, has the market cornered. The company started making chests in 1912 and has been marketing them the same way ever since--as high school graduation gifts for girls. The idea, of course, is for a young girl graduate to have a bridal chest where she can store things until she's married--fine linen and lace, love letters, blankets, china, crystal, you name it."

I reached for a folder of ads which had been ripped from magazines, held up several for them to see, then passed the folder around.

"The company didn't invent this idea in 1912--cedar-lined chests date to the Egyptians. By the Middle Ages in Europe a new bride was expected to bring a trousseau chest with her when she went to join her husband." I turned to the next page of the flip chart. "This map of the United States was generated by our market research people from a syndicated computer data base. It's color coded to indicate where sales of cedar chests are hot and where they are cold. Red indicates a high number of sales per hundred thousand population. Then hot pink, light pink, yellow, light blue and finally, dark blue--for a low number. Look where sales are hot . . . in the deep South, and in Utah--a bright red state in a field of icy blue."

"I can understand the deep South," Ben Haley said with his baritone voice. "Strong traditions, right? But, why Utah?"

"A good question," I said. "The answer has to do with the large Mormon population in Utah. Mormons tend to be traditional, and if I'm not mistaken, fewer Mormon woman go to college than the general population. They also marry earlier."

Paul Williams had been hunched over doodling on a pad. He picked up his creation and admired it, then leaned back in his chair and pointed his pencil at me eraser first. "Know what? I say who gives a shit. We need to go make ads, not contemplate our navels about who buys cedar chests and why. Our target customer's Rita Maloney, not some 19 year-old in Provo. I'm telling you--Rita's going to buy glitz." He held up one of the competitor's ads, which pictured a wholesome-looking girl in her late teens obviously dreaming about Mr. Right. "Look at this shit. For Chrissake, you think Rita Maloney's going to buy crap like this? She'd go into apoplexy if she saw crap like this from us."

Paul didn't even have to act like an asshole to tick me off, so at that moment it was all I could do to keep myself from coming across the table, grabbing him by the lapels of his flowered Hawaiian shirt and slapping him around. But I chose an indirect slap instead and spoke to him the way my fourth-grade teacher, Mr. Brand, used to. He could make any kid in the room feel like Lowly Worm. I said, "No Paul, I don't think Rita will buy advertisements that are like this. Her competitor has been very successful and built a multi-million-dollar business with this approach. She's not going to take away that business by imitating what has already been done. The sort of ad you are holding, Paul, is the hallmark of the dominant brand--the one she needs to position herself against and be perceived as preferable to."

"Yeah? Well, okay--at least we agree on something."

"But frankly, Paul, I'm not so sure she'll buy glitz

either." The volume of my voice continued to increase. "What we need is an approach that's strategically smart. One that sets Benton apart from the competitor without positioning our brand so far away it becomes irrelevant to people in the market for a chest." My voice reached a crescendo. "We will have something worth showing Rita, Paul, when we come up with an idea that has a link with tradition but positions Benton as the cedar chest for today, rather than for a time when young women married at 19--which is how the competitor has positioned himself."

"Glitz. Glitz is the way," Paul said.

"It's one way--maybe," Ben Haley said. He could have been an announcer with that voice. "What are your thoughts, Brian, on how to identify the best position?"

"We need research. We need focus groups among gift-givers--mothers and grandmothers--and gift receivers--girls. We need to find out how the fact that more and more go to college fits into the equation, and how the fact that many work for a while before they marry--move out of their parents' houses or never return once they go away to college. As we all know, many get their own apartment, or share one with a girlfriend. So we have to ask, is there a practical side of this new lifestyle we can capitalize on? Storage space is always at a premium in an apartment, and cedar chests provide storage space. They save room because they can double as coffee tables, you can even sit on them. Plus they are a heckuva smart and practical place to put wool sweaters and blankets in summer to protect them from moths. The bottom line is, in today's world a cedar chest doesn't have to be used strictly as a place for a trousseau for it to make a lot of sense."

"Sounds as though you've already come up with a position," Mary MacMann said. "Why do we need research? Research costs money."

"For several reasons," I said. "To find out if what I've just said makes sense to potential givers, and if it does, how to focus it in a way that sells Benton and not the competition. But, perhaps more important than anything, we need the research for our presentation--to prove to Rita that our recommendation will work." I was getting excited now and leaned toward Mary as I spoke. "What we can do, you see, is video tape people in the groups while they're talking and edit the tape into clips that make points to support our case. I've done it in other presentations and I can tell you, when a client sees her customers telling her the best way to sell the product to them, it's awfully hard for her to argue because it's no longer simply someone else's opinion."

Paul Williams had turned bright red and looked as though he was ready to explode. He slapped his hand on the conference table. "You want consumers to create the ads?" he bellowed. "Jesus Christ, now I've heard it all. Whatever happened to creativity? Why the hell would Rita even need an ad agency if she could do that? I'm telling you, Rita Maloney's going to go with what she likes and not with what some 65 year-old grandmother from Farmville, Virginia, says."

In my most controlled fourth-grade teacher voice I said, "I'm not suggesting our focus group respondents help design ads or even that we show them ads for that matter. If you will recall, I said we need to find out what *selling message* will appeal to them the most. Then, it will be your job to come up with a creative way to put that message across in advertising."

Paul did not respond but I thought I saw smoke rising from his ears.

"How much is it going to cost?" Mary MacMann asked.

"I would say we need a minimum of two focus groups with each segment--girls, mothers, grandmothers--in two different parts of the country. That's a total of twelve groups." I pointed to the map. "One set of six ought to be done in a red area, and the other in blue to see if anything can be done to warm up people who are cool to the product." I scratched my nose. "With travel, video taping, editing, I would say we're looking at about 60 grand or so--out of pocket."

"Sixty thousand dollars? Good Lord," said Mary MacMann. For a second I thought she was going to clutch her heart.

"Couldn't we conduct some of the groups here in Richmond, Brian?" Ben Haley said. "Richmond's not bright red, but it is hot pink."

"I suppose," I said. "That would save several thousand dollars in travel costs, and we could hold the groups here at the agency. That will save the cost of renting a facility."

"And the time our people would spend getting to Alabama or Arkansas and back," Ben said.

"This is all such a crock of shit," Paul said. "You guys are jerking off. I can't believe this--12 focus groups? For God's sake, it would take two weeks and we don't have two weeks. The presentation is next Monday morning."

Today was Friday. "It's in ten days--a *week* from Monday," I said.

"Good Lord, that's Halloween." Larry Negus was looking at his pocket appointment calendar.

"We have time if we bust our butts," I said and turned the page of the flip chart. "Here's a time line. The groups can be recruited over the weekend and conducted Monday and Tuesday nights, three a night--five o'clock, 6:30 and eight--and we'll conduct them simultaneously in two cities."

"We can do one set here in the agency and the other in Chicago," Ben said. "We have a helluva good relationship with The Research Institute and there's a good flight schedule back and forth."

"Good thinking Ben," I said, even though I had already figured on Chicago. "That will give us Wednesday to come down on strategy. Paul, you and your department will have Thursday, Friday, Saturday and Sunday to develop creative executions. At the same time we'll be editing video tape of the focus groups and getting slides made for the prologue and set-up to the creative part of the presentation."

"We can meet here Sunday afternoon and put it all together," Ben said. "I think we can do it."

Paul looked as though he'd just taken a whiff of something rancid. "Four days to come up with an entire campaign? That's putting a shit load of pressure on. I'd rather get started now and have ten days to work on it."

"Put the whole department on it, Paul," Ben boomed. "You've got 30 people. Thirty times four is a 120 man days--surely they can come up with something in that length of time."

"Something--sure. But it's not like a 120 days that are back to back," Paul said. "You want something good don't you?"

"It's one helluva lot of money," Mary said. "We're talking about blowing 60 grand out-of-pocket, for Chrissake. That's a years's salary for a decent copywriter. You do realize it takes $400,000 in billings for the agency to make 60 thousand bucks to chuck it can down the drain. We operate on 15 percent, remember?"

"Your concern for the bottom line is appreciated, Mary," I said. "And your concern about having enough time to do the job right is valid, too, Paul. We won't have the luxury of a false start, but think about this. We're talking about a thirty million dollar account. Four hundred thousand compared to thirty million is a rounding error. And the scary part is, if we lose this account, this company might be thrown into a tailspin we can't pull out of." As words poured from my mouth I made eye contact with each one of them in turn, thinking of the way Rita had done that so effectively. "Now, what do you think The Martin Agency and Arnold are going to do? Think they're going to run off to their offices and do some pretty ads? Or do you think they're going to bust their butts, do their homework, talk to customers and get out into the marketplace, work nights and weekends to put together one heckuva airtight case for whatever they propose? You can be sure that's exactly what they're going to do because they're going to do everything they possibly can do to win. *We* cannot do any less. If we hope to win, we damn well better do more than they do."

"Amen, brother," Ben Haley said.

"We've beat the bastards before and we'll beat them again," Paul said. "And whether we do research or not, we're going to be working nights and weekends. That's nothing new."

"If we lose the account, we're going to wish we had that sixty grand," Mary said. "I'm all for hard work but spending that kind of money is something else."

Larry stood and began pacing along side the conference table. I wondered what had taken him so long.

"You've been awfully quiet, Larry," I said. "What do you think?"

He stopped and put his hands on the table palms down. "I like the idea of being able to stand up there and say, 'Look, this is not just our opinion, this is what your prospective customers said. It's what your customers want and what they're telling us will motivate them.'" He started pacing again. "But that's a helluva lot of money. A helluva lot." He stopped and looked at me. "Why do we have to do twelve groups for Pete's sake? Can't we poor-boy this thing? You know, do a group or two, talk to some dealers, shoot some video tape--hell, we have a couple cameras over in audio visual--we even have some women working here who are the right ages. When we get to the presentation, can't we *say* we did twelve groups?"

"What do you mean, Larry?" I couldn't believe my ears. "You mean you want to *lie* to her?"

"Just a little white lie. I mean, let's think rationally about this. Instead of two, we do three groups. Yeah, that makes more sense. Grandmothers, girls, mothers. That gives you what you need for your video tape. Edit to your heart's content. Then we tell her we did twelve. She'll never know, and anyway, we've done a zillion focus groups before to make sure the findings were consistent. Every damn one of them come out exactly the same."

"I don't believe this," I said. "Do you always *lie* to your clients?"

"We can't do it that way, Larry," Ben said. "Think about this. What if she found out? What if word slipped out to somebody over at Martin or Arnold and they tipped her off? You know the people here and the people at those shops all go to the same watering holes. Loose lips, Larry. Our credibility would be shot to hell. We'd be dead meat."

"Yeah, but sixty thousand clams," Larry said. "That's a helluva lot to give away. And it's only a presentation. Everybody knows a presentation is just show. So we do three groups--for show. If you really think she might find out, then tell her we only did three. We can say she may want to have more done to verify the findings."

"We're talking about a $30 million account, Larry," I said. "We're arguing over peanuts and the Titanic's got a great big hole in its side. We have to do what it takes to plug the hole and it isn't going to be with research that's suspect, research that has to be *verified*. Good Lord, do you think the other agencies would present something lame like that?"

Larry stared at me without speaking. "So maybe we shouldn't do the research at all. Paul makes a damn good point. If we do the research we'll only have four days for creative. As you said, there will be no room for false starts. We've come up dry too many times on short notice when we're under the gun."

"Larry, Larry, give up," Ben said. "You know as well as I do Brian's right. Without something concrete to base our recommendation on we're just some hot shot ad agency shooting from the hip."

"So what the fuck is wrong with that?" Paul said. "What the fuck is wrong with being a hot shot ad agency? Creativity is what sells, creativity's what works, it's what we sell here--or hadn't you guys noticed? God knows we're not in business to sell research." He looked at me. "Or are we?"

I ignored his question and looked at Larry, who sat down, leaned across the table and spoke in a low voice, as if sharing a secret. "You have to admit, he has a point." He opened his hands. "Let's say you've got research. People have told you the best way to sell cedar chests is to tell them it's a damn good looking coffee table that will protect their sweaters against moths." He shrugged. "As an ad that could be boring as hell, and if we show Rita Maloney boring ads, we're dead--deader than dead--research or no research."

"So, what do you suggest, Larry?" I said.

He threw up his hands. "Do it both ways. Spend the fucking money, but do it both ways."

"Both ways?" I said, and the others echoed my words, "Both ways?"

"Maybe you were right earlier, Brian," Larry said. "This presentation is too damned important not to. So let's do the research, and in the meantime let Paul cut loose his guys and gals to come up with as many harebrained ideas as they can." He looked at Paul. "If I know your people, they'll come up with plenty." He looked at me. "Once we have the strategy nailed, they can put all their energy into executing it. If nothing good comes out of it, we'll have the off-the-wall stuff to fall back on."

Ben said, "Sounds like a good plan to me."

Mary said, "I still say sixty thousand is one helluva lot of money, and I don't like spending it one bit, not even this much." She held a finger and thumb close together. Then she shrugged. "But I guess I'll have to go along, under the circumstances."

Paul said, "And I don't like making my people jump through hoops, but it looks as though I don't have a fucking choice."

I said, "Let's get moving," folded up my flip chart and walked out of the room before they could change their minds.

Heads turned, and the predictable rubbernecks bobbed

as I weaved through the agency. Just about everyone was curious about what we were going to do to save our biggest account. People were worried about their jobs. The rumor was out of inevitable layoffs if the account went south.

My first stop was Jill Lathermill's office. I closed her door. "You were right about Paul Williams. He obviously could care less about strategy and research."

"He could care less about almost anything except winning some award show or other," Jill said. "You should see how he blows budgets. It's caused more than one rift with the client, and me more than a few ulcers. I thought old Arthur Fletcher was going to blow a gasket one day. Wouldn't be surprised if that's what made him drive off that cliff."

"Even so, we won, Jill. With Ben's help, they all agreed to do the research--even Paul, although very reluctantly, I can assure you. Larry wasn't an easy sell, either. Thank goodness Ben saw the value in it."

"Hallelujah. My son, my banker, my dog, and my grocer thank you. I thank you, too, but then I knew you would do it."

"You might want to get together with your staff," I said, "and brainstorm some selling positions. Then you and I need to get together with the research department."

"Will do." She gave me a two finger salute.

I stopped at the front desk on the way back to my office and checked my messages. To my surprise Roger Normandy, the president of Flint Advertising, New York, had called. I called him back as soon as I got to my office.

"Brian, thanks for getting back to me," he said. "Listen, I just saw about your uncle in *AD DAY*. I wanted to offer my condolences."

"Thanks, Roger, you don't know how much that means to me." Roger was a certified big shot who hobnobbed with the CEOs of Fortune 500 companies and was hauling down more than a million bucks a year in salary, bonuses and stock options.

"So, how do you feel about being back in the hometown now? Your uncle's death changed anything?"

"Now that you mention it, Roger, my uncle's death has changed the situation here in Richmond more than you might imagine. We were very close at one time and I thought it would be a chance for us to get reacquainted. It was a major reason I took the job."

"That is a shame. Oh, by the way, I guess you heard that Greg Farley left Flint for the number two spot at Omnimessage International."

"No kidding?" Greg Farley was my old boss, an executive vice president who was in charge of all the non-package goods business, which included the airline, the car rental company, a Caribbean country, the big computer manufacturer. Billings he controlled totaled over half a billion--more than six times those of Durston Negus. "Must have been a really good opportunity for him to want to move."

"I suppose it was. He'll be in line for the top spot over there, and I'm sure you know, old Randy Pendergast will be reaching retirement age in a year or two. *Ad Age* speculates Greg already has been promised the job. We hated to lose him though."

"Greg's a very capable guy"

"How about you, Brian? Interested in moving back to New York?"

"I hadn't thought about it, Roger. Anything particular in mind?"

"Greg's job, Brian. If you had stuck around you'd be in it already. But, I know. Your uncle lobbied hard for you to join him. You found it difficult to turn him down. But it occurred to me that your situation has changed. I thought it would be worth seeing how you might feel now about coming back."

I actually took the receiver off my ear and stared at it,

then returned it to my ear.

Roger continued, "The title is executive vice president. The salary is $300,000 a year to start. There are the usual stock options, the executive bonus plan, which is a step up percentage-wise from the one you were already participating in. There's no guarantee, but chances are good your compensation will add up to more than half a million a year."

Half a million a year? "Which accounts are we talking about, Roger?"

"Same ones Greg had--we're not going to mess with any of that. In fact, the beauty is, you already know the people at Trans International and Avent. And don't forget the little serendipity you'd get in the Grenadine Tourism. They have their planning meetings during the height of the season--January--so you'll get the flavor of the place. The schedule is arranged so you have plenty of time to check out the beach, and the beauties *aprés* beach at the bar."

"I could get used to that."

"Do we have a deal, Brian?"

"What about a contract?"

"The usual. For an Exec. V. P."

"What does the usual say about severance if things don't work out?"

"You'll get a two year no-cut guarantee and six month's notice after that."

Two years, guaranteed? Six month's severance?

"It's a good offer and I'm flattered, Roger, but it's so sudden. I hadn't thought about leaving. I guess I need time to think."

"Jobs like this one don't come down the pike every day, Brian. Oh, I forgot. You'll be on the executive committee. One of the top five guys--well, four guys plus Betty Pryer--who set policy."

"Can you give me time to think, Roger? It sounds good. Really good. And you know how much I like Flint. But my mom always said to look before I leap."

"Sure, sure. I didn't think you'd say yes on the spot."

"I'll need a few days at least," I said.

"I'm anxious to get this position filled, but I wouldn't want you to get here and then realize you'd made a mistake. Tell you what, take up to a week if you need it. This is Friday, so let me know no later than the close of business Thursday. If you make up your mind sooner, let me know. I'll get a contract out to you by Fed Ex so you'll have it to review Monday morning."

"Fair enough. I'm really flattered that you thought of me, Roger."

"You're the first person who came to mind, Brian. Is it okay to send the Fed Ex package to your office?"

"Just put it inside an envelope marked confidential. No one will open it."

"Talk to you soon, Brian."

"Right, Roger. Thanks."

7

Three hundred thousand bucks a year. Twice what I'd been making before, probably as high as my salary would ever go at Durston Negus, even as CEO. I'd be able to live like an Arab sheik. Plus, Roger had said it might go to half a million with stock options and bonuses. Heck, I might even be able to start accumulating some net worth.

I thought back to the reasons I'd had for leaving New York. Doing my own thing had been the primary one. Now doing-my-own-thing looked to be in serious jeopardy. But I had new reasons to want to be in Richmond. First, there was Soho. He'd be miserable in a big city. And a misery to live with.

Wait a minute, I told myself. Imagine turning down half a million a year because of a dog.

But I'd never had a dog before. My mom had been into cats.

Then there were the plans about settling down that had begun to form, a development I'd have been hard pressed to convince myself a few months earlier would happen so soon. But Nickie had started me thinking. I wasn't getting any younger and I didn't want to open my eyes some dreary morning in a cold dark city, dogless, wifeless, childless--a bachelor who was set in his ways, cynical probably, maybe bitter--at 50 or 60 or whatever. A rich nihilist who took pleasure in giving the boot to small, stupid-looking dogs. I'd seen guys like that.

I'd had plenty of girlfriends, of course. Women I'd actually become fairly serious with. Ultimately, it always came down to 'Shit, or get off the pot, Durston.' Up until now I had always followed the latter course. I'd only been out with Nickie a couple of times, for goodness sake, and I had to admit she was a little odd. I never could get through *Metamorphosis*. Bean sprouts were okay on a side salad. But, she intrigued me. Life with her would be interesting. Who knew what might develop?

Now that I thought about it, I had no regrets about the former loves of my life--except one: Rachel Linden. Looking back from age 32, it was hard to believe she had only been 19--a sophomore--and I'd been a senior in college, but I'd been crazy about her. Smitten. It was like some unseen force had reached out and pinned my eyes on her the first time I'd seen her--same as when Nickie stood in my doorway--only Rachel had been coming down the steps of Randolph Hall at Sweet Briar College. Not Maggie the Cat, that time. Far from it. More like the blithe spirit from the poem by Shelley. It was her who-gives-a-shit, I-can-deal-with-anything mentality that had snowed me. A veritable blizzard. She'd possessed a lucid sanity that prevented her from taking anything too seriously. Nickie had the same quality.

Yet, I'd let Rachel Linden slip away.

Slip away? Who was I kidding? There was no use trying to soothe my ego about what had happened. She had dropped me like a red hot enchilada at the end of the school year. She'd looked up, moisture in her eyes, the smile nowhere to be seen. "Let me know if you're ever down Sweet Briar way," she'd said.

In my gut, I experienced the initial drop of a high-speed elevator. "What do you mean? We'll be shuttling back and forth a couple of times a month."

She looked at my chest. "Not a good idea, Brian."

"I don't understand."

"College is such a special, carefree time, and I've got two years left. Football games, dances, midwinters at UVA. Pot parties. A long distance romance between Sweet Briar and New York is not the way I want to spend it."

Nickie might take the same position. New York, Richmond. The difficulty of nourishing a long-distance love affair. It would probably come down to shit or get off the pot in a matter of weeks.

Like it or not, Soho and Nickie each gave me pause about accepting Roger's offer.

On the other hand, people did have dogs in New York and long distance romances could work out. Reportedly, a guy at Martin was married to a woman who worked for Delta and lived in Atlanta. They saw each other on weekends, professing to the world that absence makes the heart grow fonder. Shoot. Who knew? Nickie might even agree to follow me to the Big Apple. She was from Long Island, for Pete's sake.

So there I was. In a matter of minutes I'd arrived where I started. No matter how I looked at it, the hardest pill to swallow, the one I saw no way to overcome, was that I'd have to give up my dream of being in control of my life. I'd had a month or so to get used to the idea and I liked the way it felt. The old clichés were dead on. I wanted to be master of my fate, captain of my ship. No Les Greenhill breathing down my neck telling me I had to do stuff that was either dishonest or stupid. The problem was, I might end up with Larry breathing down my neck instead. If I had to have someone back there calling the shots, between him and Roger Normandy, I'd have to pick Roger.

I spent the rest of the morning in the research department with Jill Lathermill working out details of the focus groups. We wanted to be sure we tested every plausible appeal, from the traditional trousseau chest given as a high school graduation gift to that of a practical piece of storage furniture for a young woman just starting out on her own. Jill and her group had already come up with a number of ideas and we held another brainstorming session with the research people and came up with even more.

"Okay, so we do the groups in Chicago and in Richmond simultaneously," I said. "Who goes to Chicago and who stays?"

"I'll go to Chicago," Jill said.

"I don't mind," I said. "I don't have a family to look after."

"My husband will take care of Johnny. It makes sense for you to be here at the groups in Richmond."

"Why do you say that?"

"The Chicago groups might be a bust," she said. "It's more likely the Richmond folks will be receptive to our selling ideas. You're going to present this research to Rita, so it's better for you to witness the good groups firsthand."

Jill had a point, but her willingness to make sacrifices drove home how much she was counting on me to keep her out of the unemployment line.

"Wait a minute, I just thought of something," I said. "You were going to Benton on Tuesday to present the bedroom furniture promotion, and I was going to tag along, remember? This way, you'll be in Chicago on Tuesday."

"I'll get Mark Macon to go with you and to make all the arrangements. Mark's the account exec on consumer and normally the two of us would have gone together, anyway. With you there, they won't even notice I'm missing. Actually, it works out better this way."

The funeral was to be held at St. Paul's Episcopal Church at one o'clock, but you would have thought the mayor of New York had died and it was St. Patrick's Cathedral. Normally, a cannon could be fired down Grace Street at

12:45 and maybe a pigeon would have been hit. But not today. Uncle Rod had drawn so much attendance at his funeral three cops were directing traffic, one of them on horseback.

St. Paul's in Richmond is at the edge of the downtown shopping district near Capitol Square, and ever since the advent of the suburban shopping mall, where you can park free and shop in climate-controlled comfort, there hasn't been a problem at any time of day or night finding a parking place on the street at a meter. But the entire advertising community had turned out, from printers and newspaper space reps to tv and radio time sales people, to the CEO through vice president level of every ad agency in town. There was even a camera crew from Channel Six, which said to me it must really be a slow news day. Anyhow, the area was so jammed I had to park three blocks away.

I hunched my shoulders, turned my collar against a cold wind that whipped through the man-made canyons and did my best to think of something besides dead bodies lying in caskets as I walked by the Carpenter Center, where plays and musicals stopped on their way from Broadway to the boondocks. Built in the '20s when Art Deco was in vogue, it once had been a Loews Theater, the place where *Gone With The Wind* had premiered in Richmond in 1939. During a performance the ceiling looked like a starry sky because of tiny recessed lights. Hidden projectors added to the effect by throwing up clouds that moved slowly by.

My thoughts turned to Nickie. That comment about the train had seemed so out of character. But what if she had meant it? What if she really was a vulnerable little girl under the self-assured veneer? That might mean she actually felt something for me. Could I be something more to her than a juicy hunk of beef?

Okay, wrong metaphor.

I thought back to the way she had looked standing in the doorway of my office that first time. What had she said at the bar? She was going down the phone list. Now she'd sampled the Ds. With my luck, she'd simply decided I wasn't good enough in bed. Now she was putting on the brakes; looking for an exit.

Horns honked, engines raced. I pulled up to wait for one of Richmond's finest to stop traffic so that those of us waiting on the curb could cross. I stared at Saint Paul's Church, a white rectangular box with columns like the Parthenon, except it had a steeple. I wondered if it had been inspired by the Capitol, fifty yards away, which Thomas Jefferson had designed with ancient Greek democracy in mind.

The cop blew his whistle, cars came to a stop. I walked across and up steps surrounded by familiar faces I'd seen at the one Richmond ad club meeting I'd attended the week before. I slipped into the back of the sanctuary and stood for a moment looking around for someone who might be able to point out Miss Saran Wrap. My gaze took in the polished wood casket in front of the altar. The church was filling up.

Then I spotted Ham Sheldrake, the comptroller of the agency. "Ham, good of you to come." We exchanged small talk about the size of turnout and how nice the church looked. "Oh, by the way," I said. "Will you point someone out to me?"

"Sure."

"I'm curious about a woman named Lauren who left the agency four or five months ago. Have you seen her?"

"Lauren?" His brow wrinkled, then his eyes lit up. "Oh yes, Lauren. Blond, slim." He cupped his hands in front of his chest and faked a whistle. "Haven't seen her."

"Oh, well," I muttered.

"There's Paul Williams over there," Ham said. "Late, as usual."

"Oh, I've been wanting to ask you something, Ham. The talks with Transpublic, I never really got a chance to speak to my uncle at length about them. We talked about them some, of course, but our conversations were always brief." I waited for my nose to grow but it didn't. "I'm curious. Were all the partners for it?"

"Larry and Ben were doing most of the talking with them as far as I know--so I imagine they must have been. Funny, though, your uncle didn't seem all that enthusiastic, but you probably know better than I. I've no idea what Mary and Paul thought."

Maybe Uncle Rod was trying to block the Transpublic deal. Then it struck me, could Roger's offer for me to come back to Flint somehow be connected?

"Do you know whether the agency was to be folded in to one of Transpublic's existing properties?" I asked. "Flint Worldwide, for instance?"

"You're talking to the wrong guy." He touched my arm. "That woman halfway down the aisle. That's Lauren McGee--the lady you asked about."

I took one look and knew instantly that Uncle Rod had been making it with her. Thin, long legs, a slit up her skirt. At a funeral yet. At least the skirt was black. Her hair was too blond and she had on too much makeup, but she was a certified knock-out in a tawdry way. Also a candidate for breast reduction surgery.

I imagined her wrapped in Saran. Whoa.

Uncle Rod had been a red-blooded American egotist who thought the rules applied to everyone but him. He'd have found it nearly impossible to turn down the advances of this one.

She could be the shooter all right--a woman scorned, as the saying went. Or, maybe she'd been blackmailing him and he had threatened to turn her in. Who knew? Or maybe Sally had blown out Uncle Rod's brains just for looking at her too hard. Either way, it fit.

Ham Sheldrake cleared his throat. "I'd better sit down," he said. "Guess you're up front with the family, right?"

I said I supposed I was, thanked him, and started up the aisle. I walked along and glanced over the sea of heads and another thought suddenly shouted at me for attention. It had to do with my impromptu question about the possibility of folding Durston Negus into Flint. It had sprung forth as though it had been lying impatiently beneath the surface of my conscious mind, itching to be examined. Transpublic International owned Flint, and Transpublic had been negotiating to buy Durston Negus. A Tarot card reader once had told me that coincidences didn't exist. No doubt about it. Something was fishy.

As funerals go it was as good as they come. I joined Sally and the girls on the front row. Eulogies were given by some of the top advertising people in town including Harry Jacobs, Chairman Emeritus of The Martin Agency and Tim Finnegan, likewise of Arnold. This belied the idea I'd gotten somewhere that Uncle Rod had made enemies of them.

As I sat and listened I was so moved by what they said that I felt compelled to stand up myself and say a few words about the fact that Uncle Rod had taken me under his wing when my father was killed and how he had always set a fine example for me. I also said how much I'd looked up to him and would miss him now that he was gone. Funny what emotions can do.

I was a pallbearer, of course, and after we slipped the casket into the hearse I made a beeline for my car. The procession to the cemetery was sure to be long and I didn't want to be the last in line. I weaved downhill as fast as I could through the crowd on the sidewalk.

Someone grabbed my arm. "How about some company, lover boy?"

"Sure," I said.

Nickie fell in step beside me.

A few minutes later we were headed out Main, about twenty cars back in a long line.

"What you said in there was touching," she said. "This

must be difficult for you."

"He had a big influence on me."

We rode in silence for a while. That hollow feeling came over me and I tried to shake it off. "Ham Sheldrake pointed out Miss Saran Wrap to me," I said to put my mind somewhere else.

"Tell me about her."

I gave her the full description. I also told her about my woman-scorned idea.

"Could be," Nickie said. "Women who make themselves up like that are usually insecure underneath."

"Another thought is that maybe she was blackmailing him and it turned ugly. He threatened to come clean and go to the police. She decided to do him in so he couldn't rat on her."

"Anything is possible with the type of woman you described."

"So how are we going to find out?"

"I'll check around and see if she has, or had, any girl friends at the office. Women love to talk. Especially about men. Speaking of which, want to hear what I've learned so far?"

"About the partners? Which?"

"All three, of course."

"No kidding. How?"

"Paul was easy. After all, he's the head of my department. Actually, I knew a lot about him already. One of those catty, chatty girls in accounting told me about Mary. Now, Larry was more difficult."

"Who told you about him?"

"Mavis Alfonso," she said.

"His secretary? How indiscreet."

"Amazing what you can find out if you ask."

She touched a button on the center console, cracked the window on her side and drew in a breath. "Who do you want first--Paul, Mary, or Larry?"

"Tell me about Paul." He was my preference for who

did it.

"Grew up in California. His father was in films, though the stories differ on exactly what his father did. Some say he was a director, others that he was a set maker." Nickie glanced out of the window again. I admired her profile. "Anyway, Paul grew up around movies and had an aptitude for art, earned top honors at the Pratt, took a job back on the West coast with Chiat Day. He was brilliant, won all kinds of awards, but has the dubious distinction of being one of the only creatives anyone knows about who was actually fired from the place." She caught my eye.

"Fired?" I cut my eyes back to the road. "I thought they coddled award show winners like golden geese."

"Apparently he never brought a job in on budget once. But by itself that probably wouldn't have done it. The last straw was he got in a fist fight with his supervisor."

"That would do it."

"Anyhow, he came to Durston Negus right after that. They were willing to take a chance on him because they needed a big name--the agency was still in the start-up mode. Your uncle hired him, at least that's what I've been told."

"Has he any particular need for money?"

"I don't think so."

Something about the way Nickie's skirt wrinkled around her thighs kept drawing my eyes. Unfortunately, she noticed and smoothed it out. I forced my eyes back on the road and couldn't help thinking that Nickie looked like Maggie the Cat, and sometimes she acted like Maggie the Cat, but that maybe she was the one who was insecure--as she'd said about Miss Saran.

Pot? Kettle?

"His family's still on the west coast," she continued. "Nobody knows much about them. He's not married--no children. The rumor--which he's been known to fan--is that his salary is right below whatever your uncle's was. Makes more than Larry Negus. The buzz says he bragged to a client the other day that he's now top dog on the payroll."

Paul's status on the payroll was not all that surprising. The creative director often was the most highly-paid executive in an agency.

"Cocaine, maybe," I said.

"I don't see any signs. No runny nose. He's manic but consistently so. No big mood swings."

"Uh-huh. He's consistently a jerk."

We were cruising through one red light after another. The cops were doing a good job.

"Tell me about Larry," I said.

"Let's save him for last. First, I'll dispense with Mary MacMann."

"Shoot."

"Mary's home-grown. Born and raised in a nearby burb called Glen Allen. She went to high school there, then to the College of William & Mary in Williamsburg on an academic scholarship."

"A smart one."

"So it would seem. Majored in English and journalism. She also has a master's in English from the University of Richmond. Started her career in PR at The Martin Agency, switched to the ad side and shot up the corporate ladder." Nickie played with a strand of her hair. "A real workaholic, they say--had a reputation for getting things done. Was enticed away by a client, then the company she was with went through downsizing and she was out on the street along with a few hundred other middle managers. Your uncle persuaded her to come back to the agency side with the understanding she wouldn't have to do account work-- apparently she'd had enough. She's been the top administrative dog at Durston Negus ever since. From all accounts she's done a top notch job. Has the respect of both the creative and the account people, although she's thought of as being overly anal. Runs traffic with an iron hand, keeps a tight rein on budgets. Has at least one run-in a week with Paul over blown production estimates."

"Married?"

Nickie shook her head. "She's lived with the same girlfriend for fourteen or fifteen years, or so I'm told. Grapevine says they're a couple."

"I see. Either of her parents need a heart transplant?"

"Both are in good health. Frankly, I think we can cross her off the list."

The procession was rounding the corner onto North Thompson Street by the state-run store where I stocked up on Dewar's. If you were in Virginia, wanted a bottle of liquor and didn't know what ABC stood for, you were out of luck.

"So that you won't be disappointed, I've saved the best for last." I heard the whisper of nylon rubbing against nylon as she uncrossed her legs. "It may be that Larry Negus is our man."

"Ah-ha," I said, proud of my powers of concentration. Nylon? What nylon? "Why would it not surprise me if Larry did it?"

"He's an old school ad guy--a relic. As you can tell by looking at him, he's been banging around in this business a long, long time."

"Forty years, I'll bet."

"He's made a lot of money and he's lost a lot. This is the third agency he's been a partner in. The first one did quite well, and he sold it. The second one went bust and took what he made on the first one down the tubes with it--as the story goes. He had a few accounts that were loyal to him, though, and that's why your uncle went into business with him."

"Benton Industries?"

"No, some little ones. I don't think they're still with the agency. Rumor has it, your uncle was the guy who brought in the Benton account--right after he and Larry hung up a shingle."

"So why do you think Larry has a motive?"

"He has a definite need for cash."

"How so?"

"The slime-ball is divorcing his wife of thirty some years for what has become known in the current vernacular as a trophy bride."

"And he needs money."

"Big time." She looked out the window. "Aside from alimony that will keep her in the style to which she no doubt wishes to remain accustomed, wife number one is entitled to at least half of everything, and everything's all tied up in real estate, stock in the agency, and a 401(k) retirement plan that he can't touch without getting killed by taxes. And, according to Mavis, this trophy bride he is so hot to marry is a money-grubbing little tart who will drop Larry like a smelly anchovy if he can't keep her all the way up to her silicon tits in diamonds and furs."

Such vehemence. But then I like a woman with a touch of venom and verve. "Looks like Larry's our number one suspect," I said.

"We can't rule out Ben and Paul. Or Miss Saran Wrap. Or Sally the Wife, for that matter."

The procession turned onto Patterson. Darned if it wasn't starting to rain. "I'm also reluctant to rule out Mary, too, at this point."

"She's only a remote possibility."

"What we need now is find out where Larry was between seven-thirty and eight last Tuesday night."

"It would be a good idea to check out the other three while we're at it. And I don't think we should quit with the files and the computer." She crossed those shapely legs again. I had to force myself to concentrate on the road ahead.

I watched Sally all through the grave-side ceremony. She seemed so stoic that I couldn't help wondering again if she hadn't found out about Miss Saran and done in good old Uncle Rod. How else could she appear so cool?

The insurance money, I kept telling myself. She'd have

staged it another way.

Her two girls, on the other hand, looked so forlorn and tearful that my heart went out to them. I wanted to comfort them but what could I say that could possibly help?

When the crowd began to disperse, I made my way through and met Sally. She looked up at me with hollow eyes. "Oh, Brian, I'm so depressed, I'm numb. I can't even cry, anymore. We're going to have to sell both houses and retrench. I may even have to pull the girls out of the school they've gone to all their lives. Both are devastated. I am, too."

"Why, Sally? Didn't Rod have insurance?"

"Yes, of course he did. But, Brian, I learned something. A shocking lesson. Insurance companies don't pay, at least most don't, if the insured commits suicide."

"You didn't know that?"

"How would I? I never suspected Rod to take his own life."

I sat in silence most of the way back into town. Nickie respected the need I had for reflection.

Finally, I said, "You know, if Sally did it, I don't think I want to find out. Those kids have been through enough. Even two million bucks wouldn't make up for what it would do to them to learn that their mother killed their father."

Nickie looked at me out of the corner of her eyes. "I understand what you're saying. Besides, if she did knock him off, he probably had it coming."

The frantic chirping of birds woke me on Saturday. The temperature had been perfect for sleeping with the window open, so I'd left it up. I laid in bed and stared into the burnt orange leaves of the old elm and wondered what someone who lived in SoHo would have thought if a gaggle of feathered creatures trying to coax the sun over the horizon had awaken them from a sound sleep. Then Nickie's face flashed before me. It was becoming a permanent fixture. Even so, I was starting to wonder if I shouldn't try to forget her and move on. She seemed to be giving me the cold shoulder treatment. Before we even made it to the cemetery I'd asked her to go to dinner with me. She'd said she was behind schedule on her novel and preferred to take a rain check. I had the impulse to fall on my knees. Instead I said, "Oh, I see. Well, how about tomorrow? Can you come over and help me go through the files?"

"It's not that I'm trying to put you off, Brian, really. But I made a promise to myself I'd spend free Saturdays and Sundays working on my novel. Paul has already warned us we will be working on the Benton pitch next weekend."

"That novel is awfully important to you, isn't it?" I

hoped to heaven it really was the novel. Maybe it was my penchant for red meat. Heck, I could become a vegetarian if that's what it was going to take.

"As important to me as your dream of running an ad agency," she said.

"Okay, but what about Saturday night? You're not going to work on Saturday night. You've got to take a break sometime. How about spending it with me?"

"What do you have in mind?"

"Dinner at my place." I held my breath.

She shrugged and nodded. That impish smile appeared.

That Friday evening I had a candlelight dinner with Soho, and another lonely night. Saturday morning came and I had all day to comb through those files and look at documents on the computer. Of course, I also needed to clean up the mess in the living room, finish painting if at all possible and go to the store. First, though, Soho and I went on a long run around the lake at the U of R and he got his fill of swimming after ducks and sticks and tennis balls.

I had high hopes of setting a tender trap for Nickie, and I wanted to cook one of my specialties. Steak was out, so I settled on *coq au vin*. That should impress her, and perhaps serve as prelude to what I hoped would be my demonstration of sexual prowess. Soho seemed to approve of my plan. I'd need red wine, brandy, mushrooms, salt pork, onions, and herbs to make a *bouquet garni*. And the chicken. You need the right kind, an old one that's tough as leather so it would withstand the stewing. The name of the dish even implied the type of bird. The French word *coq* means rooster.

By seven when Nickie was scheduled to arrive, I'd accomplished everything I'd set out to do except paint the living room. I'd found an interesting and incriminating memo in Uncle Rod's files. The *coq au vin* was ready for the chafing dish. The table was set with a red linen cloth. There were new candles in antique silver candlesticks. I'd even taken time to brush Soho until his coat shined. A ten year old bottle of merlot was open and breathing, ready to rush down the gullet and into the bloodstream--where I hoped it would loosen inhibitions, perhaps even stimulate desire.

The doorbell rang. I felt a hint of butterflies in my gut.

Nickie handed me a bottle of chardonnay as she walked in.

"Yes, I'll have some, thank you," she said in her deadpan way. "What a day, what a night. It's great to take a break."

"Busy?" I gestured to the sofa. "Oh, by the way, there's cold chardonnay in the frig."

"Cold would be wonderful." She sat and exhaled. "I worked until three this morning, was back at the keyboard at eight. Signed off an hour ago."

As I fixed drinks she told me how she had been in the flow, as some athletes called it when they were clicking--their game at full potential. She hadn't even taken a break for lunch.

I handed her a glass of chardonnay--the cold one I already had open--and sat down next to her.

"Two chapters. Two whole chapters. I've never done that much in twenty four hours."

I held up my highball glass. "To your novel. May it be a blockbuster."

She took half the glass in one long swallow.

"How did your sleuthing go?" she said as she settled back.

"Pay dirt."

Her eyebrows lifted. "Tell me."

"I went though every one of the hanging files. There's a lot of stuff in them but I didn't find anything incriminating. Only got a third of the way though the files in the computer, and that's where I found it."

"What?" She took another long sip.

"A memo from Uncle Rod to Paul Williams with a copy to his personnel file. It documented a dozen instances Paul had gone way over budget on jobs."

She yawned. "So what else is new? He had a history of that at Chiat Day. They should have known it was going to happen and padded the production estimates." She polished off the rest of the wine.

I picked up her glass and went for a refill, speaking over my shoulder. "That's what they did, at least that's what the memo inferred. Of course, Uncle Rod didn't say they padded the estimates, who would want that in writing? But he did say they allowed ample room for overruns, adding twenty to twenty five percent above what similar jobs should cost, according to 4-A averages." I returned with a full glass and the rest of the bottle, which I put on the coffee table in front of us. "Can you believe it? Even with twenty to twenty five percent more than normal to work with, he still couldn't bring an ad in on budget."

She drank. "Oh, I believe it, I've seen him in action. Changes his mind constantly and has things redone up to the minute an ad goes out the door. The changes are what cost."

"Anyway, the memo put him on official notice. It gave him six weeks to shape up or he'd be out the door."

"Whoa. When was it written?"

"Friday a week ago would have been the final day of his probation. Uncle Rod was killed on Tuesday."

"And you think he committed murder because your uncle was about to fire him?" She took looked into her glass doubtfully. "No, Brian. The guy may be a jerk, and I'll grant you he can't stay on budget. But he's also a genius. He could get another job in a heartbeat. In fact, he was bragging about an offer just the other day." She took another sip.

I was sure Nickie's was wrong, for once. "Well, I'm mildly surprised, Sherlock. Have you forgotten about the Transpublic deal? Have you forgotten about the shareholder's agreement? If Paul gets fired, the agency has to buy back his stock. Then, if the agency is sold, Paul Williams is out two million bucks, which by the way conveniently becomes three million with Uncle Rod dead."

She took the bottle and poured herself the rest. "So you think it's greed, plain and simple. That's his incentive to stay at Durston Negus?"

"Of all the partners, Paul Williams is the one I can most easily picture committing cold blooded murder."

"I think any one of them is capable."

"Of course, the one thing we don't know is whether Uncle Rod really was going to fire him. The guy may have shaped up, although I doubt it."

"Rest assured, he hasn't shaped up," she said. "I've seen him making plenty of last minute changes in the past two weeks.

The belt that'd been strapped tight around my chest for days now had finally dropped loose. I took a deep breath. Uncle Rod's murder would be avenged. The two million restored. I wouldn't have to go through life as someone else's pawn.

"There's one thing that bothers me," Nickie said.

The belt was back. "What's that?"

"Creative types usually aren't motivated by greed. They want to be free to create. That takes money, of course, but once their basic needs are taken care of, they usually stop thinking about it." A wrinkle appeared in her brow. "Paul Williams's basic needs are more than taken care of--there seems no doubt of that." She covered her mouth and yawned.

"So maybe Paul is an exception. You'll have to agree he's a jerk."

Nickie's eyes searched the ceiling. "Maybe, but I wouldn't stop looking through those hanging files. I can't help thinking you must have missed something."

"Why? Intuition?"

"More than that. You told me it was obvious someone had been going through them when you looked the first time."

"So? Maybe they found whatever they were looking for."

"If whoever it was found what they were looking for, why'd they leave the files in disarray? Why tip you or the police off that they'd been looking for something?"

"Because they were interrupted, of course."

She yawned again. "So you think they found whatever they were looking for. But they found it the instant before they heard someone coming and that would be why they didn't have time to straighten up. Pretty unlikely, I'd say."

"Okay, Okay. You're probably right. I'll keep looking. Tomorrow I'm going into the office and steal a peek at everyone's appointment calendars--especially Paul's."

"And Larry's," she said.

"And Larry's, and Ben's, and Mary's. And on Monday, you're going to check out Miss Saran."

"Check."

I stood. "Dinner's ready when you are. Another glass of wine, first?"

"Sure, why not?"

I went into the kitchen to open a new bottle. Nickie was sharp. Maybe she was sharper than me, hard though it was to admit. Nevertheless, I disagreed that Paul would not be motivated by money. This wasn't petty cash. This was millions. He'd be set for life to create to his heart's content.

I pulled the cork and returned to the living room. A low, flat buzzer sounded in my brain at what I discovered there: Nickie sound asleep.

I put a blanket over her. I had the hope, of course, that sometime during the night she would wake up, realize what happened and crawl in bed with me.

But no such luck. Sunday morning I found a note on my kitchen table that read:

> *Dear Brian,*
>
> *It's 5:45 in the morning, if you can believe that. I'm really sorry; I know*

*how hard you must have worked on dinner.
Freeze it, will you---please? We'll have
it another night.*

*You can't imagine how hungry I am.
Didn't eat yesterday, except the usual
wheat germ for breakfast, so I'm headed to
the golden arches. No bean sprouts or tofu
there, but the Egg McMuffins are great.
Please forgive me. (I'll do my best to forgive
myself.)*

Love,

Nickie

P.S. Is Canadian bacon classified as red meat?

I looked at my watch. It was eight o'clock. She'd be back home, back in front of my nemesis, the computer. Might as well go into the office and see what I could find.

A scrap of paper blew down the cobblestone street between closed shops and restaurants, turning flips like a tumble weed in an old western movie. It was hard to believe Shockoe Slip could be so transformed from what it surely had been only hours before, in the wee hours when the bars were still open. Except for three cars parked near the agency, there was no evidence of life. But the cars were a tip off I may not have the place to myself. There was a Chrysler Le Baron convertible, a late model Toyota Celica, and a twenty-year-old BMW 525i coupe. A twinge of disappointment settled in as I recalled that just such a BMW belonged to Paul Williams. It would be difficult if not impossible to have a look at his appointment calendar. Worse, I might also have to speak with the egotistical S.O.B.

The alarm was turned off but the door was locked. I used my key and went first to the lower level to see what I could find in Mary MacMann's office. Might as well get the easy ones out of the way.

Her office was austerely furnished and incredibly neat. Not a speck of dust. Her in-box was as empty as Mother Hubbard's cupboard. On her credenza was a photograph of her hugging a middle-aged couple whom I guessed were her parents.

I circled to her side of the desk and opened her appointment calendar.

It looked as though she had been in town on Tuesday. Appointments were penciled in throughout the day--nothing after four o'clock, however--and one at nine o'clock on Wednesday morning. A line had been drawn from that to Thursday at ten. Probably she had rescheduled as a result of Uncle Rod's death.

I closed the calendar. She could not be eliminated.

I turned to leave and noticed something she'd had framed and hung where she would surely see it every time she looked up: *A Penny Saved Is a Penny on the Bottom Line.*

It occurred to me as I climbed the stairs that this little homily called out for a payoff: *And after the penny has shown up on the bottom line three years in a row, you can multiply it by ten, provided you sell the agency to Transpublic International.*

I moved along a darkened corridor and slipped through the open doorway of Ben Haley's office. The place looked lived in. One wall was devoted to drawings and paintings by children, which were stuck up with thumb tacks and Scotch tape. His in-box was stacked a couple of inches over the top. Three piles of papers were on one end of his desk, probably working their way over the side into the round file. Photographs of an attractive young woman and two towhead boys under the ages of ten were turned toward him, rather than facing out for the benefit of others.

One photograph on his credenza was, however, positioned for all who entered to see: a picture of Ben in a Durston Negus t-shirt and baseball cap being carried off the field on the shoulders of his co-workers. He must have been proud to have been responsible for a big win. Home run with the bases loaded, perhaps. Would a guy who was so proud of something like winning a softball game kill the boss for a few paltry million? I wondered.

He might. He might even justify his actions by telling himself he was doing it for the wife and kids he cared so much about.

On the other hand, what would the wife and kids think if he happened to get caught? Wouldn't he consider that?

His appointment calendar was scribbled on in pencil and in different colored inks. It looked as though he'd also been in town. Nothing was on it between four o'clock Tuesday afternoon and nine o'clock the next morning.

So much for my goal of eliminating suspects.

I strolled past that gaudy reception desk in the lobby. Muffled shouts and expletives wafted from the creative department on the upper level. Paul Williams no doubt was staging one of his tirades. There'd be time enough to investigate. I was headed to have a peek in Larry's office.

Next to Uncle Rod's, it was furnished equally as lavishly, had the same twelve-foot ceiling but wasn't quite as large. Maybe it was twenty-by-twenty. It looked to me like a gentleman's library in an English manor house: Mahogany paneling below a polished mahogany chair rail, which had been ripped out of an old men's social club when the building had been razed. A red and blue Sheriz, which was too new for my taste. Dark blue leather wing chairs. A hand-rubbed antique partner's desk. The air was scented with pipe smoke and tannin. I wondered if the scent came in an aerosol can.

Larry's desk was almost bare, except for a leather blotter and a desk set boasting sterling silver fountain pens. On one corner was a photograph of the old boy himself decked out in white-tie attire, beaming, his arm around a woman in her 20s, a bride dressed in a long white wedding gown with plenty of lace. Had to be his daughter.

I tried some drawers. They were locked. Nowhere was

anything that looked even remotely like a calendar. Darn. Nothing to do but move on.

Voices grew louder as I drew abreast of the big ficus trees that stretched up toward the skylights. The sound came from the conference room that the creative staff used for brain-storming sessions.

I decided to make my presence known and poked my head in. Henry Mack and Cathy Hyman--an art director and copywriter team--sat at a round table. Paul stood before a glossy black wall splattered with dozens of sheets of sketch paper covered with lines and squiggles.

"Hi guys," I said.

Paul turned. "Well what do you know, a *suit*. Sunday, too." He beckoned. "Come in, Sunday suit. We need an opinion. These shit heads don't agree with me, and there's an offhand chance you might have more sense."

I stepped in. "What's up?"

"Got a big session tomorrow with E. C. Poppins Pharmaceuticals," Paul said. "We're presenting their new corporate ad campaign. This is your chance to put in two cents."

"Okay," I said. "But before you show me anything, tell me what they're trying to accomplish?" I was aware Poppins had come up with a budget to fund a schedule in slick magazines such as *Fortune, Forbes, Time,* and *Newsweek,* but beyond that I was only vaguely familiar with the account.

"It's a corporate I.D. thing," Paul said. "Objective's a little hazy. Ask the corporate communications guy, he'll tell you they want to goose the price of their stock. The marketing people say whatever we do should be designed to sell more pills. If they sell more pills, the price of the stock will increase automatically."

"What about their products?" I said. "Are they mostly over the counter, or are they prescription?"

"They make both. Spend more money to advertise the over the counter stuff as I'm sure you can imagine. But the fact is, they do more volume in prescription drugs."

I nodded and sat down. "What have you got?"

Paul explained that they had narrowed the concepts to two options. He pulled a sheet of sketch paper from the wall and pointed to a curvy horizontal line with a small stick figure below it.

"What we have here is a gorgeous color photograph taken on the beach at twilight, or maybe it's daybreak. The wide angle lens makes the ocean look really vast like it curves off into space. We want to capture a sense of infinity. A few whitecaps are here and there, and a soft, pinkish glow glimmering on the waves. This is a little boy walking at the water's edge, the foam almost at his feet, footprints behind him trailing off in the distance. It's like he's wondering what's out there beyond the horizon on the other side of the ocean. Okay, Cathy, read the copy."

She searched in a pile and picked out a piece of paper. "What I'm going to read is a quotation from Sir Isaac Newton. It would be the only copy except for the E. C. Poppins logo. Okay, here goes, 'I do not know what I may appear to the world; but to myself I seem to have been only like a boy playing on the seashore, and diverting myself in now and then finding a smoother pebble or a prettier shell than ordinary, whilst the great ocean of truth lay all undiscovered before me.'"

I let the quotation and the visual sink in.

"That's nice," I said. "I like the quote."

"The idea is to make people feel all warm and fuzzy about the effort Poppins puts into R and D," Paul said. "Okay, now--"

He snatched another piece of paper off the wall and held it up for me to see. The squiggles on this one looked like two heads side by side with one slightly higher on the page than the other. Underneath the lower head was what I took to be the outline of an open book.

"Okay, now," Paul said. "This is a guy in his twenties who has obviously fallen asleep and his head has landed on an open book that he's been studying. Up here is a woman, no doubt his wife, who is looking over his shoulder to see if he's awake or what. She's holding a coffee pot in one hand like she's just arrived to give him a refill." He looked at Henry again. "Don't forget the fucking pot when you render the comp, okay? There's no indication of one here."

"Right," he said, and lettered carefully on a pad: "The fucking coffee pot."

Paul continued. "The headline says, 'Evening at Home.' The copy talks about all the hard work and sacrifice that goes into becoming a doctor--the years of study, family members busting ass to make ends meet and not seeing one another as much as they'd like, the all-nighters studying for exams like this guy is doing now. You get the picture. The copy closes by drawing a parallel between all the sacrifice and determination it takes to become a doctor and the years of laboratory work needed to develop a miracle drug like whatever it is Poppins makes."

He tossed the sheet of paper on the table. "So what do you think?"

I picked up the two sheets and looked at them side by side.

"I think they're both good, and I'm impressed. But I think approach number two will sell more pills."

A corner of Paul's mouth lifted. Henry and Cathy shook their heads.

"And why do you think that?" Paul said.

"I think doctors are going to love approach number two," I said. "I mean, it seems like all they do is catch crap about making so much money. This gives them a pat on the back by pointing out how hard they worked to get where they are."

"And?" Paul said.

"And that means they're going to like E. C. Poppins. A doctor will look at an ad like that and say, 'Thank God someone's finally recognized all I've been through to get where I am today.' As a result, he'll be more likely to prescribe E. C. Poppins pills when there's a choice between two brands."

"Thank you, Mr. Durston," Paul said. "You heard the man, Cathy, Henry. A totally unbiased third party opinion. Guess that settles it."

"I'll bet it wouldn't have been settled if he had picked the other one," Cathy said.

"Little Miss Sour Grapes," Paul said. "I know. You thought you'd get a trip to Florida or California to take the shot on the beach, right? Tisk, tisk. This time you lose, but I'll try to make it up to you someday."

I stood. "Thanks guys."

"Anytime, Durston," Paul said.

"By the way," I said. "Are you going to be at the focus groups for Benton Monday night?"

"Afraid I can't make it," he said. "I'll be there Tuesday, though."

"I'm sure our paths will cross before then," I said and exited the room.

I went straight down the hallway to Paul's office, figuring he would either be arguing with them or crowing about this victory long enough for me at least to have a peek at his appointment calendar.

I had to admit that I hadn't expected Paul to possess the marketing savvy he'd just demonstrated. A creative person with an art background such as Paul could usually be counted on to pick aesthetics over smart marketing any day. The ad with the boy on the beach certainly was more pleasing aesthetically than the one with the doctor. But there could be no doubt that relating to doctors would pay more dividends to Poppins Pharmaceuticals than enigmatic ads with beautiful shots of oceans and sunrises. What surprised me was that Paul Williams agreed.

The walls of his office were covered with layouts and ads that had been ripped out of magazines and taped up. Papers and books were piled on his art table and strewn on his credenza. Some also were stacked underneath his computer stand. It took me awhile to find his calendar under all that debris.

How much longer did I have?

My pulse raced when I saw he'd had an appointment with Uncle Rod at 4:30 that fateful Tuesday afternoon. An ice cube dancing to the rhythm of Chopsticks darted up my spine as I read what he'd written in parenthesis under the notation: "Six-week review." Plus, there was no indication he'd gone out of town or had anything else going on that evening.

I hadn't ruled out Larry. In my book he was sleazy enough to have bumped off his own grandmother. Ben was a possibility, too, whether or not I liked it. Mary's love for pennies on the bottom line certainly caste doubt on her. Sally and Saran also remained possibilities. Nevertheless, I was convinced now that Paul had the strongest motive. It was one that spanned centuries and traversed cultures. Even Christ's trusted disciple, Judas, had betrayed his master for a measly thirty pieces of it: Good old fashioned money.

9

Midway through Monday morning, as I sat at my desk and wondered how in the world I could nail Paul Williams, another matter broke through to compete for attention. It had to do with the Fed Ex package I'd just received from Roger Normandy. Thursday was the deadline to let him know whether I would accept his offer.

If only there were some way to hold back the hands of the clock. But no such luck. They just kept moving--one tick at a time. If I decided not to return to New York, if I did not accept Roger's offer, I had only until a week from Wednesday to come up with more than $500,000 to buy Uncle Rod's stock. This realization gave me hot flashes. Beads of sweat formed on my brow.

The phone rang.

"Sorry about Saturday night, lover boy."

"Not to worry, you're forgiven," I said. "And in luck, too, because I froze the *coq au vin*. Too bad we probably won't have a chance to sample my culinary skill until after the Benton pitch. It's going to be a marathon around here--focus groups tonight and tomorrow night. I also have to squeeze in a trip to Benton to schmooze Rita

Maloney and find time to put the pitch together."

"*Coq au vin?* I'm impressed."

"Not nearly as much as you will be when you taste it. Fortunately, it's one of those dishes that's better the second time around."

"I cannot wait. By the way, how did the snooping go?"

I filled her in on Sunday morning. "So it appears that any one of the partners could have done it," I said. "At least according to their calendars."

"But you think the evidence points to Paul because of his appointment with your uncle on Tuesday afternoon. Still doesn't feel right to me. Tell you what. Maybe I can find out from Heather Hamilton what his record has been lately for staying on budget."

Heather was our production manager. Her job included keeping records of actual expenditures on ads versus what had been estimated.

"Good idea. And help me think of a way we can prove he did it if we do find out he was about to get the ax."

"That's easy. Let him discover--surreptitiously in his mind, of course--that you're on to him. Then watch your backside very carefully while you see what he does."

That ice cube played Chopsticks on my spine again.

"Oh, and I've been trying to find out who knew Miss Saran," she said. "No one does, by that name."

"Of course not. It's Lauren McGee."

"I know, silly. My attempt at humor. Anyhow, her closest friend at the agency is Ellen Rowland."

"You mean, the ditzy mini-skirt? The plot thickens."

"The good news is that Ellen likes to talk. The bad news is that she and Miss Saran are off on a little vacation together in Cancun. She'll be gone all week."

"Ah-ha. With Sugar Daddies in tow?"

"So rumor has it. Seeing as how she's got a new one already, maybe it was over between her and your uncle."

"She still could have been blackmailing him."

"Perhaps. Picked a good time to exit the country, too.

Anyway, I'll arrange a little impromptu chat with Ellen next week when she gets back."

"I'd been hoping to have things solved by then. I guess it can't be helped," I said.

"Something tells me she didn't do it, anyway. You know, Brian, I've been thinking. We don't know about Larry, yet. Even though you're gunning for Paul, even though Lauren Saran is probably capable, even though Aunt Sally didn't know about the suicide clause--Larry has my vote. The man must have a calendar. Maybe his secretary keeps it."

"Could be." I fiddled with the corner of a scratch pad. "I'll ask Mavis."

"Oh, another by the way, Brian. My computer at home is on the blink. Crashed this morning in the middle of a sentence."

"Sorry to hear that, Nickie."

"Thank God it hadn't been long since I'd hit the save button. Anyway, I'm taking it to the repair shop today at lunch. If it takes a while to have it fixed, which no doubt it will, how about letting me use your uncle's--the one you snatched from his office? I could use mine here, of course, but I'd rather keep my novel and my copy writing separate. Otherwise, I start interspersing phrases in sex scenes like 'Batteries not included' and 'Now, for a limited time only,' and, oh yes, one of my all time favorites, 'Free gift.' Did you ever get one that wasn't? Anyway, I spend all together too much time in this place, already."

"Sure." I tore at the paper some more. "What would you do, come over to my place to use it?"

"If you don't mind. I promise I'll be as quiet as the mouse at the end of the wire connected to the keyboard. I'll even take Soho out for walks."

"Okay, that'd be good." I had to struggle to control the glee in my voice. I was delighted. "Tell you what. The easiest thing would be for me to have a key made. Then you can use the computer anytime you like."

"Oh, please don't go to any trouble." She paused. "Tell you what, I'll have it copied at lunch. Just leave it at the front desk in an envelope. I'd like to use the computer tonight--and you have focus groups, right?"

"Right." I tossed the top sheet of the scratch pad in the trash. "No problem."

I left the key for Nickie on my way through the lobby to the northeast corner. Mavis Alfonso looked up as I walked her way. I stopped in front of her desk.

"Is Larry in, Mavis?"

"Sure." She reached for her phone. "Want me to get him for you?"

"No, no, don't bother him. Maybe you can help. Do you keep his calendar? I want to see when he'll be free for a meeting I need to schedule."

"Sorry, Brian, I don't. He does that himself."

"Really? I was looking for it the other day and didn't see it anywhere."

"No, you wouldn't. He has one of those small diaries he keeps in the breast pocket of his jacket. Pulls it out every five minutes to look at it. Says he'd be lost without it."

"Oh, right, I've seen him do that. Don't bother him now. I'll catch him later." I turned away.

How on earth was I going to get a look?

Then it occurred to me. Larry was supposed to be at the focus groups. Maybe he'd take off his coat.

Before I returned to my office I stopped in to see Mark Macon, the account exec on Benton consumer products. Jill had already left for Chicago and I wanted to know about the arrangements for our trip to Benton.

Mark was two years out of the master's of advertising program at Northwestern, curly blond hair, baby blue eyes, a bundle of energy. He was the kind of young hunk who made the teeny boppers swoon. Bulgy biceps. He sat behind his desk in a cubical located in an area of the agency known as the bullpen. I sat across from him.

"I have the Beech Baron reserved at eleven tomorrow morning," he said. "It's an hour flight. Sam Trenton, the ad manager, will meet us at the airport and the three of us will go to lunch."

"What about Rita Maloney?"

"I asked Trenton if he could have her join us, but he said she's busy. Fact is, we may not even see her."

"Damn." I could ill afford half a day out of the office if I wasn't going to have the opportunity to score at least a few brownie points with Rita.

Mark shrugged. "Rita's just not the hands-on, nose into any and everything to do with the advertising type her predecessor was. But Trenton said he'd do his best to get us into her office for a visit."

"This Trenton--is he on our side?"

"He's pulling for us. But he says he won't have any input into the decision. Fact is, he's worried about his own job. Rita's an unknown--too soon to have a handle on her, he says. He's afraid he's identified with the old guard and if she goes with a new agency, she might decide to replace him, too."

"A new broom sweeps," I said. "So what are we presenting?"

"A tv spot and a couple of print ads for the Chelsea bedroom furniture promotion in January. Buy a room of bedroom furniture and get a mattress and box spring free. The tv will run in markets where there are participating dealers. The print has room at the bottom for dealer names and addresses. Borax stuff."

"Let's have a look."

"The storyboard and layouts are in creative. They're putting the finishing touches on them." Mark picked up some typed sheets and handed them to me. "But, here's the copy."

"Say Hello to a Chelsea Bedroom Suite and Bid Farewell to Morning Backache," I read aloud. "Morning Backache?"

"Surveys show most people are sleeping on old, worn out mattresses and box springs. I guess their friends and neighbors don't see them so they don't replace them, but once those things start to sag, they're murder on your back."

I read some of the copy, which urged people to take advantage of the offer and do their backs a favor.

"Has Jill seen this?" I asked. "Does she think they'll go for it?"

"No sweat. Jill's given it her stamp of approval and I'm pretty sure Trenton will buy it. He won't be seeing any surprises. We walked through it on the phone. Of course, I have no idea how Rita will react and neither does he. That is, if we even get to show it to her."

"Okay," I said. "We'll keep our fingers crossed."

Before I left Mark's office we agreed to meet in the lobby the next day at twenty to eleven.

I was in the lobby at about a quarter to five, checking messages, when the focus group participants began to arrive. The first group was scheduled for five o'clock and would be among grandmothers of young women between eighteen and twenty-two years of age. A research department staffer led them to the large conference room. I ducked down a different hallway into the adjacent viewing booth.

It was not large, but certainly adequate: two rows of swivel chairs--the second one elevated--positioned in front of a large window. The other side looked like a mirror but from this side we could watch what was happening in the conference room. I couldn't see anything now, though, because the lights were on and the blinds were drawn.

Ned Tandy, the guy in charge of audio-visual equipment, was in the midst of setting up a video camera.

"How's it going?" I said.

"Fine, thanks." He screwed in a wire and shoved a

three-quarter inch cassette into the deck. "That about does it."

I turned off the lights and raised the blinds. Grandmothers were filing in. Some searched for their names on tent cards positioned in front of chairs around the table. A gray-haired lady helped herself to one of the soft drinks on the sideboard in front of the two way mirror, pausing as she did to inspect her makeup. She leaned close to the glass, pressed her lips together, then puckered like a goldfish.

Ned looked through the viewfinder of the camera and adjusted one of the controls.

"Where is the switch for the mike?" I asked.

"Next to the door, this side--about half way up."

I rotated it clockwise until I heard a squawk, then turned it back a notch. The murmur in the other room was now audible. The voices had a metallic quality. I sat in a front row chair and took a pad of paper from a stack in the middle of the writing shelf.

"How's the insulation?" I asked. "Are we sound proof?"

"No problem," Ned said. "Two pieces of glass, vacuum sealed with an inch and a half of space between them. Sand in the walls. Don't worry, they can't hear."

Ben Haley walked in. "Am I late?"

That baritone, announcer's voice always startled me.

"Still filing in," I said.

He took off his jacket, hung it on a hook on the back of the door, then sat next to me. "Haven't had a chance to tell you, Brian, how glad I am you're heading this pitch," he intoned. "These focus groups are absolutely the right way to go--Paul was all wet about that. He's a damn talented guy, but sometimes he lets his ego get in the way of good sense. One thing I will say for him, though, he can be terrific with clients, believe it or not."

I was going to have to see that firsthand.

"By the way, who is supposed to be here watching with us tonight?" Ben asked.

"Larry should arrive any minute," I said. "Paul said he couldn't make it, but that he'll be here tomorrow. And I guess this isn't Mary's thing. At least that's what she told me. Oh, and Freddie from research will be here."

"Mary's content to remain behind the scenes, making sure things run right," Ben said. "Darn good thing she does. Who went to the groups in Chicago?"

"Jill Lathermill. And Blake Burns from research went, too. This is the place to be, though. We have more of a chance people in Richmond will be interested in cedar chests. The Chicago groups have the potential to be real duds."

I thought about Jill as I looked over at Ned Tandy, who was still fiddling with the video camera and equipment. For her sake I prayed we got what we needed tonight. The thought of her out of a job made me sick to my stomach.

In a low voice I said, "I've been meaning to thank you, Ben, for coming to my defense when Larry tried to scuttle this research."

A smile appeared between the beard and mustache which puffed those puffy cheeks. "Ganged up on him, didn't we?"

"Double-teamed him is what we did," I said. "I'd have been seriously out of luck without you. Paul sure wasn't going to give me any help, and all Mary thinks about is how *not* to spend money."

"Larry is old school," Ben said. "The consummate flimflam ad man. Thank God guys like him are dying out." He paused. "Oh--sorry Brian. You know I didn't--"

"Don't worry about it, Ben. Tell me. Think Larry will retire anytime soon?"

"He's getting there," Ben said. "But I don't think he's got any plans."

"Who do you think is going to take over as CEO?" I figured if I bought Uncle Rod's stock then naturally it would be me since I would have forty percent. But I wanted to see what Ben would say.

Ben's acorn-filled cheeks bulged a couple of times as he collected his thoughts.

"Why, I assumed it would be you, of course," he said with those smooth pipes. "You will be the largest shareholder, right? I can tell you one thing, I'm glad it won't be Larry. We need a dynamo like you in the job to lead us. Advertising is a young person's business, and this firm is no exception. The leader of a group like ours needs to be youthful--someone the others can relate to and respect. Not only that, this company needs someone who is up to date--not a two martini lunch, wine and dine with one hand while the other is up to the elbow in their pocket anachronism like Larry Negus."

I laughed. "Thanks, Ben. I appreciate how you feel and I appreciate your confidence. It means a lot to me."

I realized at that moment that I liked Ben. He was intelligent, witty, a good ally. It even occurred to me I might be able to enlist his support to help me prove Paul Williams did it. Of course, I would have to think about the possible ramifications of bringing him into my confidence.

"What do you think Paul and Mary will say if I become CEO?"

"I think Mary will be delighted. As for Paul, we might have a problem on our hands. But I tell you what, Brian, he'll just have to accept it. The guy is good at what he does, damn good. But unfortunately, as you and I know, he isn't without flaws, serious flaws. Has some you don't even know about."

Like murdering people, I thought.

"If push comes to shove. I assure you, you'll have my vote," he continued. "And if we have to replace Paul--hire another creative director--well then, that's exactly what we'll do."

"I'm glad to know I can count on you, Ben."

Freddie from research slipped into the room, nodded to us, and took a seat on the other side of the camera.

"Oh, Brian," Ben said. "Just so you'll know. I have to slip

out after the second group--got an obligation at home."

"Sure, I'll fill you in tomorrow on what happens."

Just then Larry came through the door in a flurry, his white hair mussed, his liver spots as pronounced as ever. I noticed he wasn't wearing a jacket--probably had left it hanging in his office. I'd have to slip out to the john at some point and have a look at the contents of the breast pocket.

"Have I missed anything?" Larry took a seat next to Ben. "Look at that woman eyeballing the mirror." He stuck a thumb in each ear and waved his fingers at her. His jowls seemed to flap.

"They're getting ready to start," I said.

The moderator, Sheila Crockett, walked into the room and positioned herself by a chair at the head of the table, her back to the glass. She stood while the few women standing took their seats. Then she sat down.

"Thanks for coming this afternoon," she began, and went on to explain the purpose of the session and the ground rules.

"And behind me," she continued, "is a cleverly disguised two-way mirror." Everyone laughed. "Some people back there are checking up on me, making sure I do my job correctly. Oh, and I also should tell you, this session is being recorded so that I won't have to take notes as we go along. That way I can go back over the tape to refresh my memory about what was said this evening. You see, I have to write a report. But don't worry, what you say will be in confidence, I assure you. You are not going to see yourself in a television commercial or on the evening news, or hear yourself on the radio."

There was a chorus of "aw-shucks."

"We're here to discuss graduation gifts for girls who are finishing high school or college," Sheila said. "I believe each of you has a granddaughter who has just finished one or the other. Can you tell me what sort of gifts you thought about giving, what you actually gave, and if it pops into your head, what your granddaughter got that she particularly liked?"

Sheila went around the table and let each woman talk. It was a way to get them warmed up and into a discussion. Unfortunately, no one mentioned cedar chests, so after a while Sheila brought up the subject.

"I got one of those when I finished high school," one grandmother said. "Hinton's Furniture Store used to give a miniature chest to every girl in our high school as soon as they became a junior. Then their parents would give them a full-size chest when they reached graduation. It's a shame that tradition has died out."

"It was a hope chest," another said. "You were hoping you were going to be asked to get married, and it's where you kept all the special things you were collecting for when that day finally arrived. Girls nowadays don't want to admit they'd like to catch a man, or that it even crosses their minds. Bunch of hypocrites if you ask me."

There was a round of laughter.

"You know, a cedar chest is a practical place to store certain items," the lady continued. "I still use mine for blankets and sweaters. Had it more than 40 years. Keeps them from getting eaten up by moths in summertime."

"It's too bad, but things have changed since we came along," the gray-haired grandmother who had checked her makeup said. "Most girls these days go on to college. Then they get a job and find their own apartment."

"That's right," a mousy little woman said. "My granddaughter did just that and she told me, 'Grandma, if you're gonna give me something, for goodness sake make it something practical. Something I can use.'"

Sheila asked, "Would you consider giving a cedar chest as a college graduation gift? Or to a girl setting up her own apartment?"

"It's a remote possibility," one lady said. "If they didn't think it was hokie. Maybe this ad agency here could do some advertising to convince people it's an up-to-date idea."

"If you tell them it's a practical place to keep wool in the summer, they'd go for it . . . maybe," the gray-haired lady said.

"Whatever you do, don't say it's a hope chest," said another.

The discussion continued along these lines and the participants bantered back and forth about the practicality, or lack thereof, of a cedar chest as a gift. The consensus seemed to be that it was a gift whose time had come, and gone.

Finally Sheila said, "I have some posters here which have been prepared to solicit your reactions to a variety of selling messages for cedar chests. Now, please don't think of these as ads, but rather, as different approaches designed to encourage you to think about giving a cedar chest as a gift to your granddaughter. Here's the first one." She held it up for them to see, and read the caption which was printed in large block letters, "'It's not just a very nice gift, it's a tradition.'" Then she read the copy that went with it.

"I like that," one lady said. "That's the meaning of the hope chest--the tradition."

"I'm sorry, but I don't think it appeals to the young women of today," another said. "When they see tradition, it doesn't mean anything to them. It brings back the old hope chest idea, and I'm willing to bet you dollars to donuts they don't like that. They're thinking about going to college or getting a job. Lord help them, they want independence instead of a man. At least that's what they want you to believe."

"Amen, sister," said a third.

Sheila put another poster in front of them and read the caption. "A cedar chest holds more than just keepsakes. It holds hopes and dreams." Then she read copy that supported the traditional hope chest idea.

One lady said, "I'd like to see young girls get back to the tradition, but I don't believe it will ever happen."

Another said, "If you want my opinion, even I think it's

dumb. For goodness sake, what year is this anyway?"

Larry leaned over to Ben and said, "Jesus, these old biddies are tough. You guys talked me into going along with spending sixty grand for this? We can't show the client this shit. It's not what they want to hear."

"It may not be what they want to hear, Larry." Ben appeared to do his best to keep his voice from booming. "But somebody needs to show them what they are up against."

"For Chrissake, you don't do that now," Larry said. "After you have the account, that's when you tell the truth--maybe--and then only to cover your ass. Jesus. You tell them what they want to hear when you're trying to sell them, goddamn it. They want to hear how much product they're going to move if they use your ads instead of somebody elses." He pointed his index finger at his temple. "Am I missing something? What gives here anyway? Were you guys born yesterday, or what? For Pete's sake."

I leaned toward Larry. "Relax, Larry. This is just the beginning of the first group. It's going to be okay, trust me. First we scare the pa-jesus out of them with some of these quotes we've been hearing. Then we show them an approach that will work. Believe me, we'll have Rita Maloney eating out of our hand."

I hoped to heaven I was right.

"He's right, Larry," Ben said.

A lady in the group was saying, "My oldest granddaughter is twenty. When she graduated from high school I suggested she choose her silver, crystal and china patterns for her hope chest, and she thought I was completely out of my mind. 'Get with it, Grandma,' she told me."

"Christ Almighty," Larry said. "We're screwed. Totally screwed. There's no way in hell, just no way. Sales, sales, sales--that's what clients want. Not some double-talk from a bunch of old women. What on earth were you guys thinking of? I knew I shouldn't have listened. Damn."

Sheila pulled out a card with another approach and read it. The group beat it into the ground, then kicked it a few more times for good measure.

Sheila whipped out a board touting what a practical gift idea a cedar chest could be and read, "Announcing the cedar-lined closet for the girl who's brand new apartment is barely large enough for a chest of drawers," then read body copy supporting this claim.

The group looked at the poster without speaking, their collective brows wrinkled.

"Maybe, just maybe that would do it," one lady finally said.

"If they just didn't think it was a hope chest. That's the danger," said another. "No one wants to be thought of as old fashioned."

I was thinking to myself, please, please say something positive, but most of the comments were negative and only a few were even lukewarm.

"Of all the approaches you've shown us," a lady said finally, "this is the one that makes the most sense. It has some merit, I guess, but I'm quite sure my granddaughter would still rather have a CD player."

"Or a VCR," said another.

I felt slightly sick to my stomach. Perspiration was forming on my brow. It was time to get some air, and to check Larry's coat pocket before he decided to bolt. I stood.

"Be back in a second, guys. Got to take a whizz," I said and was out the door and down the hall.

Mavis was long gone from her desk, her computer draped in plastic and her reading lamp turned out, but light shone from Larry's office. I felt a flutter in my stomach and a tingle down my spine as I crept inside, my eyes darting from one side of the room to the other. Every little sound and creak sent the hairs of my neck on end.

His jacket hung on a polished brass coat rack. I gently lifted it by the lapel. There it was, the pocket diary.

I opened it to last week. What a mess: barely legible scribbles, many scratched through--some resembled hieroglyphics, no doubt a code known only to Larry. It appeared, however, that he'd had a meeting at five-thirty, or thereabouts, on Tuesday. The entry said, "Ad 2, Omni."

Ad 2?

Ad 2 was a club for advertising professionals under the age of thirty. Maybe he had been their speaker. It certainly would be easy enough to find out--a job for Nickie.

I replaced the diary and exited his office; breathed a sigh of relief.

My mind worked as I walked back to the observation booth. If Larry had been the Ad 2 speaker Tuesday night it was doubtful he could have made it back to the agency in time to do in Uncle Rod. They probably had cocktails for forty-five minutes or an hour before the speaker went on. If so, he would have started at six-thirty, and if he talked for an hour, that would take it to seven-thirty at least. Most clubs had dinner before the speaker went on, and that would push it back even farther.

I remembered the police lieutenant checking my watch. The murder had been committed between seven-thirty and eight.

Old Larry had an airtight alibi. Fifty people could probably testify he was at the podium when the murder was committed.

What time had I called him that night? Well after the police arrived. I hadn't looked at my watch, but it was just before ten when I arrived at Sally's. Probably around nine o'clock then. He must have just gotten home.

I pushed through the door to the booth, careful not to let in too much light, which might be seen by the focus group participants on the other side of the mirror.

Ned Tandy still stood behind the video camera taping away. Freddie from research furiously scribbled notes on a pad. Larry wore a scowl, a little black cloud over his head. Rain was almost visible.

"Where's Ben?" I said.

"Had to leave," Larry said. "And I think my time has come as well." He stood. "If you want to know what I think, I think we're up shit creek, that's what. Our only hope is that Paul will come up with some spectacular creative work. Jesus, this research is a bust. Of no use whatsoever."

"Don't jump to conclusions, Larry," I said as I took my seat. "This is only the first group. We have two more tonight and three tomorrow. Things will turn around."

But they didn't. Surprisingly, the girls were not as gloomy about cedar chests as their mothers and grandmothers. Some even liked the idea of practicing family traditions, although most agreed the hope chest idea was hopelessly outdated.

One said, "I like that idea. Neither my grandmother nor my mother had one as far as I know, but it would be a tradition I would have the opportunity to start."

Of the cedar closet in an apartment idea, another said, "If my mother or grandmother saw that, she'd be inclined to go out and buy it for me. I guess it'd be something I could keep and remember, but I can tell you, I'd much rather have a microwave or a ten speed bike."

"Or a Nautilus machine," someone chimed in.

"How about a Nordic Trak?"

"There's a lot of furniture I need before a cedar chest would make sense," one followed up by saying. "How about a sofa or a dinning room table and chairs--for openers?"

By the time the last group was over, I was totally dejected. But I told myself that maybe there was some way to edit what I'd seen so that it would work in the presentation. It would be a challenge, but unless the groups tomorrow night or the ones in Chicago came out very differently, I had no choice but to try. None of the appeals we had tested on the participants were strong, but the practical storage-furniture approach--mixed with an ounce of tradition and pinch of sentiment--looked like the best way for Benton to sell the turkeys.

I wondered if Nickie would still be there working as I pulled into the garage I'd rented behind my apartment. No light was visible in the rear window, but my place encompassed the entire first floor. The room with the computer was toward the front.

I walked through the walled garden, past the huge old elm, up three steps to the back porch, fumbled with my key and was surprised to find the door wasn't locked. I gave it a push. Something caught and held it. I looked closely. A chair was wedged under the knob, holding it shut.

I knocked and called out, "Nickie, are you there?"

The light in the kitchen flashed on, and in a moment Nickie had the door open.

"About time you got home, lover boy."

I moved inside. "What's with the back door?"

"Attempted break in." She gave me a little peck on the cheek. "Scared the tofu out of me."

"Attempted what?"

"I was at the computer, beginning the part in chapter fourteen where the guy who has been after the heroine seduces her. Really erotic scene. Anyway, all of a sudden I hear this loud cracking noise. And Soho goes berserk. It startled the daylights out of me so I called out, thinking, no--check that--hoping it was you coming home early. Next thing I hear the door slam and the pitter-patter of feet scurrying down the back steps. Soho was practically throwing himself against the door, barking his head off."

I took a close look at the door. It was splintered.

"I figure he or she used a crowbar," Nickie said.

"He or she?"

"Whoever killed your uncle did this. I'm convinced of it. They knew you were at the focus groups. What they didn't know about was Soho. Fact is, he probably scared them off."

"Because of the files?"

"Because of the files. Didn't I say that whatever they were looking for is still there?"

A thought struck me. "Paul Williams. Of course. He was probably looking for that memo putting him on notice."

Nickie shook her head. "I wouldn't bet the ranch. I still don't buy that he would do it because of greed."

"Larry and Ben were at the focus groups. What time did it happen?"

"Seven-thirty, maybe."

I tried to remember what time they'd left. It'd been before the first group ended.

"Took me an hour to get my head screwed back on right," Nickie said. "Lost the mood of that sex scene completely."

10

After Nickie left, I stayed awake until two o'clock combing through the hanging files. Then crawled into bed alone once again, alas, convinced nothing in them could implicate anyone in Uncle Rod's murder. It must have been Paul who tried to break in. He'd been after Uncle Rod's copy of the probation memo. It just made sense. He wanted to wipe it off the hard drive and to check the files to make sure there wasn't a duplicate. That was probably what he'd been doing when he was interrupted and left the files in disarray.

The window was open and I could hear the sounds of the city at night: a horn, the screech of brakes. A bottle crashed on pavement. Someone walking down the alley shouted an obscenity. Outside my window, the leaves and limbs of the big elm formed a patchwork pattern of black against a cloudy sky. Soho sniffed my hand. He was getting the hang of the set-up. Wait till Brian was lying down, feeling lonely. Ask innocently if he could offer solace.

"I know I'm going to regret this later, buddy," I said.

I let him jump onto the bed, which shook as he landed.

I went back to thinking about Paul. Somehow, I needed to check his personnel file, which would be kept under lock and key. Mary MacMann would know where. I would have to think of a good excuse before she would let me have a look, but I was willing to bet a paycheck he'd stolen Uncle Rod's memo from it. If it had disappeared, that would be more evidence to hang him with. With my arm around Soho, I managed to fall asleep unplagued by nightmares for the first time in a week.

By mid-morning, Tuesday, I was in my office, the employment agreement Roger had sent staring me in the face. It was time to have a closer look.

An awful lot of whereas and wherefores and parties of the first part were contained in it, but the salary was spelled out in black and white: three-hundred big ones. I'd have stock options which would give the ability to buy certain numbers of shares at today's prices at specified dates in the future. Also, a formula was spelled out for calculating an annual bonus based on an incentive pool to be generated by profits over a targeted amount. I made a mental note to ask Roger how often and by how much past profit goals had been exceeded. That is, if I decided to consider the offer seriously. Then we'd negotiate.

I knew I needed to read the whole thing carefully, but tossed it aside for now. If Paul was the culprit and if I could prove it, maybe, just maybe I wouldn't have to read the darn thing at all. Of course, there was the potential loss of Benton to consider, and the almost certain nose dive the agency would be in if that unfortunate possibility came to pass. The focus groups I'd seen the night before did not give me any reason to be optimistic. To the contrary, the only hope seemed to be that tonight's groups would be better.

All in all I should have been delighted about Roger's offer. Didn't I like money? Hadn't I promised myself never to allow myself to be poor again?

That thought reminded me of the mental note I'd made to send my Mom some money. I pulled out my checkbook and wrote her one for a thousand dollars, jotted her a note and stuffed it and the check in an envelope. Then I rummaged in my top drawer for a stamp.

Something about me had changed since I'd been in Richmond. When I forced myself to think about returning to Flint, even for five hundred thou a year, I felt a little sick to my stomach. I hadn't realized before what a rotten taste I had in my mouth about the place because of what Les Greenhill had made me do. Plus, it would be the death of a dream. D.O.A. Defunct. Just like Washington & Lee and the brand new ten-speed bike I never got. I'd be back there working for corporate bean counters and anonymous shareholders instead of for myself.

Enough with the negative thinking. It was time to get rolling. I wondered if Nickie had found out anything. Before she'd left the night before, I'd told her about Larry's appointment at the Ad 2 meeting and she'd agreed to confirm with someone in the club that he was there between seven-thirty and eight. She also owed me confirmation from Heather Hamilton that Paul was still in the budget-busting mode. That bit of information interested me the most.

I picked up the phone and dialed.

"Nickie D'Agostino."

"Hello, lover girl. Find out anything?"

"Well, Brian." She paused, maybe to shut her door. "Did anyone ever tell you what a sexy voice you have?"

"No headache this morning?"

"Seems as though the only time I ever get them is at night."

That being the case, I wondered what she would say to lunch at my place, but thought better of it. I'd be up to my eyeballs all day long. There wouldn't be time to do the number on her I had planned.

"Speaking of night," I said, "let's have dinner this evening."

She paused. "I thought you had focus groups. Besides, I'd planned to write."

"After the focus groups, after you've put in some quality time at the keyboard. Meet me at the Border around ten. We'll split a bowl of chili."

"Obviously, you've never actually tasted their chili. I have and my advice is, have a fire extinguisher ready."

"Well, we don't have to pick from the Mexican side of the menu, there's always the German dishes. Potato pancakes are a safe bet. No meat in them either. You should like that."

"Naw, cheese enchiladas in verde sauce. Tastes great and can be counted on to induce incredible dreams," she said. "No one says healthy food has to be bland."

I suppressed the image of half-digested enchiladas and verde sauce on the carpet the night I discovered Uncle Rod. "What about tofu?" I said. "How do you spice that up?"

"You don't. It's one of the crosses we health nuts have to bear. Oh, on another subject, you will be interested to know that Heather says Paul's record on budget busting has not improved. Not much, anyway. She said he's been on his good behavior the last few days but that last week your uncle was on the warpath about it--had her put together a detailed report of the prior month and a half, which she gave to your uncle the day he died."

I felt a rush. "I would say the pieces are falling into place."

"I still have doubts."

"Maybe it's time to let him know--surreptitiously, as you suggested--that I'm on to him."

There was a pause. "I don't know, Brian. I think you need more evidence."

I told her about my theory of the personnel file. "As soon as I hang up, I'm marching down to Mary's office. I've thought of a ploy that will get me access."

"It's definitely worth a look. Let me know what you find."

"You mean, what I don't find. If the memo's not there, and with Larry's airtight alibi, I would say it will be time to leak to Paul that I'm on to him."

"We're not certain Larry has an airtight alibi. Not yet. I've asked three people, but none were at the meeting last Tuesday night."

"No? But you'll keep working on it?"

"Of course," she said.

Before we hung up, she said she'd meet me at the Texas Wisconsin Border Cafe at ten o'clock. Then I grabbed a file I'd been collecting on possible staff to work on Benton and headed for the lower level.

Mary sat at her desk, reading glasses perched precariously on her nose. She was hunched over a stack of job dockets from which she appeared to be intent on ferreting out an extra percentage point of profit.

She looked up.

"Mary, do you keep the keys to the personnel files?"

"Sure. Which do you need?"

"I don't need just one. When we present next Monday I want to give Rita a rundown on who will work on her business. I'm putting together a brand new team. You'll agree, we need an all-star cast. If I could have a look through the files, I'll make sure our best are on the list."

Her nose wrinkled; the glasses teetered. "*Give* you the key? I don't know, Brian. Those files are confidential. Now, if it were Jill Lathermill's file you need, or someone else's in your department--"

I smiled and nodded. "I'm glad we have someone in charge of administration who takes the job as seriously as you do, Mary. Of course those files are confidential. Silly me, why should I think I would be privy to them? Maybe it will be all right for me to look at them after I buy Uncle Rod's stock and own 40 percent of the agency. In the meantime, I'll just *guess* at who should be on the team."

I turned and started down the hall.

A few seconds later I heard, "Brian, wait a minute."

I spun on my heel. "Yes, Mary?"

She was at her door, holding up a key. "Here, let me show you where they are."

Cabinets containing confidential information, mostly financial records, were arranged in two rows and formed an alcove in a corner of the basement a few feet from the entrance to the accounting department. I had to stoop, the ceiling was so low. Four of them were marked "Personnel."

Mary explained that a table and chairs positioned in the middle had been placed there for auditors.

"We've had a rash of them lately," she said.

"Really? IRS?"

"Transpublic International," she said. "But I'm sure you know all about that."

"Didn't know it had gotten so far--not all the way to due diligence. The deal must have been ready to close."

"The whole thing moved very quickly. Transpublic doesn't waste time once they decide they want something."

I studied Mary's face. "How did you feel about the sale?"

"I was against it. Personally, I like being independent. But Ben and Larry were so gung-ho it was hard to argue. When and if it came down to the wire I was planning to go along with whatever your uncle wanted."

"What did he want?"

"He never said, exactly. Not to me. But at the very least I know he wanted to retain a residual interest, so those of us who remained with the firm would still have a stake in it."

"I see." Perhaps this residual interest was what he planned to turn over to me, although I wondered if maybe he hadn't been planning to scuttle the deal altogether. I supposed I'd never know, now.

Mary left me alone with the key and I sat down with the file folder I'd brought that contained, among other items, the company phone list. I studied it for a few minutes with the idea there might actually be one or two people I would want to look up in addition to Paul. What I'd told Mary was true. I was putting together the Benton team. But I didn't need the personnel files to do it. In the first place, I was surely going to keep Jill on the account. In my book she was as good as they came, and whether I liked it or not I had come to feel an emotional stake making sure she kept her job. I sure as heck wasn't going to be responsible for putting the only breadwinner in that family out of work. Besides, Rita had commented that she had gotten good reports on Jill. She had said herself that the ad manager at Benton relied on her.

So it was media and creative where I thought I might switch a few bodies around. I planned to use biographical sketches our public relations director had given to me to decide which ones.

My eyes came to rest on Nickie's name. It seemed to stand out to me, like it had been written in colored ink. Why not take a peek in hers? Of course, there would be sensitive stuff, like her salary, but it wouldn't actually be snooping. She should be considered for the team, but she had been with the agency such a short time our PR man had not yet prepared a bio on her.

I located her file and Paul's, pulled them out and opened Paul's first. I was itching to see whether that memo was there or not and could feel my heart thump as I sorted through the contents.

The guy made major dough. Why did the creative types always have to be the Daddy-big-bucks of the business? It was apparent from what was before me, though, that Paul did have an impressive record of creating successful ad campaigns and winning awards. He was like a baseball pitcher who'd won twenty games a couple of seasons in a row--a simple matter of supply and demand. As was the case in most lines of work, there weren't enough talented people to go around.

As I continued to peruse, I realized the baseball analogy was apt. Damned if they hadn't given him a signing bonus.

Oh, it was only $25,000, but that was $25,000 more than Uncle Rod had given me. Perhaps my buns wouldn't have felt so fried if Paul was not such a jerk.

Was there no justice in the universe?

I went through the entire file a second time; then a third. But no memo putting him on probation. Nada. Zilch. Goose egg. The file had to have been tampered with. All the documentation was totally free of negative comment. He was my man, and it was time to allow him to prove it. I was going to set a trap.

I felt sleazy opening Nickie's but kept telling myself it was honest research.

First, I noticed she made a nice salary, almost two-thirds what I did. Another talented creative, darn it.

Lord, she was only twenty-eight, four years younger than I. I hadn't made that much money when I was twenty-eight.

She was born and raised in a town somewhere on Long Island. Way out. Graduated *summa cum laude* from Bard in upstate New York. Double major in creative writing and drama. Acted in a lot of plays--Blanche in *A Streetcar Named Desire*. A 3.8 GPA. First job was at Flint Advertising, New York.

Flint? She'd never said anything.

Only there a short time. Left before I arrived on the scene.

Why hadn't she mentioned it?

Fallon in Minneapolis was her next stop--a hot creative shop, especially while she worked there. As she had told me, Hill Holliday Connors Cosmopolus in Boston was where she'd worked most recently.

Her list of awards was impressive. Best in Show in Minneapolis, a Gold Lion at Cannes. When a creative person won big awards like that and jumped around, she could pump up her salary pretty fast.

Now, here was something. Damned if she hadn't

worked on a furniture account: Lounge-King Recliners. Won a Gold Pencil for a tv spot she'd created for the brand. Maybe she did belong on the Benton team.

I went back to my office and gave her a call.

"You didn't tell me you worked at Flint."

"You looked in my personnel file."

"It was right there along with the others, and I was wondering if maybe you had something in your background that would make you a logical member of the Benton team."

"You couldn't just ask?"

I started scribbling on my memo pad. "You also didn't tell me about Lounge-King Recliners."

"True. And Lounge-King won me a Gold Pencil. But Flint, on the other hand, is a time in my life I would rather not discuss."

"It was that bad?" I drew the outline of a man. Then, in front of him, the bars of a jail cell. I scratched them out.

"Damned account executives write the headlines," she was saying. "That is, if the research department or the clients don't write them first. The joint stinks."

Needless to say, her assessment of my former--and perhaps future--employer made me uncomfortable.

"Must have changed since you left," I said.

"Fat chance. Roger Normandy still runs the place, doesn't he?"

Maybe it was better to move on. "The Paul Williams memo was missing," I said.

"No kidding?"

"Not a hint of anything negative in the whole file. I wonder if he didn't purge more than just the memo."

"If the memo ever made it to his file in the first place," Nickie said.

"What do you mean?"

"I mean, maybe it was never put there."

"Nickie, dear, take a look at the memo on Uncle Rod's computer. There's a copy directed to Paul's personnel file."

I tapped the pen on the pad for emphasis. "Says so in black and white."

"Okay. But you and I both know a memo like that in someone's personnel file is a pretty damning thing. The only reason you would actually put one there is to set up giving the guy the boot."

"Precisely." I put down the pen. "That's why Uncle Rod put it there, and that's why Paul took it out. If Paul were fired now he would be able to say he wasn't properly warned. Chances are good he'd win his share of the proceeds of the sale to Transpublic International. Punitive damages, too."

"I have a difficult time believing Paul's the murderer and I don't think your uncle was on the verge of firing him."

"Am I hearing this correctly? You told me an hour ago Heather said Uncle Rod was on the warpath. He had her prepare a detailed memo on budget busting that covered the last six weeks."

"I know, I know. But tell me, would your uncle or anyone else fire a creative director of the stature of Paul Williams with the firm headed into a pitch for its biggest account? Wouldn't that send an awfully negative signal? Wouldn't it raise some eyebrows by calling into question the stability of the agency?"

I picked up the pen again, tried to snap it with the fingers of one hand but couldn't. "He was probably going to wait until after the pitch."

I could almost see Nickie roll her eyes. "What a way to motivate a guy. Tell him that right after he helps keep the big account, he's out on the street, sans his share from the big sale to Transpublic."

I let this thought sink in. "Uncle Rod was a stubborn sonofabitch," I said. "He usually took a while to decide something, but once he did, it would be a cold day in hell before he'd change his mind. I think he had made his decision on Paul a long time before the account went into review."

"It's possible, I suppose. Some people do have suicidal tendencies."

"No black humor intended?"

An uncomfortable silence followed.

"Well, then," she said, finally. "Let it slip to Paul that you think he's the shooter. The worst that will happen is he'll think you're crazy. But if you're lucky, he'll try to knock you off in the parking deck."

Once again. that ice cube played Chopsticks on my vertebrae. "Now that you see it my way, got any idea how to go about it?"

"Have any memos to write that need to be distributed to the partners?"

"The one giving my recommendation on the Benton team. The partners have to go along."

"I've been thinking about this," she said. "Make sure Paul's copy has a paper clip on it. Then slip a note under the clip on the backside of the memo. He'll think it got stuck there accidentally. Happens all the time."

"What do you think the note should say?" I started drawing a heart, caught myself at it, tore off the top leaf and crumpled it.

"Make it to Mary saying you found a memo about Paul in your uncle's files and that it has made you suspicious. Tell her you want her to check to see if the copy is in the personnel files where it is supposed to be. If he's done what you think, that'll get him riled up."

"Good idea."

I went to work on my word processor as soon as I hung up. My recommendation took several pages because it gave my rationale for why I'd picked each individual on the team, which included Nickie as copywriter. Then I took the scratch pad and scribbled a bogus note to Mary:

Mary,

In going through Uncle Rod's files I found a memo to Paul Williams, a copy of which should be in Paul's personnel file. Would you please check to be sure it's there? I know this is an odd request, but it may be very important. The memo is dated September 2.

Thanks for letting me know as quickly as possible.

Best,

Brian

I made copies of the account team recommendation memo, clipped the note to the back of Paul's as Nickie had suggested, and made the rounds to deliver the document to all the partners myself. My pulse raced wildly and my skin felt tingly as I walked along the hallway toward Paul Williams' office. What if he were there?

I would just hand it to him, say a couple of words and bolt.

I was going to need eyes in the back of my head because he'd soon be gunning for me big time if he really had murdered Uncle Rod.

Was this a smart thing to do? Lord, I'd better decide right now.

An image from my nightmares rose to mind, only this time I saw myself as I'd seen Uncle Rod and my father-- half my head blown away. Sweat broke on my forehead. I wiped it with the back of my hand.

His office was empty--only the usual chaos.

I wanted the share in the agency that was coming to me, didn't I? So, I was taking a chance. When would I ever get another opportunity to run my own show?

I wanted to lead the troops into battle. That couldn't be done without risk.

You've got to. If you're wrong you're wrong, but if you're right, you've got the proverbial brass. Lock the doors; look both ways before you cross he street. Don't talk to strangers or accept any unwrapped candy. Look before you leap. Fasten your seat belt. Don't pee in your pants, and certainly not into the wind.

I placed the memo on top of the pile in his cluttered in-box, checked that the note was still attached, and let it go.

As I strolled nonchalantly back to my office I looked at my watch and realized I was supposed to meet Mark Macon in the lobby in five minutes to leave on the trip to Benton. I'd be out of the office all afternoon and back just in time for the focus groups. At least I could relax until then.

Less than half an hour later I sat in a Beechcraft Baron on a runway at Richmond International. The pilot gunned the engines--to make sure they still worked, I guessed. The twin engine plane had seats for a pilot and copilot and four passengers--two abreast that faced each other. Mark Macon sat in one across. I had to tilt my head so it didn't press against the headliner. My legs were cramped.

The engines roared; the pilot released the brake. I felt my stomach lurch as we shot down the runway. We lifted off and banked.

The roar settled into a drone.

"How long does it take to drive to Benton?" I said.

"A little over two, maybe two and a half hours," Mark said. "We usually drive, but I knew your schedule was tight." He explained that Benton was west of the Blue Ridge Mountains in a village that straddled a tributary of the Shenandoah. We'd land near Waynesboro, the largest town nearby, where we'd have lunch.

I went over the layouts and copy with Mark for the Chelsea promotion and we took a close look at the proposed media schedule. The one-week promotion would set Benton back just over $5 million, so it seemed to me that Rita would be interested in reviewing what we had planned. By the time I'd finished playing devil's advocate with Mark to make sure we had answers for every possible objection, we were high over the Blue Ridge, starting down.

It struck me that the foliage in Richmond was still radiant but that here the leaves were past the peak. Probably the altitude, I thought.

Mark pointed out the window. "That's Wintergreen. See the ski slopes? Two golf courses? One's in the valley and the other's on the mountain." He tapped with his finger. "That's Arthur Fletcher's 10,000-square-foot bungalow perched at the top. It's not far from the fourteenth tee."

"Some bungalow," I said.

"Plus a five car garage. He collected cars. Had a '54 Rolls Royce Silver Shadow, a '37 Cord--remember that old movie, *Topper?* Like that one. And a '56 Jag roadster. That's what did him in, you know."

"The Jag? How so?"

"The house is up really high. There's a steep driveway with a sharp curve before you get down to the road. Anyway, old Fletcher decided to drive the Jag to work one day, hadn't had it out for a month or two. Apparently, the master cylinder had a leak and the brake fluid had seeped out. Didn't make the curve. Went straight off the edge and took a 900 foot free fall before he came to an abrupt halt on a bolder. I've seen where it happened. Great place for hang gliding."

The plane suddenly dropped a few feet and my head bumped against the ceiling. A flock of butterflies took flight in my stomach.

"You get these up-drafts over the mountains," Mark said.

"That was more like a down-draft."

The plane went into a slow bank and descended fast. Before long, the pilot leaned between the front seats and asked us to be sure our seat belts were fastened. A few minutes later, we touched down on a grass landing strip and taxied to a building with a wind sock on top.

I recognized Sam Trenton, whom I'd met at the agency

once before. He leaned against a big black Oldsmobile--a big, hulking guy about forty who had played first string tackle for Virginia Tech. A kind of Gentle Ben, but a bear, nonetheless. One I wouldn't want angry with me.

When the airplane's engines shut down, we got out and walked over to him. He stuck out his hand. "Good to see you, Brian. Thanks for coming."

"It's a pleasure, Sam."

I sat in the front seat next to him, Mark got in the back, and we drove into Waynesboro.

"Thought we'd hit the Purple Foot for lunch," Sam said. "It's one of Waynesboro's finer eateries. Doubles as a wine store."

Towns similar to Waynesboro can be found all up and down the Valley. I guessed it had a population of maybe eight or ten thousand. Five or six stop lights. Two main drags ran through. One had a strip shopping center with the usual collection--Rose's, a grocery, Radio Shack. The other was a more traditional small town main street with a thrift store, a Tru-Value Hardware, a Dollar General.

The Purple Foot was in an old storefront building. We walked inside, passed case displays of wine and found a seat at a table in the back. We each ordered a glass of the vintage of the day. While we waited for our meal, I pumped Sam for information about Rita.

"How do you read her?" I asked.

He shook his head. "She's strictly business--hard as nails from what I see, but in a very different way than her predecessor."

"What do you mean?"

"Mr. Fletcher made every decision in the company. The rest of us were there to carry out his orders--it was simple as that. Rita expects you to make all the decisions to do with your job. Then she'll hang you if whatever you decide doesn't work."

"At least you get to run your own show," I said.

"Sure. Just don't dare screw up. Tell you what, I liked it

better with Mr. Fletcher. He could get mad as hell at you, but at least you knew where you stood. He would tell it to you straight."

"Got mad at the agency a few times," Mark said.

"Cost overruns," Sam said. "Cost overruns came damn close to being the end of you guys."

"I understand that was a problem, but I also understand that it has been corrected," I lied. "There is something I don't get, Sam. If Rita is such a delegator, why is *she* picking an agency? Shouldn't that be your responsibility?"

"Frankly, that's one of the things that has me worried. The guy that buys wood and glue picks his own suppliers. The woman in charge of office supplies picks hers. Of course, if they screw up, it's off with their heads. But anyway, why shouldn't the ad manager pick his main supplier? I have this feeling the answer is that she plans to replace me once she selects which agency she wants. She may even be waiting for the new agency to be on board so they can help her pick my replacement."

I could see fear in Sam's eyes. "So help us keep the account, Sam. And we'll tell her she already has the man she needs."

"You better believe I'm doing everything I can."

We had a good lunch and then got back into Sam's car so he could drive us to Benton where we'd go over our recommendations.

Rolled bails of hay were scattered in geometric patterns across the yellow stubble of undulating fields. Purple mountains formed a backdrop on each side, Appalachians to the west; Blue Ridge to the east.

"How's Ben Haley doing?" Sam asked. "Haven't seen him since old Mr. Fletcher's funeral."

I thought about what Jill had told me, that Ben's mother was dying of cancer, but that he didn't want it to be known.

"He's doing okay," I said.

"He was one of the few people who could deal with Mr.

Fletcher," Sam said. "Both of them came from southwestern Virginia. Coal mining country."

"Talked us out of more than one or two scrapes," Mark said from the back seat. "Proved how much it helps to have a close relationship with the big cheese."

"I guess after Mr. Fletcher died there really wasn't any need for him to come, anymore," Sam said. "I get along fine with Jill and Mark." He glanced at me. "I depend on them both, Brian. They've always come through."

"That's good to hear," I said.

The car rounded the bend and started down a hill past a sign that announced, "Benton, Virginia, Population 348."

Sam must have seen me looking at it. "More people work in this town than live here. We have five plants in Benton and six more scattered across the United States."

A few minutes later we pulled up to a red brick building that appeared to have been built around the end of the nineteenth century. It was situated along side a muddy river--at least that's what they called it. Looked more like an oversized creek to me.

"This is the original factory building, built in 1888," Sam said. "Only, nothing is made here anymore. It was converted into the executive offices back in 1964."

We went inside and made our way to Sam's office where Mark went to work presenting the layouts and the storyboard and the media schedule. I threw in my two cents worth every now and then, but for the most part it wasn't necessary for me to do anything except watch.

After about an hour, all the details had been covered.

"Looks good to me," Sam said.

"Shall we take it to Rita?" I said.

"Now's as good a time as any," Sam said. "Pack it up and follow me."

We rode an elevator to the third floor and then took a hallway to an expansive reception area where a young man sat behind a long mahogany desk.

"Is Miss Maloney free?" Sam said. "She told us to stop

by."

The young man picked up a phone, pressed a button and mumbled into the mouthpiece. He looked up. "Yes. She'll see you now."

I led the others into a large room, about thirty-by-forty, with a ceiling that must have been fifteen feet high. It was furnished in eighteenth century colonial style and had a huge plate glass window that showcased a view of the creek-size river. Rita looked up from behind a personal computer, no doubt the one she had gotten to replace Arthur Fletcher's.

She stood and came around her desk, looking smart in a worsted navy blue suit, a white silk blouse and red silk tie with dark blue polka dots. Her intense eyes stared at me through tortoise shell rimmed glasses. I took her hand.

"So good of you to see us, Rita. I think you're going to like the promotion we have to show."

"Thanks so much for coming, Brian, but I'm afraid I haven't time. I'm putting together a report for the shareholders. But I did want to say hello. Perhaps I'll have Sam show me the promotion tomorrow."

"Sam liked it," I said. "Does that mean we can run with it?"

"As long as Sam's in charge of advertising, if he says so, it's all right with me."

In the airplane on the way back, Mark said, "You still have a lot of friends and connections at Flint, right?"

"Sure do," I said.

"Do you think they need any account executives who have a master's degree from Northwestern and two years of experience on the job?"

11

It looked to me as though old Sam Trenton was a goner, all right. If the guy could make decisions as long as he had the job, why wasn't he given any say-so in the selection of a new agency? The choice of an agency was the most important advertising decision of them all.

The question, of course, was whether it was also a forgone conclusion there would be a new agency. This, apparently, was what Mark Macon thought, but I was determined not to give up without a fight. For the rest of the trip back I tried to think of different ways I might present the new account team to Rita, ways to make the various aspects of their backgrounds even more appealing and compelling-- by showing examples of their work that related to what Benton was trying to accomplish, for example. Such as Nickie's commercial for Lounge-King that had won a Gold Pencil.

As I reviewed my notes on Nickie, I began to have the feeling that something wasn't right, like the time I discovered a girl I'd been dating in college had been going out with one of my fraternity brothers on the sly. Neither of them had had the guts to tell me. Oh, I knew something was wrong but couldn't put my finger on it. No doubt this had to do with what shrinks affectionately call denial. I didn't want to look Truth in the face. Not then. Certainly not now. Even accepting as only a slight possibility that Nickie might be using me made me feel sick and lost--the way I'd felt at the supermarket when I was three and looked around for my mother and didn't see her. But I couldn't shake it. Nickie had been at Flint. Nickie must have known Roger Normandy. Nickie said she didn't like Flint or Roger, and gave them both the finger when she left. But, if I were trying to hide something, like maybe that I was somehow in cahoots with someone in that organization, what would be the quickest way to cast doubt on the possibility of a connection?

Who did I know in creative at Flint that might remember Nickie?

It was four-thirty before I was back at my office. I picked up the phone and dialed.

"Flint Advertising, Worldwide," a female voice said.

"Tony Lavantos, please."

I heard a click. I'd forgotten how operators in New York usually didn't even say something like, "One moment, please."

"Mr. Lavantos' office."

"Is he there?"

"I'm sorry, he's in a meeting."

"Ask him if he can he talk to Brian Durston, would you please?"

"One moment."

I waited about fifteen seconds.

"Brian, old buddy. So you heard about Greg Farley, right? I say go for it, Brian. You'd be perfect for the job. Want me to put in a word with Roger?"

"Thanks, Tony. Maybe I will, but that's not why I called. Put on your thinking cap, will you? Five or six years ago. Cub copywriter by the name of Nickie D'Agostino. Dark hair, blue eyes, slim."

"Who'd forget a dish like that? You're slipping, Brian. You forgot the hooters."

I actually blushed. I also had the impulse to tell him not to talk that way about her. But instead, I said, "What else do you remember about her, Tony?"

"We just said most of it. A tad nutty, I guess. She had talent, too--you know, copy writing talent. Unfortunately, she was one of those types who never paid attention to the creative briefs you account guys always shove down our throats. Got sideways with the brass on more than one occasion over that battle ground called marketing versus creativity. Never did learn that the definition of creative at Flint was whatever the client would buy. So she followed my advice and went where they don't give a shit what clients like. Chiat Day, Fallon. I see her name in the books all the time. Damn good advice, it was. Probably makes more now than I do."

"Who was she friends with?"

"Nobody. Lots of guys wanted to be friends with her, if you get my meaning. But no luck."

"Really? Nobody?"

"Not that I recall. Like I said, she was kooky. Guys around here were probably too straight for her."

"How well did she know Roger Normandy?"

There was a pause. "Can't say that I recall, Brian. Probably one of the brass that she butted heads with. Two people could not be more different."

Yes, and sometimes opposites attract, I thought. "Thanks, Tony," I said.

We finished the conversation with some small talk. Then I hung up.

I sat for a while staring at the wall. That creepy feeling would not go away. Eventually, the face of a girl from my high school history class flashed before my eyes: Tina Jaspersen, a petite beauty with icy gray-blue eyes, blond hair, and pale, almost translucent skin. We'd been at the same party on New Year's Eve along with about fifty other teenagers. My best friend and I shared a bottle of Jack Daniel's and I ended up on my back, holding her hand, kissing it, telling her how pretty she was, how maybe the two of us could go steady and eventually get married. Brother. You should have seen me slink into history class on the fourth of January.

I felt that way now.

No, that wasn't exactly true. Somehow this was different. It was hard to put my finger on. I mean, I think I have a fairly good head on my shoulders. Yet time and again I'd noticed that Nickie was a step or two ahead of me. Like she knew what I was thinking and what I was going to say before I said it. Now this--this thing with Flint and Roger Normandy and corporate intrigue. To tell the truth, it frightened me. I realized I had fallen under her spell and she could be the shooter. I could be her stooge. Ever see that movie with William Hurt and Kathleen Turner called *Body Heat?* Check it out at Blockbuster.

You'll get the picture.

So what now? How could I find out? And what was I going to do about it?

Nothing I could do at that moment. It was almost time for the focus groups.

Larry didn't show up that evening. But Ben Haley sat on one side of me and Paul Williams on the other. I kept Paul in my peripheral vision the whole time. He didn't say anything or let on he'd seen the note, but of course I hadn't expected him to. He acted normally, like the jerk he was.

The feeling it gave me to be right there beside him caused me to remember a bully in junior high I'd offended one time. Must have made a face or looked at him too long when he was pushing someone else around. He saw me and came to kick my butt, but the bell rang and the teachers came out just in time.

I resolved to defend myself, to knock the block off the S.O.B., but telling myself I could handle him didn't help the way I felt. I spent the day sweating through my classes as though it was a hundred degrees outside, the windows were down, and there was no AC. Yet, strange as it may seem, I felt chilled at the same time.

After class, Biff or Butch or Bubba or whatever his name was shoved me in the chest. I staggered backwards.

"Why'd you look at me like that, pretty boy? Think you're hot shit, don't you?"

He swung and missed. I came in low, led with my right. It glanced off the side of his face. This really made him mad. His eyes grew round and he snorted, but then he stepped back and said, "Ah, can't you take a joke, Durston? Can'tcha see I was only kidding?" He smiled and stuck out his hand.

So he wasn't going to kill me after all, I thought. I moved forward to take his hand.

Mistake.

Next thing I knew, I had caught one on the jaw. Until that moment, I'd thought stars circling one's head were an invention of some cartoon maker.

So there I was right next to Paul, who as usual was doodling on a pad. I looked down at his hands. At least he didn't have on any rings.

The first focus group was held among grandmothers and started at five o'clock. The mothers came on at six-thirty and were talking now, and the girls would begin at eight o'clock--same schedule as the night before. It was midway through the mothers group. A spirited discussion had unfolded among the women in both groups with some pithy and feisty comments along the way. Unfortunately most were as negative as they'd been on Monday night. The mothers had just been shown the poster that positioned cedar chests as a romantic but practical item that would be ideal for a husband to get for his wife as an anniversary or birthday gift.

Sheila Crockett, the group moderator, finished reading

the copy and the women stared at the board, shaking their heads or rolling their eyes.

"I'd rather have a piece of jewelry--that's what I call romantic," one of the mothers said.

"My husband better not go out and buy one of those things without me there to pick it out," another said.

"That's right, you could trust my husband to get something really gaudy--you know? When it comes to furniture, his taste is in his mouth."

"I can think of a dozen things he could get me that I'd like better than a cedar chest. How about a weekend in Washington and a play at the Kennedy Center?"

"For the love of Pete," I said.

Paul Williams patted me on the back. "Fucked up, huh Durston? Sixty grand down the drain. Yep. An absolute disaster. Too bad, my friend. All I can say is, you should have listened. Glitz may not sell the biddies on the other side of this glass, but it'll sell Rita Maloney. Trust me."

Ben Haley revved up his announcer's pipes. "Glitz is not the way to go."

"These focus groups may look like a train wreck," I said. "But you haven't seen my edit job."

I hoped to heaven I really could pull something off--make a silk purse out of a sow's ear, as the saying went.

"It's true, I've witnessed the wonders of electronics create more than one or two miracles," Paul said. "I've even done it myself a few times, but from what I've seen tonight you're gonna need Jesus Christ Himself before this crap'll work."

I said, "Benton needs to sell these chests as gifts from a mother or grandmother to a girl who's starting out--a gift that'll provide her with practical storage space she'll appreciate, but one that still has a touch of sentiment and tradition."

"Practical storage is dead on," Ben said. "And I think you're onto something with that touch of sentiment and tradition, Brian. Picture an older woman trying to decide on a gift for a younger woman. She's getting on in years, she knows she won't be around forever. She'll want to give something that'll last and be passed down to future generations. Sentiment and tradition are an unspoken part of it. What do you think, Paul? How sentimental is a microwave or a Nautilus machine?"

"Can't go overboard with sentiment, though," I said. "It shouldn't be sappy."

"You'll need to doctor the tape to make it come out that way," Paul said. "For my money, glitter is still the way to win the account." He stood and pushed his chair aside. "I've seen enough of the bullshit going down on the other side of that glass. I'm outa here."

He left.

"Don't listen to him, Brian." Ben Haley's voice was deep and melodious. "You're right about the strategic position Benton should take. From what I've seen of these groups, it may be difficult, but I think you can build a case."

"We have the groups from Chicago still to come, too," I said.

"Believe me," Ben said. "You'll see things when you go back over the tapes that you didn't the first time around."

Ben's words and his confidence made me feel one helluva lot better than I would have otherwise. We suffered together through the rest of the mothers group and all of the girls', and when the time came to leave I wondered if he'd like to stop for a drink on the way home and chat about what we'd seen. It was only nine-twenty-five and Nickie wasn't supposed to meet me at the Border until ten.

"Headed west?" I said as we walked to the front door of the agency.

"Way west--Brandermill."

"I'm meeting someone at the Border at ten. Want to stop on your way for a drink? There's time."

He agreed.

The place where we were to meet was located at Plum

and Main Streets and my apartment was in a three-story former single-family residence two blocks away between Plum and Lombardy on Grove. So, rather than risk having the top slit, I parked in the garage, and walked.

The Border was in an old brick storefront on the corner, painted blue and gray--the significance of which was not lost on me. On the side that faced the street was a huge cutout in the shape of the United States, top half blue, bottom half gray. Through the middle on a white strip edged in black dotted lines was written, BORDER CAFE.

Inside, smoke floated against a high tin ceiling from which hung antique fans, turning lazily, powered by a network of pulleys and belts. Rednecks, college students and refugees from stock brokerages crowded near the bar and filled the air with chatter. I made my way through the assemblage, inhaled the odor of hops, rice and best barley malt, and found a vacant table near the the restrooms. Practically every inch of wall was covered with license plates from Texas and Wisconsin, photographs of heroic characters such as Pancho Villa and a guy who was hanged because he stole somebody's Stetson, or the work of taxidermists. This bordered on art, demented though it was, and ranged from a cow's head to a buck, raccoon, ram, wild boar, duck, goose, a couple of bob cats, and a rather puny deer's rump.

I caught a glimpse of Ben as he weaved through the crowd to join me. With that beard and those acorn-stuffed cheeks, he should be sure to steer clear of the taxidermist who'd gotten hold of that deer.

I ordered a Corona and Ben asked for iced tea.

"Don't sleep well if I drink," he said.

"I don't know if I'm going to sleep thinking about how to edit those tapes."

"You're right about the position, Brian. When you go back through to pull out quotes, you can throw out the negative stuff. I think you'll have enough positive comments to accomplish our objective."

"I hope you're right." I had serious doubts. "At least we can use some of the negative stuff to show Rita what Benton shouldn't do."

Ben chuckled. "I hope Martin and Arnold recommend campaigns directed at men that sell the idea of a cedar chest as an anniversary gift."

"Talk about a gaping hole in their canoe," I said.

We both had a good laugh, and it occurred to me that Ben was really something. His mother was dying of cancer but you certainly couldn't tell.

A waitress came with our drinks. I pulled the wedge of lime from the Corona tall-neck and dropped it in an ash tray.

"Cheers." Ben held up his tea.

"To victory," I said and took a swig.

As I placed the bottle on the table, I wondered if I should say anything about his mother. I wanted to comfort him if I could. Then I remembered what Jill had said. I didn't want to betray her confidence. So I decided now might be a chance to get more background on Paul.

"What do you think of Paul Williams?"

Ben rolled his eyes and took a sip of tea.

"Come on now, don't sugar coat it."

"He's a pain in the ass, but that comes with the territory, doesn't it? You have to pamper the creatives if you want to keep them happy and productive." Ben placed his glass on the table. "You know, I could live with Paul, might even sing his praises if he didn't constantly blow budgets. Problem is, I'm the guy who has to explain cost overruns to clients."

"I understand Uncle Rod was on the verge of firing him."

"Really? Didn't know it had gone that far."

"I found a memo in Uncle Rod's file putting Paul on probation. The time was up the day Uncle Rod was killed."

Ben's eyes narrowed. "What do you mean, *killed?*"

My scalp crawled. Time to backtrack. "Well, I don't

know," I said. "It's just a theory. Frankly, it's one reason I've been searching through Uncle Rod's files. To see if anything there would point to a motive. The probation memo does, but--"

"You don't really think--"

"Probably not. But if Paul is fired, it'll cut him out of the Transpublic sale."

Ben stared at me. Why did I have to have such a damn big mouth? "But then, he probably wasn't going to fire him. With Benton in review, it wouldn't have been a smart thing to do. Pretty far fetched, really."

Ben nodded. "Shame about Benton. If that hadn't come up, there'd be a few more millionaires in the world right now."

"Uncle Rod really never talked about it much," I lied. "How do you suppose he felt about selling the company?"

"Rod's main thing was he wanted his cake and to eat it too. He was demanding to keep a considerable stake in the agency."

That must have been what he was planning to give to me.

"How'd you feel about keeping a stake?" I said.

"I was ready and willing to sell every single share. Ever since I was old enough to know what money was, I've wanted to be a millionaire. Would be, too, if it weren't for Arthur Fletcher. I was gonna take the money from the sale and invest it, you know? I've never thought an ad agency was a good place to tie up all your money, and for once it looked like I was going to have some. Let it work for me, instead of the other way around."

I recalled Nickie's profile of Ben. Things had been rough for me and my mother, but I imagined poverty in Appalachia was even worse. "Arthur Fletcher?" I said. "Rita Maloney was the one who threw the account into review."

Ben's brow furrowed. "Did I say his name? I guess because Arthur had some problems with the agency, too. You've heard, I'm sure. Blown budgets, a campaign for bedroom furniture he says we rammed down his throat. He could be a feisty S.O.B."

"I understand you were pretty close to him, that you got us out of more than one scrape."

Ben shrugged. "I suppose. All I did was reason with him. Anyway, I think we have a good opportunity to keep the account. Select the positive things said in those groups, Brian. Whatever will support our position. Show them a few negatives, each strategically picked. I can still hear that woman, 'You can trust my husband to get something gaudy.' Sounds like something my wife would say."

"How long have you been married?"

"Since college. We've come a long way together."

"Kids?" I knew he had two boys but didn't want to let him know I'd been snooping.

"Two terrific little boys. Well, not so little anymore. They're headed into the terrible teens. I'm not worried, though. They're both good guys."

There was something warm in the way Ben's mouth curved and the gleam that shone from his eyes. It made me nostalgic for the time before Dad died.

"You worked for a while in Baltimore, didn't you?" I said.

"Yeah, but I'm glad we moved to Richmond. The wife and kids love Brandermill--it's got everything. Good schools, recreation, no crime or drugs. I thank my lucky stars every day your uncle persuaded me to come to Durston Negus."

He paused and looked into his tea. "Your uncle was one helluva guy. I looked up to him--he was a mentor."

"I was hoping to get some mentoring myself."

"What happened is really tragic. But, you're way ahead of where I was five years ago. You don't need mentoring." He looked me in the eye. "Shoot, Brian, you're going to be our next CEO. It's time for you to do the mentoring."

"Thanks, Ben. But you know, there's something I've been wondering. Don't you want the job? To be our CEO, I mean?"

"It's not surprising you'd be wondering that. I'll bet every guy with your leadership qualities assumes everyone wants the top job. Truth is, it isn't so. I know my limitations. I don't have your charisma. Fact is, I'm a good second man. Why should I kid myself by thinking otherwise? I've done all right, I've come a whole lot farther than anyone else in my family ever did." He shook his head. "I sure as hell don't want to lose what I've got."

"We'll get the agency back on track. First thing tomorrow I'll get together with the researchers who were in Chicago. We'll comb through the tapes to be certain the position we talked about makes the most sense, and that we can support it with clips."

"What time's the strategy session?" Ben asked.

"Three o'clock. All the partners should be there. We need to agree on the position and on the team that we'll present on the account."

Ben looked at his watch. "Getting on toward ten o'clock." He took a few bills from his wallet and tossed them on the table. "I enjoyed talking with you, Brian. You're a good man. I'm glad we've gotten to be friends." He stood. "See you tomorrow at three, old buddy."

I sat amid the smoke and the din and the stuffed animals as I waited for Nickie, thinking about Ben. How many people did I know who actually knew their own limitations? I recognized a few of mine, but doubted I'd identified even half. What must it be like to know you don't belong at the top?

I took the last sip of Corona and looked up. Nickie was making her way though the crowd. I thought of my conversation with Tony Lavantos and experienced a sense of sleaziness mixed with a healthy dose of uncertainty. Something else tugged at me, too. It was brought to my attention by that doggone ice cube playing Chopsticks once more time. Its icy presence lingered on a spot right below the back of my neck.

Nickie wore that Rachel Linden smile that seemed to say she knew something she wasn't telling, that she could hardly refrain from laughing outloud about how she had me totally, completely fooled.

"How's your backside, lover boy?" she said as she sat down.

"Backside?" I said. "Oh, right, Paul. To tell the truth it's the sweaty palms and the nervous stomach that are gonna do me in. Not him."

"Trust me, he didn't do it." She looked past me over my shoulder. "Still, if I were you I'd make sure my back was to the wall."

I glanced behind.

She giggled. "Sorry. Couldn't help it."

A waitress arrived with menus. We both ordered enchiladas in verde sauce without looking. I asked for another Corona.

"Oh, and would you melt the cheese on my chalupa, please," Nickie said.

"How's Soho?"

"Took him for a half hour walk. Well, more like an involuntary run. He pulled me the entire way."

"I should probably send him to obedience school."

"And the focus groups?"

"More of the same." I told her about my idea for the selling position and how I was going to have to be creative in editing the tapes.

She tilted her head as if to let the idea sink in. "A gift for a young woman starting out on her own, with a little sentiment attached?"

"That's right."

She frowned. "Not from my mom. My mom was a certified hippy--flowers, Haight Ashbury. To her, tradition is an anathema. No doubt she's why I turned out the way I did."

"Doesn't have to be the mom."

Her eyes darted toward the ceiling. "Yes, you're right. Grandma would go for the tradition thing. Acts as though she's hard as nails--says my mother made her that way. I imagine Mom drove her nuts. Grandma also maintains that she is one adult in our family who is practical and down to earth. Has hope for me, though. Suffers from the delusion she and I are cut from the same cloth and that Mom dropped in from outer space. . . . I never have had the heart to tell her I can't stand meatloaf or mashed potatoes. Peas, either. . . . Uh-huh. She'd go for tradition." Nickie shrugged. "It's funny. We are alike in a way. Just not the way she thinks."

"You mean you're not practical and down to earth? What about tofu? What about bean sprouts? Practical food if ever there was. Oh, that's right. I forgot about Kafka. Well. I was encouraged when you went for the Egg McMuffin."

"No doubt. But I've regretted it ever since. No, practical and down to earth are not the way to describe me."

"Nevertheless, you are as hard as nails."

She smiled. "So it may appear to you, but believe me, it's a front. The way we're alike is that we both project a tough exterior, but under the façade, we're sappy and sentimental. Don't laugh, it's true." The now famous smile returned.

"You are kidding," I said. "Say it isn't so."

She shook her head.

The waitress placed our food on the table.

I looked at hers. "Darn, why didn't I ask for melted cheese?"

"Next time you'll listen."

We ate and talked. She told me where she was in her novel. I filled her in with details about the focus groups. I considered confiding in her about my offer from Flint, but I already knew what she thought of the place. And, on the other hand, if she was in cahoots with Roger Normandy and was Uncle Rod's killer, maybe she already knew about the offer. Either way, it was better to put off the discussion.

It was just before eleven o'clock when we finished and quite cool when we walked outside. Orange light from sodium vapor lamps reflected off black asphalt. Lights in windows of high-rise office buildings downtown were visible in the distance. Horns honked, engines raced. I heard the sound of a bus's air brakes and remembered that I'd parked the car in the garage. Nickie had also walked to the Border. When there was an opening we darted across Main, then strolled arm in arm on the brick sidewalk along Plum.

She certainly hadn't complained of a headache. I could feel her breast pressed into my arm. She had to feel it, too.

What about Normandy? What about a conspiracy?

Boy, was I confused.

We stepped off the brick sidewalk to cross Grove. Something flickered in my peripheral vision. I turned and saw the high beams flash on of a car parked on the opposite side of the street. The engine roared, tires screeched and headlights lunged at us, rear wheels spinning like a slingshot drag racer. It came like a huge, swooping owl with claws open to tear us apart, yet somehow, inexplicably, in slow motion. I wrapped my arms around Nickie, put my shoulder to her like she was the pad on a blocking sled and ran, leaped forward into space and time--falling--as visions flashed: Rachel Linden telling me it was over, Tina Jaspersen laughing at my silly, sappy sentimentality, Uncle Rod bent over with his head in a pool of blood, My dad in uniform, The flag as it was handed to my mother, rifles discharging, Nickie standing in my doorway that first time. The top of Nickie's head.

I heard the wind rush out of me, a gigantic crash, a tinkling, the spray of tiny shards of glass, the roar of an engine receding. Then--silence.

"Are you okay?"

I opened my eyes. Nickie was on top of me, her face inches away. I sucked in air. "Are we dead?"

"What? I look like an angel? Thank you, Brian. No one ever told me that before."

I struggled to my feet and pulled her up; felt pain in my leg below the knee. "Did you see him? Was it Paul? The license number, you got it, right? Let's call the cops."

"You're bleeding." She bent down, found a hole in my trousers, ripped it larger. "Blood's all over."

"I'll be okay." My leg buckled.

"Give me your arm." She pulled it over her shoulder and pushed upward. "Ha-ha! Imagine me, supporting a jock. A true athletic supporter. . . . If we only had the Jockey Underwear account."

"You got the license number, right?" We moved toward my apartment.

"I'm sorry, Brian, but the light over it was out."

"What kind of car was it?"

"Sorry, I don't know. To me Caucasians and cars all look alike."

We started up the steps.

"What color was it, then?"

"Don't know that, either. Maybe some paint came off on that lamp post. It hit pretty hard--broken glass everywhere."

I limped through the front door with her help, and into my apartment.

Soho came running.

"Down, boy, take it easy."

I flopped on the sofa. Nickie ripped my trouser leg open the rest of the way, felt above and below the knee.

"Doesn't appear to be broken, but it's a deep scrape--like sliding on asphalt into third. Let me get a wash cloth."

I watched her leave the room. Soho climbed on the sofa and licked me in the face.

"Thanks boy. Yeah, yeah, I know, you can see I'm upset. You'd be, too, except you'd have gone after the sonofabitch, wouldn'tcha?" I stroked him, roughed him up a little around the neck. "Better get down now, Soho. Get down.

That's right, lie down. Don't let Nickie see you on the furniture. Could be a neat-nick, you know."

She returned with some gauze and tape from the medicine cabinet in one hand, a warm wash cloth in the other, knelt in front of me and went to work.

"That was scary as hell," she said. "I know I joked about it--you being a jock and all. It was my way of getting through it. Almost scared the you know what right out of me. Dear God. We came within an inch of eternity. I'm still shaking."

"Yeah, it was close, all right. A lot closer than someone would make it who simply wanted to have it look like they weren't part of a conspiracy."

Her brow wrinkled. "Sorry, I don't follow. Mind running that one by me again?"

"It's isn't important," I said. "But I will say this. One more thing I thought was a myth has turned out to be true."

"What, that I'm a suppressed Florence Nightingale?"

"No. That your life flashes before you. The highlights, anyway--ouch. That hurts."

She worked intently. I gritted my teeth.

"Almost done," she said at last. "Now, these highlights. Anyone I know in them?"

"How can you be over this already?"

"I'm not." Her lips parted in that smile. "But a close call like that does make a person appreciate being alive, doesn't it?" She dropped the gauze and the tape and moved closer, stopping one or two inches from my face. Softly, she said, "I wanna know what's important in your life." She cleared her throat. "More specifically, I wanna know who's important. Tell me, what, or rather who, did you see?"

I looked into those dark blue eyes, shifted to get comfortable, enfolded her in my arms. "A lot of stuff from my childhood." I paused. "Let's see. . . . Okay, I saw you. I saw you the way you appeared to me that first time. You were standing in the doorway of my office."

The smile. "Totally brazen, wasn't I?" Jet black hair

framed her face. White translucent skin glistened with tiny, almost imperceptible beads of moisture. I inhaled the musky scent of her perfume, felt the warmth of her breath.

It was my turn to smile. "Shameless, barefaced, brassy, impudent, and tawdry. . . . Precisely how I like my women."

She came closer. "And oversexed . . . . You like 'em oversexed."

Our lips met in a long, slow, unhurried, deeply passionate kiss. That testosterone gland swung into gear, dumping every last drop of a load that had been building up for days. A warm rush started in my toes and rose upward, engulfing my calves, thighs, hips, gut, chest, neck, arms, head, until my entire body was one gigantic organ of pleasure, quivering in rapture, all the while longing for more and more and more.

But even in the midst of that overwhelming joy I did not forget my pledge to set aside my own selfish desires and to do one heckuva number on her.

You gotta believe I did.

12

As I drove north on Ninth Street past the Marshall House, it struck me how out of place an eighteenth century brick colonial looked smack in the middle of an urban setting of late-twentieth century office buildings. Tinted glass, chrome, white and gray marble everywhere, the bed towers of The Medical College of Virginia a couple of blocks away. John Marshall had been the first chief justice of the United States and a Richmonder whose house somehow had escaped the blaze of 1865. That was why it still sat where it always had.

I circled the block and found a place to park. I thought I was headed to Police Headquarters but frustration turned out to be my actual destination. Although Lieutenant Ryan was very polite and cordial, he was also firm.

"I'm sorry Mr. Durston, but there's nothing I can do. The case is closed. I'm afraid you haven't told me anything that amounts to the kind of hard evidence we would need to reopen it. Nothing that would hold up in court. I'm sure you understand."

"But someone tried to run over me. If I had turned my head a second later, I'd be dead."

"I'm sorry that you were almost hit by a car. I've no doubt it must have been frightening."

"What about the memo?" I held up a printout. "The one that put him on probation?"

"Look, Mr. Durston. People get in jams with their bosses--it happens, you know, all the time. They don't automatically turn around and kill the boss because of it."

"The stock? The sale to Transpublic?"

"There's nothing that links the two in any solid way. You've heard of a small technicality called reasonable doubt? What you've told me doesn't come close to what would be necessary to overcome that."

There was nothing to do but move on. It was obvious I'd have to come up with airtight evidence. In the meantime, I had a presentation to put together. The only thing I could think of was to try to find Paul's car and see if it wasn't banged up from from having crashed into that lamp post, which by the way, did not have any paint rubbed off on it. Of course, I really didn't expect his car would be anywhere I could find it. He was too smart to still be driving it, probably already had it in some body and fender shop halfway between here and who knew where. It would be interesting, though, to see how he acted toward me when we saw each other. I'd better keep the eyes peeled that I'd grown in the back of my head.

By nine-thirty I had cased the parking lot, and as I had suspected, no 20-year-old BMW. I was back in my office. Jill Lathermill sat across from me.

"I hope you had more luck here in Richmond than we did," she said. "The Chicago groups were a bust."

That feeling of being slightly seasick took hold, the one I had come to associate with thinking about Jill out of work. For a second I had the image of her balanced on the edge of a cliff about to fall backward into the abyss. I wanted to reach out and grab her.

"The Richmond groups could have been better, as I'm

sure you'll hear, but I think I can do something with them." This was more optimism than I actually felt, and my words served to put even more pressure on my ability to pull a rabbit out of a hat, but there was nothing to be gained by making her even more upset than she must already have been.

I explained the selling position that Ben and I had discussed: practical storage mixed with a pinch sentiment and an ounce of tradition. "I think I can build a solid case for it at least in Richmond and areas like it. How does it fit with what you saw in Chicago?"

"To tell the truth, I think Benton should save its money and not advertise in the blue areas. From what you tell me, there's some basis for the tradition-sentiment approach in areas like Richmond. But frankly, I didn't see it where I was."

"Almost all the grandmothers remember hope chests, and some mothers do, too," I said. "The local furniture stores used to give away miniature chests to every girl in the eleventh grade, probably up until the '60s. A lot of the older women got full size versions as gifts--still have them, actually. There seem to be some fond feelings, but I'd say they're mostly latent."

"Those feelings can be stirred up among the gift-givers," Jill said. "Your position makes sense in that context. The problem in Chicago is, there isn't that subconscious base to work with. No tradition, no nothing. It's not there. Hope chests are almost laughable."

This wasn't what I had been hoping to hear.

"Ten million dollars isn't that much of an ad budget when you spread it nationwide," I said. "I'm glad we did the research in Chicago even if all we got from it was an indication we should concentrate our efforts elsewhere--use the money in parts of the country where there's hope it will bring the client a return."

"I would say we got that message loud and clear."

"What about the poster that sold the idea of men giving

a cedar chest as an anniversary or birthday gift?"

Jill chuckled and shook her head. "That one got all kinds of hoots and howls. The idea of men picking out furniture without their wives along. Brother. If I'd had my female hat on instead of my account supervisor hat when we came up with that one, I could have predicted what was going to happen."

"Do you think I need to watch all six Chicago groups?"

"No. You might want to watch the grandmothers from Monday night and the girls and mothers from Tuesday. They're the best of the worst."

"You'll pull some quotes for me that support a recommendation to stay out of blue?" I said.

"Right. Fish where at least some fish are swimming."

My eyes rested on her for a moment. That seasick feeling was still with me. "What are you going to do, Jill, if we don't keep this account?"

She stiffened, took a breath. "To tell the truth, I don't know, Brian. I haven't started looking, yet. I've been too busy trying to keep the account going--we can't let any balls drop now." She shrugged. "Mike's got an interview next week with Central Fidelity--in the trust division. Maybe our luck will change."

"I hope so, Jill. Say, I have a friend at CFB in commercial lending. I'll give him a call and see if he he knows anyone who might help. Anyway, don't worry--don't even think about losing Benton between now and then. We're going knock Rita on her heels. Just wait and see."

My nose didn't grow; that was a good sign. I sure as heck could have used one.

By Wednesday afternoon I had viewed three groups from the Chicago disaster, and was in the editing booth with Ned Tandy going over the Richmond tapes for the second time. Nothing had changed, but I was beginning to feel that maybe I'd be able to do something with them. Every now and then, someone would say something positive, although it was usually surrounded by negative comments.

There was a round of laughter from the monitor. Then a woman said, "You know, a cedar chest is a practical place to store certain items. I still use mine for blankets and sweaters."

"Copy that, Ned," I said. "From where she says, 'You know,' through 'sweaters.'"

Ned nodded and went to work.

A little later, another grandmother said, "If you tell them it's a practical place to keep wool in the summer, they'd go for it . . . maybe."

"Hold it, Ned. Back up a little. Hold it right there. Now, let's get what that lady said--only cut it before she says the word, 'Maybe.' Can you do that?"

"I can cut out a syllable if that's what you want," Ned said.

We kept on wading through, picking out pearls and leaving the negative stuff behind. Ben had been right. Although I wasn't convinced I could make the silk purse we needed to win the account, there were a few positive comments if I looked hard enough. For example, referring to the practical storage idea one of the girls said, "If my mother or grandmother saw that, she'd be inclined to go out and buy it for me. I guess it'd be something I could keep and remember, but I can tell you, I'd much rather have a microwave or a ten speed bike."

I had Ned copy that through the phrase, "Keep and remember." When I got around to putting all this together in an effort to put the best spin on it possible, I sure as hell wasn't going to include anything about a microwave and a ten speed bike. Not that I was thinking I'd pull the wool over anyone's eyes, I planned to tell Rita what a tough sell she had ahead of her, even if Larry did maintain we'd be better off to say only what she wanted to hear. I wasn't going to lie. On the other hand, when it came to convincing her of the tack she should take, I didn't want to clutter her mind with a lot of negative banter.

By the time I left the editing booth, I was convinced the marketing position I'd decided on with Ben was the right one for Rita to take, even though I still had doubts about my ability to sell it to her on Monday morning--given the sow's ear I had to work with. Doubts or no doubts, though, I would have to keep a positive face if I was going to persuade Larry, Paul and Mary.

I had ten minutes before the big strategy session in the large conference room so I went to check my messages. Nickie had called and so had Roger Normandy.

I returned Nickie's call first.

"Hold onto your seat," she said.

"No lover boy? No hot lips? No how's your backside?"

"Sorry, I've been incredibly keyed up, wondering when you were going to call. It might have been Larry, Brian. I finally found someone who was at that Ad 2 meeting. The meeting started at 5:30, there was a social until 6:30 when Larry started his speech, and he was out of there by 7:15--according to Beth Osborne, and she should know. She's the program chair."

"And the meeting was held at the Omni, which is a two minute walk from the agency."

"You got it, Watson."

I thought for a second. "Yes, but what about the attempted break-in? You know, Monday night during the focus groups? Larry was there with me, remember?"

"I've been wondering about that, too," she said. "Then I remembered. Didn't you tell me Larry left early? What time did he leave?"

I had seen the groups two more times now and they were fresh in mind. I scribbled *grandmothers, mothers, girls* on a scratch pad.

"It was during the group with grandmothers." I put a check by it.

"And what time was that?"

"Well, the grandmothers came on first, so it started at

five. Then the mothers came on at six-thirty," I said. "So--"

"The break-in took place at seven-thirty. I knew it wasn't Paul."

"We don't *know* it wasn't Paul."

"But don't you see? It could have been any of our candidates. And Larry's got a motive."

"Yeah, but so do the others. Mary, Lauren Saran Wrap."

"I don't think it was Mary," Nickie said. "No motive. And it couldn't have been Miss Saran. She's in Cancun."

"How right you are." Sally's face flashed in my mind, but I kept my mouth shut."

"So what are we going to do? Damn. I thought we had this thing narrowed down."

"What did the police say?"

"As you suspected, not enough evidence. Nothing that will hold in court. Obviously, they're right, considering this latest development. The case is still closed."

I wrote the names of the partners on the scratch pad. "We have to find out where each of them was that night. Larry left the Omni at seven-fifteen. I called him about nine to tell him about Uncle Rod. There's almost a two-hour hole. The others we know zip about. Nada. Nil."

"And you've looked at their calendars."

"Aside from asking each of them, what more can we do?"

There was a long pause.

"Unfortunately, I don't think we've heard the last from the killer," Nickie said at last. "Whatever he thinks is in those files must really have him worried. He missed last night, but only by inches. Oh Brian, I'm getting scared, scared for you, scared for me."

She was right.

"I could bring the files back to the office," I said.

"Oh, Brian, maybe you should."

"No, I'm not going to do that--I'm determined to catch him. So, he's going to do one of two things. Try to knock me off, or try to get into the apartment and get whatever it is that's got him all riled up."

"Is it really worth dying for? Think, Brian. Think about it hard. There's almost nothing worth dying for."

I circled Paul Williams' name on the pad. "My guess is, he probably knows I went to the police. Anyone in their right mind would go to the police after what happened last night. So, he has figured out that if he should be successful in knocking me off, the cops are going to be damn suspicious. I've told them what I know, about the partners and the stock and the sale to Transpublic. If something happens to me, the cops are bound to reopen the case."

"True. But you can't let down your guard. Whoever aimed that car at us last night and mashed on the gas is desperate. He or she is capable of anything."

I folded the top sheet of the scratch pad and put a crease in it. "Don't worry, I've already grown eyes in the back of my head. My guess is, he'll be back after the files. We need one of those surveillance cameras like the ones they have in banks."

"Our friend knows about Soho, now," she said.

"If he's smart, and I know damn well he's smart, he'll wait until nobody is home--including Soho. Like when I take him out to the lake for a run."

I looked at my watch; it was five minutes to three. "Listen, Nickie, I've got to run. The strategy meeting is in five minutes and I've one more call I need to make. Do me a big favor, though, will you? Look in the yellow pages. See where we can get a surveillance camera. We're going to catch the S.O.B."

"Aye, aye, chief. Promise you'll be careful?"

We agreed to meet in the lobby at five; I hit the flash button and dialed Roger Normandy's direct line.

"Mr. Normandy's office."

"Brian Durston here. Is Roger in?"

"I believe so, Mr. Durston. He's been expecting your call. One minute, please."

There was a click.

"Brian?"

"Yes, Roger."

"Good to hear your voice. Listen, I don't want to be a pest, but I wanted to make sure you had everything you need to make a decision. How close are you?"

"I'm getting there, Roger. I'll let you know before the end of the day tomorrow, as we agreed."

"Did you get the employment agreement?"

"Yes. And there is one question. The target profit goal, the one that has to be met before the bonus pool starts to accumulate . . . how realistic is that?"

"I've been at this with Flint for eight years now, Brian, and I can honestly say we've exceeded our profit goal every year. In fact, for the last two we've doubled it. There's no reason to think we won't continue to hit numbers like that. If you will plug in the math, you'll see that you'll be entitled to a bonus in the $250,000 range if we can keep the same level of profit."

I looked down and realized I was drawing dollar signs on the pad. Then I thought about padding invoices and Les Greenhill and it brought me down.

"And the stock options?" I said.

"No one can predict the future price of a stock, Brian. But if you were to review the history of Transpublic over the past ten years you'd see it has climbed from about 30 a share to about 60 and split two for one every two or three years. If we can maintain that kind of performance you'll be a millionaire before the age of 40, I can assure you."

I drew a dollar sign, followed by a one and six zeros. Then I added the commas.

"One more thing, Roger. Were you aware Transpublic had been negotiating to buy Durston Negus?"

There was a pause. "To tell the truth, Brian, I knew talks were going on. But I also knew they'd been called off because of that big account of yours--what is the name? Benton Furniture? The truth is, although I didn't say so before, the potential loss of Benton was another reason I thought you might be interested in returning to Flint."

"I see. I guess you could say it is a cause of concern." I tore the top sheets from the scratch pad and crumpled them. "You know, Roger, it wouldn't be right for me to leave here in the middle of preparations for a pitch. We're smack in the midst of putting it together."

"Of course not," Roger said. "When is it?"

"Monday."

"No problem, Brian. I wouldn't expect you to give anything less than the customary two-week notice. But I do need an answer from you by tomorrow afternoon. I can't let this position go unfilled for long. You know how clients are. They get antsy, think you're sitting on your hands. But if you decide to come back to Flint--and I think you'll see the wisdom in it--we won't say anything publicly about your decision until after the Benton people have decided on an agency. Believe me, I understand the delicate nature of your situation, Brian."

"Thanks, Roger. You've been very helpful. And, you've given me a lot to think about. I'll call you tomorrow before five o'clock."

"Talk to you then, Brian"

It was three on the nose when I walked through the conference room door. Ben, Mary, and Paul were already there, seated. Paul was doodling as usual.

I felt my skin crawl as I walked to the head of the table. "Anybody seen Larry?"

"He's on his way," Ben said in that baritone. "Did you review the tapes?"

"Yes. And you were right."

"How did Chicago come out?" he asked.

"No help."

Larry and his white hair and liver spots came through the door. He pulled up a chair next to Ben. They were all here now. I was almost certain one of them had tried to run over me last night. Then Sally's face appeared in my mind.

Something in my stomach twitched.

"Thanks for being on time, everybody," I said. "This is the meeting where we decide on strategy."

"Those goddamn focus groups were a fucking disaster," Larry said.

Mary looked his way. "You mean we chucked sixty thousand dollars down the drain?"

"Now wait just a minute, Larry," I said. "You saw about three-quarters of one group. I can assure you what you just said simply is not true."

"Paul filled me in on last night," Larry said.

"Paul saw one and a half groups," I said. "I saw all six Richmond groups. Lord, I've seen them three times now. And I've seen three of the Chicago groups and been thoroughly briefed on the rest. I can say unequivocally that we have what we need to support the position that Ben and I have been discussing." I hoped to heaven it was true. "I'm absolutely certain I can put together a very convincing case to use in the presentation."

Larry stared at me as though waiting for me to blink.

"You're just going to have to trust me, Larry," I said.

Paul picked up his legal pad and admired his doodle. He tossed it back on the table and looked up at me. "Practical storage mixed with a spoonful of sentiment and a dash of tradition. That's what you said, isn't it?"

"Very succinctly put," I said.

"And potentially boring as shit," Paul said.

"These chests, how much do they cost?" Mary said.

"Three or four hundred bucks," Ben said.

"Who's going pay four hundred bucks for storage space?" Mary said.

"Moths don't like the smell of cedar, Mary," Ben said. "You put blankets and sweaters in them during the summer."

She rolled her eyes. "How many boxes of moth balls can you buy for $400? For Pete's sake."

"I think you make a good point, Mary," I said. "That's

why we can't forget the sentiment and the tradition. They add value."

"And it's also a nice piece of furniture," Ben said. "I mean, how much does a new coffee table cost these days? My wife saw one she wanted for two thousand bucks."

"What was it, gold plated?" Mary said.

"Brass, mostly. And glass."

"Jesus, you people are so full of shit," Paul said. "How boring is storage? I'm telling you, at least I'm trying to tell you but no one will listen--we've got do something with sparkle. As the old cliché goes, you sell the fucking sizzle, not the fucking steak."

"Do you have something specific in mind?" Larry asked.

"I thought you'd never ask." Paul stood. "We've been working on this in creative, and my direction to the troops has been glitz, glitz, glitz, give me some glitz." He shoved his chair out of the way and rubbed his hands together. "We've come up with a bunch of stuff, as you'd expect, but let me just pick out the creme de la creme. Picture a series that's based on old movies--old movies with lots of glitz and lots of glitter. You see them all the time on AMC, like Fred and Ginger, and *Forty Second Street*." He nodded my way. "Old meat head here gave me the idea when he talked about how he was going to work miracles with that focus group tape through the wonders of modern electronics. Anyhow, what we do, see, is take characters out of these movies and insert them into our commercials. Fred and Ginger dancing on top of a cedar chest. We'll even colorize them." He did a little tap dance step--kicked an imaginary top hat with the heel of his foot. "God, I can see it now, that kind of stair-step pyramid-like thing that swings around with all those gorgeous chorus girls dressed up in feathers 'n' shit. We'll put the cedar chest right at the top of that fucker." Then he put his hands on the table and leaned forward like he was going to share something really special. "My personal favorite, though, is *Breakfast at Tiffany's*--you know, that flick with Audrey Hepburn and

George Peppard from the story by Truman Capote? Remember that part in the beginning when Holly Golightly's in the cab--real early in the morning, headed down Fifth Avenue? It's dawn--remember how the light is kind of bluish-gray?--but there's still traffic, of course, and this terrific music is playing. Baa, baa, baa-baa-baa, chinka, chinka, chink. The name of the tune is 'Hubcaps and Taillights.'"

"Where does the cedar chest come in?" I asked.

"Oh, I don't know, that's a fucking detail. Maybe we have Holly sit on it and kick back--right in the middle of Fifth Avenue."

"You could put it in the window of Tiffany's," Larry said. "You know how she gets out of the cab and walks over to the display window with her brown bag in her hand?"

"Great fucking idea," Paul said. "She pulls out her cup of coffee and her donut and her eyes light up behind those dark glasses when she sees this magnificent hope chest on the other side of the glass."

"How much is all that going to cost?" Mary said. "Sounds expensive to me."

"Another fucking detail," Paul said. "Would you quit with the fucking how-much-is-it-gonna-cost crap? They said the budget was ten fucking million dollars. They can fucking well afford it."

"I have a problem with it," Ben said. "It's been done. Diet Coke--with Jimmy Cagney and Humphrey Bogart."

"I remember that," Larry said. "Didn't they use Cary Grant, too?"

"Bet that was expensive," Mary said. "You would really have to pay top dollar for names like that."

"Lintas? Yeah," said Larry. "Didn't Lintas go down the tubes after that? Interpublic merged them into Ammirati & Puris--"

"Aw for Pete's sake," Paul said. "Every fucking thing has been done. But goddamit, it hasn't been done the way that I have in mind. In those commercials they pulled the characters out of the old flicks and put them into current live action stuff. I'm talking about doing it the other way around."

"I've got a monumental problem with it," I said.

Paul looked at me and frowned.

"I'll admit that it's creative, and there's no question it'll get noticed and talked about," I said.

"What fucking more could you ask?" Paul said.

"There needs to be some reason why you would want to buy the product," I said.

"Aw bullshit," Paul said. "Did those Diet Coke spots give a reason to buy? How about the Nike commercials? Just Do It, man."

Larry said, "Advertising is the business of raising people's awareness--getting people to think about a product because a thought is what leads a person to action. These commercials do the trick in spades."

"You make a good point, Larry," I said. "But there's a difference between Diet Coke and Nike and cedar chests. People are constantly making decisions about which soft drink to buy. It's an impulse thing, so whatever is on their minds is what they buy. The same goes for athletic shoes, except maybe to a lesser extent. A person is in the store and they're going to buy one brand or other, and something in their brain says, 'Well, if it's good enough for André Agassi and Tiger Woods, it's good enough for me.'"

"So what's your fucking point?" Paul said.

"If there's one thing the research tells us, it's that people are not itching to rush out and buy a cedar chest the minute a girl is about to graduate from high school or college or to set up her own apartment. Maybe they're thinking about buying some kind of gift for her, but it's more likely to be a microwave, or a VCR. We need to sell the *idea* of a cedar chest, not just get them to select our brand instead of the competition. We even need to get them to go to a different kind of store."

"Wait a fucking minute," Paul said. "I distinctly heard Rita Maloney stand right there and say she was planning to take the market away from the other brand. That says to make Benton top of mind, ahead of the other one. We're not trying to sell the idea of buying a cedar chest, we're trying to take sales away that would have happened anyway--just like Nike and Diet Coke."

"He's right," Larry said.

"That's what she told us," Mary said.

"Somehow, I think we need to do both," Ben said.

Paul looked at Ben and shook his head. "For Chrissake, this is not *War and Peace* we're creating here. We're talking thirty second commercials. How much do you think you can do in thirty fucking seconds?"

"Just think how many graduation gifts, and house-warming gifts are probably purchased every year," I said. "Just think about all those VCRs and microwaves. Cedar chests are probably an infinitesimal percentage of the total. What would it take to double the percentage? What would it take to triple it? Why should Benton be content with just taking away market share? Why shouldn't they create *new* sales while they are at it?--take sales away from stuff that has no sentimental or traditional value whatsoever?"

Paul flopped down in a chair. "I don't know. But I do know, I like the fucking campaign we've already come up with."

I sat down as well, and looked from Mary to Larry to Ben.

Larry leaned forward. "Both you guys make good points. Now Paul, you have the old movie campaign practically in the can. Why don't you have some of the spots you mentioned fine-tuned and maybe put into rip-o-matic form for the presentation? In the meantime, give a couple of other creative teams Brian's selling proposition and let them see what they come up with? We'll decide on Sunday afternoon what we will present. Hell, maybe we will present both of them."

"Sounds good to me," Ben said.

"Why not cover all the bases?" Mary said.

What was going on here? "There's just one little problem," I said. "I'm doing the research and strategy part of the presentation--the build-up for the campaign we recommend. I have more than twelve hours of video tape to edit down to a few precious minutes. Obviously, I'm going to want to do it one way if we present Paul's campaign and another if we use mine."

"So do it both ways," Larry said.

"Larry, twelve hours of tape whittled down into a couple of minutes. Have you any idea how long that's going to take?" I exhaled. "Actually, we're not talking about just two ways we might go in this presentation, we're talking about three--practical storage with tradition and sentiment, the glitz-awareness-grabber, and the one where Rita gets to take her pick of the two."

"You have my sympathy, Brian. No kidding," Larry said. "But this presentation is a matter of life and death for the agency. Suppose Paul's people don't hit pay dirt on the tradition thing? We have to be able to fall back on glitz."

I looked at Ben. Why wasn't he coming to my defense?

Ben said, "He's right, Brian. I agree with your strategy, but if we don't have the creative to go along with it, we're dead. It's as simple as that."

"Can you help me, Ben? Can you take the glitz tack and edit the tape to support it?"

He frowned. "I wish I could, but something has come up. I'll be lucky to make it back here by Sunday afternoon. In fact, I was going to tell you guys to write me out of the presentation. I'll be there, of course, but don't give me a speaking part."

"What's the matter?" Larry said.

"It's personal," Ben said.

Everyone agreed that I would just have to do the first part of the presentation however many ways it took so all our bases were covered.

After the meeting Ben pulled me aside.

"I didn't want to blast this out in front of the others, but you and I've become close, so I wanted you to know."

"Right, Ben. What is it?" I could see sadness in his face, and his skin looked a little ashen to me.

"My mother died," he said.

"Oh Ben, I'm sorry."

"It wasn't unexpected. She'd been battling cancer for more than a year. Anyway, I'm driving the whole family to Galax. The funeral is on Friday."

I didn't know what to say. The poor guy looked so sad.

"We should be back Sunday. I'll do my best to make it to the meeting."

"Thanks, Ben. You know how much I value your friendship and support. If you can't make it Sunday, don't worry. We'll see you at the presentation Monday."

13

It occurred to me while I was standing on the Heriz in the lobby, waiting for Nickie and staring up at the the light coming through the ficus trees, that I'd spent a good deal of my working life trying to second guess clients. Oh, I always start by telling them what I think they need. Unfortunately, though, that's usually not what they want to do, even when I know in my heart I've recommended the best way to sell the most widgets. They seem to have this nagging feeling their problem is slightly different, somehow unique, that I cannot possibly have identified the proper course of action. I lead them to water but they just don't drink.

Of course, they can't say why.

Bring me a rock, they say instead. It must be out there somewhere, albeit engulfed in mist. The truth is, it isn't out there. It's lurking in a hidden corner of their minds.

How big a rock?

Don't know. Just bring me a rock.

What color do you want?

Get the heck out of here, will you? And bring me a rock.

But how will I know if it's the right rock?

You won't, but I will when I see it.

What size and color rock did Rita Maloney want? I could see her in my mind's eye, standing in the conference room, adjusting her tortoise shell rimmed glasses, holding court.

"The campaign that will win favor with me is the one I think will sell the most hope chests--no ifs, ands, whereas, wherefores, or buts."

God, how many times had I heard almost precisely the same words? The question was, what did Rita think would sell the most hope chests? Maybe Paul was right. Maybe glitz was the way to go. Maybe the movie campaign would catch her fancy.

Then again, she had called them hope chests, hadn't she? If she thought of them as hope chests, rather than less specifically as cedar chests, she might have a hard time picturing one in Tiffany's display window on Fifth Avenue.

And Holly Golightly wasn't exactly the best role model for a nineteen year-old. But then, neither was Madonna, and she'd sold one heckuva lot of CDs.

Nickie came down the steps from the upper level, hooked her arm through mine and we went out the door.

"Security Systems Incorporated," she said as we walked downhill and across Fourteenth Street to the parking garage. "They sell and rent surveillance cameras. I picked it for its highly creative name. It's out in the west end--Parham Road."

When we were in the my car headed west on the downtown expressway I said, "What type of rock do you suppose would appeal to Rita?"

Dark blue eyes darted at me. "You're going to give her a ring? I've heard you account guys will do anything for a client, but this is extreme. Although I guess you heard the one where the account guy tells the prostitute to watch closely--because he is only going to show her one time how to please his client."

"Of course I have. Didn't you ever hear the one about the client who asks the agency to bring her a rock?"

"Sure I did," Nickie said. "But, in my experience, they

may not know what they want but they sure as hell know what they *don't* want. Bring me a rock, and make sure it isn't shaped like an arrowhead, or have any inkling of phallic overtones. Oh, and for goodness sake, it better not be pink. I've heard it all, all right, and I stopped listening a long time ago."

That certainly fit with what Tony Lavantos at Flint had said. "You're working with Paul on the presentation, right? What do you think of the old movie approach?"

Nickie was silent. After a moment she said, "It's borrowed interest, a gimmick. I'm not a fan of that. Still, it'll get the public's attention. The judges will frown on it, though."

"We're not trying to win an award here. We're trying to win the account." We were approaching a toll plaza. I took my foot off of the gas. "Actually, we're trying to save our rear ends."

"As I said, I stopped trying to please clients long ago. Now I try to please myself. It has worked for me."

For some reason, what she said made sense. "'This above all, to thine own self be true.' Four hundred years old, but still good advice," I said. "You're right, the best approach is to tell her what *we* think will sell the most chests." I threw 35 cents in the hopper and pressed on the accelerator. "Got any great campaigns in mind that also happen to please you?"

"One's starting to incubate."

I glanced at her and noticed that little smile. "Want to share it with me?"

She shook her head. "It's too soon. All I will say is, it plays to the research. Practical and sentimental. Every award I have ever won in this business has been for something that had a layer of emotion in it. That's what intrigues me about the combination of practical and sentimental." She let out a little sigh. "But you have to be careful how you handle an emotion like sentiment. It can get cheesy."

I was glad to hear Nickie felt she was on to something, and that it played to the selling position. I would have felt a lot better, though, if it were full-blown and I knew what she had in mind. Her observation about the movie approach relying on borrowed interest was right on. I knew there was something about it I didn't like.

We both remained silent as I steered the car onto the Powhite Parkway, and then onto Interstate 64, West. My thoughts turned to Jill Lathermill and her family. Her concern about losing the account and therefore her job must have been building to a fevered pitch. She was a good person and a heckuva fine employee. I'd called my friend at Central Fidelity and he'd said he didn't know the man in charge of the trust division well enough to pull any strings. What was she going to do if both she and her husband were out of work? Unemployment compensation wouldn't even cover the mortgage payment. At least I had Roger's offer to fall back on.

Or did I? Roger wanted an answer tomorrow. I glanced at my watch. Less than 24 hours to decide.

I looked over at Nickie; her eyes were closed.

Should I discuss it with her? And if I did, what did that say about the two of us?

I looked up and saw the sign for the exit to Parham Road. Better cogitate for a moment.

"You said Parham, right?"

"Three thousand block, north," she said.

I rented a camera--why buy one? Heck, I would only need it a few days at most. At best, a few hours. I took it home and it fit nicely halfway up on the bookshelf, wedged between *The Road Less Traveled* and *Romancing the Brand*. I ran the wire behind the books and under the Kazak to a small recorder which I hid under the sofa. Then I plugged it in, tested it, and covered the little red light on the front with a small piece of black electrician's tape.

I stepped back to admire my work; turned to Nickie.

"What do you think?"

"I'm amazed. You're the first account guy I ever met who could screw in a light bulb by himself." She smiled. "Don't worry, I'm going to spare you the joke about how many it usually takes."

"Thanks." Soho jumped up on me. "And what do you think, buddy?" I roughed him up a little. "You think it's time to go to the lake, don't you? Time to chase the ducks and to let Public Enemy Number One into this room to have his picture taken. Hold on just a minute while I change into my running clothes."

I had all those tapes to edit and felt the tug of the office on me, but now was as good a time as any to test my theory that the killer would wait until both Soho and I were gone to break in and search the files. Besides, Soho needed the exercise. Heck, the tapes could wait until tomorrow. I'd hit them in the morning and stay on them until the job was done.

I made a big production of leaving. I opened the garage door and called to Soho in a loud voice.

"Come on, boy, let's go. Get in the car. Time to go."

It was crowded with the three of us in the two-seater but before long we were there. Soho jumped out of the car and made a beeline for the lake and the ducks.

The early evening sky was still light, a pale blue with a yellow undertone. Our forms and the trees caste long shadows on the grass and the walkway by the lake. Nickie and I walked hand-in-hand, breathed in dry fall air and the smell of water, ducks, and the outdoors.

The surface of the water was smooth and dark--a mirror that reflected the magnificent fall foliage of surrounding trees: the burnt red-orange of dogwoods, the brilliant yellow and orange of oaks, the fuchsia of oriental shrubs. A tune, Edelweiss, drifted to us from the brick and stone bell tower of the chapel on the Richmond College side. We didn't speak. Instead, we stood taking it in, until the chimes stopped echoing across the water. I picked up a stick and threw it for Soho, who plunged in after it.

"I've gotten a job offer," I said. "And I've been wondering whether or not I should take it."

"I see. Want to tell me about it?"

"Tomorrow is the deadline to give an answer. I guess I haven't mentioned it before because I've had a feeling how you might react." I bent down and picked up another stick.

Nickie sat on a bench a few feet from the water. "Try me."

"The offer's to come back to Flint, and it's a good one. I would be Greg Farley's replacement. He's taking the number two spot at Omnimessage."

She nodded. "Greg Farley's an executive vice president, right?"

"Yes. I'd head all the non-package-goods business. The salary is way up there--I'm sure you can guess what the top four or five executives at an agency like Flint are pulling down. Plus, there's a generous bonus plan. And stock options."

Her gaze turned to the lake. We both watched Soho take the stick in his mouth and turn for shore.

"Why did you come to Richmond in the first place? Why did you come to Durston Negus?"

"It looked good financially. The cost of living is lower here. But the big thing was, I was tired of being somebody else's go-fer, of having to do whatever someone else told me to do whether or not I thought it was the right thing. To put it simply, I wanted to run my own show. Uncle Rod was going to give me his interest in the business--I was to be his successor."

"And now that may not happen," she said.

"Not unless we catch his killer. Not unless we come home and find the killer on the tape."

"I've got my fingers crossed."

"Even so, there would still be the Benton account hanging out there. If we don't keep the business, Nickie, it may not make sense for me to invest my inheritance in the agency. The fact is, the place might go into a nose dive. We could both be out of work."

"Then you could use the money to start your own agency."

"Hey, now. I hadn't thought of that."

"And I could write my novel full-time. That wouldn't be so bad, would it?"

Soho was out of the water. Before he could shake, I tossed the other stick.

"That's another good thought." I cut my eyes at her. "But how would you pay the rent?"

She looked up. "What rent? I was thinking maybe you needed a roommate."

A warm sensation flooded over me. "As a matter of fact, that's the third interesting thought you've had in a row. What about things moving too fast?"

"I *was* worried about that. Still am." She shrugged. "You might as well know, Brian. A frightened little girl is hiding under this acerbic exterior. One who's afraid of being hurt."

"I had an inkling. But tell me, what happened to calm your fears?"

"I'm still afraid, but after our close call I gave some serious thought to a basic truth I read somewhere. An infinite number of paths exist for a person to follow in life. If you don't choose, if you procrastinate and let fate choose for you, you may not like where you end up." She paused and looked at me. "I think I know now where I want to end up."

I picked up the stick Soho had left behind. "What if we don't catch the killer? What if we don't catch the killer and Benton goes south? What do we do then?"

"We're both out of work."

"Precisely. It looks to me as though I have two choices. I can be a millionaire before the age of forty, or I can be unemployed. That doesn't seem like it should take all that much thought. It's a no-brainer. I've always been motivated by money."

She was silent. Soho reached the stick.

Finally, she said, "You underestimate yourself, Brian. Maybe I'm a better judge of you than you are." She held me with her eyes. "Let's talk about money. Most people think it will solve all their problems. But when they get it, usually they find it ranks pretty low on the hierarchy of needs--down with food, clothing and shelter. It sure doesn't nourish the soul."

"Maybe it doesn't nourish it, but you can't keep the body and the soul together as a unit without it. Oh, I know. I've even thought about what I'd do if the worst happened. I could always flip hamburgers at McDonald's, right? I don't have a mortgage and I don't have dependents." Except Soho, who was now only a few feet from shore. "But the thing is, maybe I'd like to have a mortgage and dependents."

"Uh-huh. You'd be able to afford a really big mortgage with all that money from Flint. Where would you have this huge house that was full of dependents? Greenwich?"

I picked up the stick and got ready to throw. "Greenwich might be a bit rich for my blood. You can't get anything there for under a million."

"Westport or Darien? White Plains? All the way out in Brewster maybe?"

Soho emerged huffing and puffing, water poured from him. I threw the stick as far as I could.

"Someplace in that vicinity."

"My father commuted into the city every day from Long Island."

"I'd guessed that."

"There is just one thing I wonder about. Maybe you have it figured out."

"What?"

"When are you going to see these dependents? Weekends--right? Except when you have a new business pitch to work on, which will be about two or three times a month. And you'll also be able to squeeze in some quality time between, say about 8:30 at night and, oh, 5:30 in the morning. Of course, the little ones will be asleep, you can't help that. And it'll be a shame to miss the dance recitals and the school plays, but how in the hell are you going to get back out to Brewster for something like that?"

I picked up the stick Soho had dropped and sat down next to her. "Okay. How about a six room apartment up around 60-something, a couple of blocks off Park?"

"Which will only cost about ten or fifteen thou a month, parking not included, the equivalent of which you can get around here for approximately eight hundred a month. Twelve-hundred, tops. And that would probably be a penthouse." She took my hand in both of hers. "How about my original question. What do you want out of life?"

Her hands felt warm. I looked from them into her dark blue eyes. "I want exactly what you think I want. I want to run my own show. I want to make my own decisions for my own reasons, not because the shareholders are expecting a big dividend this quarter. I want to be with you. I want to have some Durston-D'Agostino offspring who are star players in Little League. I want to live close enough to the office to come home for lunch. Nooners every now and then would be nice. I want to make you scream with pleasure and beg me to stop because it feels so good you can't stand it." I shrugged. "That's it in a nutshell."

She squeezed my hand. "Damn. It's a shame but I think you're going to be disappointed."

"About what?"

"I doubt I'll ever beg you to stop."

An icy spray fell over us, a cold shower compliments of an impatient Soho--stick in mouth. "You devil." I laughed. "You knew we were getting mushy, didn't you?" I stood and threw the stick I'd been holding; watched it hit far out in the water.

"Great sense of timing," Nickie said.

"So your advice is, be true to yourself?"

"In everything you do. Little compromises eventually become big compromises. It's the reason I left Flint."

"That's not an easy credo to follow in the ad game. Especially when the clients are paying the bills."

"If you're good enough, if what you do sells widgets by the carload, they'll indulge you. The really hot, successful agencies have that figured out. Their clients come to them because the principals of the agency believe in what they do, and what they do works. The savvy clients know they don't make compromises, but they want what those agencies are selling so badly they accept the terms."

"An enviable position to be in. And you're right. It's not one we enjoyed at Flint."

"Most agencies are in the same boat--from big ones to little two-man shops. They're in it for the money and they're scared. Scared the client's going to walk." She shrugged. "And because they're afraid, they compromise their principles, if they ever had any. They're so scared of losing the business they give the customer what they think he wants, rather than what they know he needs. And sometimes it works--for a while. But in the end it always backfires. You lose the business anyway, and you wake up one day to find out you're a prostitute."

"So stick to your principles," I said.

"To thine own self be true."

I thought about that as I threw the stick and watched Soho swim for it a few more times.

Rita Maloney . . . what did she need? What was going to sell cedar chests for her?

Practical storage with sentiment and tradition--all we needed was an idea to pull it off.

Soho emerged from the water and snorted. He'd had quite a workout.

Nickie said, "It's going to be just a little messy--wet. Yes, that's the word--wet--on the way home in your extraordinarily roomy car."

"I'll take him for a couple of laps around the lake. That

will dry him off."

Soho and I settled into a comfortable gait on the path that weaved among the trees at the edge of the jet black lake. Ducks quacked in the distance. A goose honked. Streaks of yellow lit the sky. Windows of the commons reflected on the water, glowing with incandescent light. Lovers strolled past. A father and two little boys fished from a bridge. Across the water in the twilight sat Nickie on a stone bench
At that moment, I knew I loved her.
Dear Lord, I hoped this feeling didn't turn to agony as it had with Rachel Linden.

Ten minutes later, Soho and I rounded the turn at the end of the bridge on lap number three and started on the straight stretch toward Nickie. I motioned, pointed toward the car.
"Let's go, before he chases the ducks."
When we got there Nickie rubbed her hands along his back. "I don't think I would call this dry. Damp, maybe. Dry, no."
"I'll put down the top. Then there will be room for him in the space behind the seats."

There was something dreamy about cruising along Grove Avenue with my girl and my dog, the balmy breeze on my face and hair. We passed by kids on bicycles, a mom and dad out for a stroll pushing a baby carriage, college kids in a Jeep Wrangler with the top down, music blaring. I didn't come back to reality until I backed the car into the garage.
The killer could be lurking anywhere.
I walked softly through the walled garden, under the big elm, carefully climbed the back steps, and tried the knob. Locked. No sign of a break in. I inserted the key.
"Okay, Soho," I said. "You go ahead. Check things out."

No one was in the apartment; nothing was on the tape.

Twenty minutes later, I had the *coq au vin* out of the freezer and into the microwave. We were sitting on stools at the bar in the kitchen. The table was set, a bottle of merlot breathing. Nickie sipped a glass of chardonnay. I took a long pull from my scotch.

"I really thought he'd come," I said.

"He, or she. Maybe he already got what he wanted."

"No one could have come in with Soho here. Not without our knowing it. Certainly not now with that camera on."

"You're right. My guess is whatever he wants is still here. This person knows you haven't found it. He or she probably knows what is going on at the office, knows you don't have time right now to look for it."

"I feel guilty about taking off this evening. Especially since I now have to be prepared to do the presentation three ways. Maybe, as a matter of sticking to my principles, I should insist the presentation be done my way--or not at all."

"You could do that. If you had a creative approach you knew was right," Nickie said.

"You're going to see to that, correct?"

She took a little sip and winked.

"I suspect our man, or woman," she said, "is waiting for what they think is the right time to make a move, and this evening wasn't it."

I looked at my highball glass, hefted it, took a sip. A new thought struck me. It started small, puffed itself up and came crashing into my head full blown.

"Darn, darn, darn--crap. Know what I think? I think Paul panicked yesterday--decided he had to get rid of me because I was on to him. Then he missed. He came within inches, but he missed. And he thought he was a goner. I had to go to the police, right? And I did--but nothing happened. No police came to call on him. Didn't so much as ask him a question. He knows I showed them the memo. He has to. But the police weren't interested because the case is closed. So he breathes a sigh of relief. Now there's no need for him to break in here to steal that memo and wipe it out of the computer's memory because the police have already seen it. I let the horse out of the barn, but the funny thing is--it didn't matter. So the sonofabitch has gotten away with murder."

Nickie looked at me, no hint of a smile on her face.

"Darn, darn, darn--crap, again," I said. "That's it. It all fits."

"It's possible, Brian. But if Paul Williams did it, we'll flush him out."

I felt like sitting down right there and staring at the floor, but the beeper of the microwave sounded. I forced myself to get on with dinner.

Nickie lit the candles and turned off the lights. I transferred my creation into the chafing dish--all without speaking.

I sat, took the bottle of wine, poured a splash in my glass, held it to the candle's glow. Paul had won this round. But had he won the fight?

I took a sip.

If days went by and those files were not disturbed, it would confirm my hypothesis. Once I was sure, I'd find a way to trip him up.

I poured wine in Nickie's glass, then filled mine.

She raised hers. "To victory."

I clicked her glass.

After a few sips and a couple of bites my mind began to break free of the mire. I'd get him. No way would I let him get away with it. Also, there was no way that I could sit across the table from Nickie in candlelight and stay in a rotten mood.

"I was right about one thing," I said. "The *coq au vin* is better the second time around."

"I'm impressed you know how to cook."

"Ever seen that old movie with Jack Nicholson--*Five Easy Pieces?* He can only play five pieces on the piano, but he plays them very well. For me it's four easy pieces on the stove--hamburgers, French fries, steak, and *coq au vin.*"

"A renaissance man, nonetheless." She tilted her head. "Hamburgers, steak, and French fries? Guess I'll have to share my recipe for yogurt fruit cup delight topped with a sprinkle of wheat germ. A renaissance man needs balance in his repertoire."

She looked radiant in the soft, warm light. I put down my fork, leaned across the table. "At the lake you mentioned an interest in sharing living quarters. Would that be just a practical move? To provide you some measure of insurance against a temporary loss of income?"

Her face was motionless, then came the smile. "Practical, yes--very. We wouldn't even have to have a key made. I have one, already. And Lord knows when I'll get my computer fixed. But if I move in, who cares? The one you swiped from the agency works just fine."

After dinner, I drove Nickie to her apartment. We took Soho along just in case someone wanted to rummage through the files while we were gone. He and I both watched Nickie fill two suitcases with clothes and put food items into a couple of used grocery bags.

When we got back, there was still nothing on the tape. But now at least there was yogurt and wheat germ in my frig. It sat there, right next to the club soda and mayonnaise.

14

The inside of an editing booth makes me think of a submarine. It's cramped. There are no windows, lots of controls, little dials, levers, buttons, and the air is piped in. For the next few days that was where I was--aboard a submarine. Except when I walked Soho and crawled in bed.

Only one thing made life bearable: Nickie. And she was asleep practically each time I saw her.

I was awake a good portion of every night. Sometimes I'd look at her for hours. But she wasn't the cause of my insomnia. It had to do with the limb I'd crawled way out on.

Limbs. Black shadows projected by street lamps on a pale gray ceiling. The sounds of the night. New York, Richmond. It didn't matter which. They were the same. The air brakes of a bus when it stopped across the street. A police siren. The clang, clang, honk, of a fire truck. The dull roar of traffic from the expressway in the distance, the moan of a train whistle when the wind blew a certain direction. It must have been because of old movies, or maybe it was buried in the collective unconscious--the train whistle was the most forlorn sound of all.

There was a time in every 24 hours when it was

impossible to fool myself with my own bravado. That time was now, between two and four in the morning.

Uncle Rod had said each man and woman came to earth for the purpose of overcoming obstacles, that each of us was placed here so that our souls could work out problems which stood between them and perfection. In his view the physical world was a school, an elaborate Outward Bound course constructed by Infinite Intelligence as a place to bring fledglings along in preparation for ever higher levels of existence. Maybe he was right. I hadn't thought about it much. I guess I was waiting for the time when I felt I'd reached the halfway point of my tenure on the earthly plain to examine the meaning of it.

The current crisis had accelerated the process.

I now realized which obstacle I must be on the earth to overcome. The obstacle was fear. Not fear of physical harm. I'd played football in high school and college--safety--and faced unafraid more than a few big backs who had broken through the line and come at me full speed, the tops of their helmets pointed squarely at my chest.

Bubba's threat to knock my block off had frightened me. But I'd dealt with it. And anyway, the fear I'd felt then was nothing compared to what I experienced now.

I couldn't help thinking maybe I'd screwed up, big time. It felt as though I were living a nightmare: I was running and little demons were right behind me, running hard, reaching out, their claws an inch away. I was moving my legs as fast as I could, but I wasn't gaining ground. If only I could wake up. Except this wasn't a dream. I could easily wake up a week from now and find myself unemployed and unable to find a job in a field that had undergone a dozen years of down-sizing and showed every indication of continuing on the path of less is more.

So why not start my own agency? Why not offer clients less if that's what they wanted--a cost-effective alternative to the Flints and the Martins and the Arnolds and the Durston Neguses?

Right. And what would I use for money? How would I live, not to mention pay rent on office space?

Darn it. I'd had all these thoughts before I'd made my decision, before I crossed the Rubicon. I would not go back to New York, even if it meant flipping hamburgers. Nickie's logic seemed dead right, then. I should not cop out on my dream. I should go for the brass ring while there was still time to screw up. Heck, I was only 32.

But those thoughts and the decision had taken place in the calm light of day--not now, not in the dark hours between two and four o'clock when second thoughts were at their peak, when fear crept into the consciousness along with a distant train whistle, and pried its way deep into the gut.

I thought I'd known what I was doing. I'd weighed the downside along with the upside. It had seemed crystal clear.

Why did it seem so hazy now?

Would my decision backfire?

I rolled over for the hundredth time. Nickie slept peacefully beside me, her face that of a child. If she had been awake she'd have told me that we all are adrift in a sea of ignorance and can never be certain what a decision will bring. Even so, that shouldn't keep us from taking action. We have free will. We use it to make choices and that's how we learn.

It occurred to me that contrary to what Uncle Rod believed, maybe that was why we're here. To learn. Or, at a deep level, perhaps we already know. We simply need to *remember*. Re-member. Return the wisdom to our souls so that we become whole.

To do so required action. Choices.

Doing nothing was a choice--to do nothing--to let chance determine our fate.

Anyway, Roger had needed an answer.

"Hi Roger, this is Brian Durston. Listen, I've made a decision. I find your offer very tempting. I want you to know that. For a lot of people it would be their dream job, and it would have been mine only a few months ago. But after thinking long and hard, I've decided I can't accept it."

"Really? I'm disappointed, Brian. I thought surely you would. Things must have worked out for you. The Benton account is staying, then?"

"I don't know about Benton, yet, Roger. It wasn't so much work-related, or my current job. This came down to a choice of lifestyles. I've come to realize I'm not cut out for the big corporate environment. A few years were okay. I enjoyed most of it. But that was then and this is now. It's nothing against you or Flint. I'm just not meant to be a company man."

Thick silence hovered. At last Roger broke it. "I don't know what to say, Brian. I hope you know what you're doing--"

"I hope so, too, Roger. I sincerely do. Thanks again for thinking of me."

Nickie's advice had been to stick to my principles. *Follow your dream, Brian, the course you think has the best chance of leading where you want to be,* and that was what I had done. To heck with money, to hell with security--go for it. Catch the brass ring or tumble off the wooden horse into the machinery of the carousel.

If Uncle Rod were right, Nickie was as well. If a person were here to overcome obstacles that his soul knew would come about, then confronting those obstacles was the right course of action. Using free will to make decisions that would overcome them was the purpose of life and that meant that pursuing a goal or a purpose higher than the accumulation of material wealth must be what the soul would have us do. After all, material wealth remained forever on earth, but according to Uncle Rod, the lessons learned here, the re-membering, were part of the soul forever.

By Sunday afternoon when I walked through the front

door of the agency, I had concluded that my decision had been correct. I hadn't taken the easy way and chased the almighty dollar or security. I'd made my first conscious and perhaps slightly irrational life decision based on principles. Damn the torpedoes, full speed ahead. I could bid farewell to my salad days, and hold on for dear life as an adult.

To add to the pressure, no one had come to search the files. The camera whirred silently throughout the weekend. The only beings it got on tape were me and Nickie and Soho. This made me all the more certain Paul was my man, and while my logic seemed infallible, I could not think how I would flush him out into the open.

Not that I had time to think. I had been too busy preparing for the presentation.

I entered the conference room and took my seat. Jill Lathermill was there along with Mary McMann and Larry Negus. So were Nickie and her art director teammate, Ivan Hogan. Paul Williams stood and rubbed his hands together.

"Here we are, everybody. We've been having so much fun these last few days. We've tried a million ways to execute this practical-storage-tradition thing and to make everyone's life a little easier, I've culled it down to a precious few. Hand me that stack of tissues will you, Nickie?" He picked up a sketch pad sheet from the top of a pile and held it for us to see. "This could be a tv spot or a magazine ad. What you see here is a good-looking Williamsburg colonial with a for sale sign out front. In California we might use a ranch. The headline says, 'It's Your Dream House, but It Doesn't Have One Very Important Feature.' The copy talks about the fact it doesn't have a cedar closet, but the expense of installing one should not keep you from buying the house because you can bring your own in the form of a Benton cedar chest. The logotype at the bottom says, 'The Benton Cedar Chest. Low Cost Protection Against Moths.'"

For a few seconds no one spoke. Then Larry said, "Why wouldn't you just buy a box of moth balls? That would be even cheaper, wouldn't it?"

"Yes, but moth balls smell bad, Larry. Geez," Paul said. "Okay, next." He held up another sheet. "Here we have a studio apartment--living room, dining room, kitchen--furnished in early Holiday Inn, except in front of the sofa is one of Benton's cedar chests." He looked at Ivan Hogan, the art director. "Maybe we could have everything but the chest in black and white and make the chest in color. Did you think of that?"

"It wouldn't work, Paul. It would just look weird."

"Okay, we'll talk about it later." Paul looked back at the rest of us. "This one says, 'Can You Find the Cedar Closet in Your Daughter's First Apartment?'"

No one said a word.

"Okay, okay, so it needs a little work." He tossed it to Ivan and picked up another. "Here's a tv spot. We start with a tight shot of a woman. She's pulling down the trap door to the attic. The voice-over says, 'And now the moment of truth.' The woman climbs the fold-down steps. 'It's autumn, and the day you've been dreading all summer long has come at last.' She's in the attic now, and she unzips one of those hang-up plastic wardrobes. She sees something, she looks more closely. Her expression turns to one of horror. 'Your worst nightmare has come to pass, moths have eaten holes in your expensive woolen clothes.' Cut to a Benton cedar chest. 'It needn't have happened. Make a small investment before summer comes again. In a Benton cedar chest. Low cost protection for blankets, sweaters and expensive woolen clothes.'"

Mary nodded her head. "Now that would make me think about buying a cedar chest. With that one you hit me right where it hurts--in the pocketbook."

Larry said, "I realize your pocketbook is your most sensitive organ, Mary, but at the risk of repeating myself, why not just use moth balls? You said yourself the other day they are a helluva lot cheaper than a cedar chest."

"I know, but I'd forgotten how bad they smell--and

how expensive a winter wardrobe is."

"The spot doesn't say anything about moth balls and how bad they smell," Larry said.

Paul said, "Yes, but we could run it in conjunction with magazine ads like this." He picked up another sheet, looked at it and turned it to a horizontal position. Then he held it for the rest of us to see. A squiggle ran across the top above what looked like two boxes side by side.

"What we have here is a two-page spread which would run in women's magazines. On the left is a box of moth balls. On the right, a cedar chest. The headline says, 'The Preventive Medicine on the Left Costs Less, but Brother Does It Smell.'"

Paul chuckled.

"Cedar smells, too, doesn't it?" Larry said.

"Yes, but Larry, cedar smells good," Paul said. "Moth balls smell bad."

I sat horrified while Paul held up one stupid concept after another. Visions of the unemployment line flashed through my mind. I could almost hear the sizzle of hamburgers; smell the grease. Finally, I could not take it any longer. "Wait a minute, wait a minute," I said. "With all due respect, Paul, something is wrong here. What happened to the selling strategy? What happened to practical storage with a touch of sentiment and tradition? I see the practical storage loud and clear. But there's nothing in any of this about sentiment and tradition."

"You account guys always take everything so fucking literally," Paul said. "You get married to a fucking position strategy that has all these fucking words in it and you expect to see something overt in the creative pertaining to every single fucking one of them. There's nothing wrong with any of this creative work. The sentiment and the tradition stuff is implied, or can't you see that with those little beady eyes of yours?" He picked up the sketch of the Williamsburg-style house and pointed to it. "Look at this. It could be on the fucking Duke of Gloucester Street, for

Chrissake. How fucking traditional can you get?"

I said, "I don't think you've quite grasped the point of sentiment and tradition I thought we agreed upon, Paul. You see, our research indicates that grandmothers and even some of the mothers remember when receiving a cedar chest represented a rite of passage for a young woman, a sort of coming of age. They recognize things are different today and that giving a cedar chest to hold a trousseau may not be appropriate. Our goal is to make giving one appropriate again by positioning it as something practical, as valuable storage that's at a premium in today's cramped living quarters. A place to protect wool in summer. Yet, even though it's a practical gift, there's an undercurrent of sentiment connected with the giving of it because of the meaning it once had."

Paul stared at me, then blinked. "Knock me over with a fucking feather. That's the first time I ever heard any of that mumbo jumbo. You must have dreamed that we had a conversation about whatever you just said, Durston." He looked around at the others. "Any of you ever hear any of that before? Am I going nuts or something? Is it me?"

Larry shrugged.

Mary shrugged.

"That's what I thought the position strategy was all about," Jill Lathermill said.

"Now, just a minute," Paul said. "You weren't even in the fucking room."

Jill held up a piece of paper. "Here's the creative brief I gave to traffic Wednesday afternoon. I'm sure you got a copy. It's all spelled out in here."

"Aw for crying out loud. Account executives and their fucking creative briefs," Paul said. "You hide all this shit in fine print, write it in little tiny mouse type on the head of a fucking pin, don't say a goddamn thing about it, then whip it out and gloat that it was all down in black and white. Who the fuck reads creative briefs, anyway?"

Jill shrugged. "We went to a lot of trouble to put the

strategy down in writing so you would have it to refer to. Seems like you would at least take a look at it." She looked at me. "Doesn't it seem to you they would at least take a look at it?"

"I looked at it," Nickie said.

"So did I," Ivan said.

Paul gave them a double-take.

"See. We did look at it," he said. "All this bullshit--was it in there guys? Ten to one it's a fucking figment of her imagination."

"It's in there," Nickie said.

Ivan nodded.

"No shit? Well for crying out loud. If it's in there, how come we don't have any creative that relates?"

"We did," Nickie said. "Only you threw it out. You said it was cheesy."

A light seemed to click on above Paul's head. "Oh, you mean that sappy shit with the grandmother?"

"Maybe we should have a look at it," I said.

Paul frowned at me. "I don't know, Durston. It's not the kind of work we usually do around here."

"If it even comes close to the strategy we should have a look," I said. "Everything so far has been off by a mile."

"Okay, okay. Jesus. Did you keep it, Nickie?"

"It just so happens I have it right here." Nickie reached beside her and produced a handful of sketch pad sheets. She looked at Paul. "Want to do this, or shall I?"

"Be my guest."

"Okay, what I have here is a magazine ad." She held up a sheet with two circles drawn on it in black Magic Marker. "This is a picture of an older woman, sixties, maybe seventies--gray hair, wrinkles--standing behind a girl in her twenties. The older woman has her hands over the girl's eyes like she is about to reveal a gift. Down in the corner there is an inset photo of a Benton cedar chest-- positioned as though that's what the girl is going to see. The headline says, 'Your Mother Thinks We're Both So

Practical.' The copy will say something like, 'And she's right. Which is why I'm giving you this Benton cedar chest. It will protect your woolen clothes from moths and it will give you a place to store your most prized possessions in that tiny, but attractive new apartment of yours. But what your mother doesn't know is that underneath the practical exterior of both of us, we are two of the most sentimental people in the world. That's why I'm giving you a gift you'll open many times, long after I'm dead and gone.' That last part needs some work. It's not exactly the way we will say that." Nickie looked at me. "But you get the idea."

Ivan Hogan pointed to a corner of the paper. "Underneath the inset photo I was thinking we might put something like, 'The Gift She'll Be Opening the Rest of Her Life,' in bold type. What do you think?"

"I like it," I said. "The thing about the chest being around after the grandmother is gone is right on. Maybe we shouldn't use the word 'dead' though. What about tv?"

"The tv would be similar," Nickie said. "We haven't got it down on paper, yet, but we want go get the message across that this grandmother and granddaughter are soul mates, and by giving this gift the grandmother knows a part of her will always remain with the younger woman."

"Don't you think that's overkill?" Paul said. "Really now, it makes me want to get out my crying towel and puke."

"It's an honest emotion, a universal desire," I said. "And it gives one heck of a good reason to buy. This grandmother knows the granddaughter will outlive her. The chest is a way to be an on-going part of the girl's life. Who wouldn't shell out four hundred bucks for that?"

"I understand the logic. It's just so fucking cheesy," Paul said.

"I think it's kind of nice," Mary said. "Just think. You can buy immortality for only four hundred bucks. Such a deal."

"Sometimes cheesy sells," Larry said.

"My grandmother would run out and buy one after seeing that," Jill said. "She would be breaking down doors."

"You think so?" Paul said.

"Which is exactly what Rita Maloney wants," I said. "Broken doors."

Paul looked over his shoulder. "Am I out numbered here, or what? Gang up on me, why don't you? Geez."

"So like we said before, let's present both approaches," Larry said. "The old movies and this sappy stuff."

"I've been thinking about that, Larry," I said. "And I don't believe it's a good idea. Makes us look wishy-washy. Rita said she wanted our recommendation on what would have people lining up to buy chests. What does it say about us if we tell her, 'We don't know--so here, take your pick.'"

"We finally agree, Durston," Paul said. "The old movies will blow her socks off." He winked at Nickie and Ivan.

"What are you worried about? Are you afraid it says we don't have conviction?" Larry said. "So what else is new? I've never seen an ad agency that did. I'm telling you how to win the account, for Pete's sake. We show her both, we got our asses covered. Haven't you ever played blackjack?"

"What's wrong with giving her a choice?" Mary said. "When I walk into a dress shop I expect to see more than one hanging on the rack. I expect to have a choice. Why should it be different?"

"Right on," Larry said. "At least somebody here has a brain in their head. Let Arnold and Martin hang their hats on one approach."

"We're not selling dresses," I said. "Suppose you were diagnosed with heart disease and your doctor said, you have a choice, Mary. We can perform open heart surgery, or we can wait for a donor and give you a heart transplant. Either might work. But it's your decision, so take your pick. What would you say?"

"I know what Mary would say," Paul said. "She'd say, which one costs less?"

Everyone laughed but me.

"Rita Maloney is about to spend ten million of her stockholders' money," I said. "She wants to be damn sure she spends it the right way and she wants an expert to tell her what that is. She wants the doctor to say, 'You need open heart surgery, and you've come to the right place. Don't worry, we'll have you good as new in no time.'"

"But suppose what she really needs is a heart transplant?" Paul said.

"At least she'll think the doctor knows what he's doing," Jill said.

"This is such a subjective business," Larry said. "Everybody believes he's an expert. Throw a Coke bottle off the Empire State Building, you're bound to hit one. Every client I ever met thinks he knows more about advertising than the agency."

"I'm telling you, I can feel this down to the tips of my toes. Rita Maloney wants an expert opinion," I said. "She stood right at the end of this table and said she wanted to be convinced by us of the right approach."

"She did say that, didn't she," Mary said.

"I think it's time to take a vote," Paul said.

"Now wait a minute," Larry said. "Only the partners get to vote, right?"

"You, me and Mary," Paul said.

Oh Lord, I thought. "Mind if I make sure we all agree on exactly what the three of you are voting on?" I said.

"Okay. Lay it out for us," Larry said.

"You're voting on whether or not to make a strong, definitive recommendation and present only one approach along with the strategy behind it," I said. "And that approach would be the one Nickie just showed us."

"You will develop the approach further, right?" Mary said. "Smooth out the rough edges? Develop tv? Get rid of the 'dead' word?"

"Right," Nickie said.

"And if the vote is no, we will vote next on whether to

present the old movie approach by itself, right?" Mary said.

"That would be better than presenting two approaches, in my opinion," I said.

"All right already. Let's vote," Larry said.

"All in favor of the grandmother approach?" I said.

Paul and Mary raised their hands.

A look of shock transformed Larry's face. "What's with you people? I don't believe it. This is going to be suicide."

Paul shrugged. "He had a very convincing argument."

"Ditto," Mary said.

"Boy, that's a relief," Jill said.

"Makes sense to me," Ivan said.

Nickie smiled. "We'd better get to work."

Paul stood. "Come on, guys, let's knock this out." He turned to me. "What time can you be here in the morning, Durston? We still need to choreograph this fucker."

"You name it," I said as I stood and got ready to leave. "My part's ready."

"What time do we go on--nine? How about 6:30?"

"See you then," I said.

I walked back to my office. After almost four days of working into the night, it felt strange not to have anything to do. Who could say when Nickie would finish, so I went home, got Soho and took him to the lake. Jaunts of ten minutes or less around a few blocks in the Fan were the only exercise he'd had since Wednesday, so the second I opened the door he bolted out of the car like Steve McQueen in *The Great Escape,* and headed for the water.

As I jogged after him, I couldn't help thinking about Paul Williams. What a very, very strange dude. Obviously, he was a scurrilous blow-hard, but I'd seen plenty of those. What I hadn't seen before was one of his breed who could actually see the wisdom in someone else's idea and change his position accordingly. The type usually clung steadfast to his own, no matter how insipid, long after everyone else had moved on. Of course, I'd seen him at work on the

Poppins Pharmaceuticals campaign and been impressed with his marketing acumen. He'd chosen the one doctors would love--the one that would sell the most pills--over the purely aesthetic approach. Maybe I had misjudged him. Maybe his raucous exterior had misled me and he was not the yahoo I thought.

Soho had already dived in after the ducks and sent them scurrying. He bounded up to me with a soaking wet tennis ball in his mouth, which I wrestled away and threw as far as I could.

What really had me wondering, though, was how in the world Paul could act so cool and composed, so thoroughly unruffled in a meeting with me, when he had murdered my uncle, tried to murder me, and all the while knew that I was on to him. The guy must have antifreeze in his veins. His brain must be totally pathological.

Unless . . . unless he hadn't done it. The thought came like the plunk of a cello deep down in my bowels.

But if Paul didn't do it, who did?

Larry, of course. Larry had the classic motive, greed. He could easily have left the Omni that night, strolled three blocks to the agency, pulled the trigger, and been home by the time I called to tell him about it. By then, he would have been on his third or fourth martini. My dealings with Larry of late certainly indicated the man had no morals, no sensitivity to the difference between right and wrong. There wasn't a scrupulous bone in his body.

On the other hand, why had he tried to break in to get whatever was in the files, attempted to kill us, and then given up so abruptly?

Part of it fit, though. I remembered he had been visibly upset when he learned I had taken home the files and the computer. So why was he laying low now? Did he know about the camera? With the presentation and his insistence I do it three ways, he obviously knew I would be too busy to look anytime soon. Was he simply taking his time, waiting for the right moment? Waiting for my guard to be down?

Soho was back with the ball. I heaved it as far as I could and took a seat on a bench.

Could I be mistaken about Larry?

Larry and Paul were the only two people I had seriously considered at the agency. It could have been Sally. I'd known that all along, but had refused to give her serious consideration. I didn't want it to be her because of the girls. So, maybe Sally had realized Uncle Rod was making it with Lauren--Miss Saran. Had caught them in the act and he'd said, *Well, Sweetie, you shouldn't be so surprised. All we're doing is what you and I did when I was married to Millie. Remember? I left Millie for you, too. Just the way I'm going to leave you now for Lauren.*

Oh, no you won't, she'd said. Then she'd faked the suicide.

But what was in the files that she had wanted so desperately?

The letter from Lauren to Rod?

Could be.

And why hadn't she come back after that first attempt to get the letter had failed?

Maybe she'd realized I was way off on the wrong track and had decided to let well enough alone.

Maybe so. Anyway, if she'd done it, I'd probably never know. Hadn't I already decided I didn't want to?

And what about Mary MacMann? I hadn't considered her seriously. Money obsessed her. Every other word out of her mouth had something to do with it. Would the lure of more of it in her own bank account be strong enough for her to commit murder?

Darn. Maybe she did do it--although I had trouble picturing her with a gun in her hand, pointed at Uncle Rod.

Don't move, Rod.

Put that gun down, Mary.

She would move closer.

You won't get away with it, Mary. Brian will be here any minute.

She would put the gun to his temple--squeeze.

It was possible, of course. But the thing was, she hadn't even seemed all that interested in selling her stock.

What *had* she said?

She'd said that if push came to shove she was going to go along with whatever Uncle Rod wanted.

Had she lied? You'd expect a murderer to lie--to try to throw you off the track.

Maybe. But no matter how hard I tried, it simply didn't feel right.

Who else? Ben?

A cold spray snapped me out of my thoughts. The tennis ball was at my feet. I picked it up and threw it hard. Where was something else around here to throw? I needed to keep two things alternating.

I got up, found a stick and returned to the bench.

The thing about Ben, the thing I kept coming back to was, would he do it just to increase the amount he would receive from the Transpublic deal? He wanted to be a millionaire, wanted it desperately. But would he risk everything--his wife, his kids--to make it three million instead of two?

I'd grown up poor. I knew what it was like. Maybe if I had had enough in the bank, I wouldn't have gone along with what Les Greenhill had demanded of me. I'd have told him to take a flying leap off the thirty-nineth floor.

How much would it have taken for me to do that? Numbers clicked over in my head. Two million? Two million and I'd have done it in a New York minute.

If not Ben, then who? Were there other candidates I'd overlooked?

I shook my head. For a moment I'd even thought it might be Nickie. Okay, it had been more than a brief moment. But that close call. It would have been crazy to put herself at such great risk. And, Roger Normandy had readily admitted to knowing about the Transpublic talks, and about the deal being put on the shelf because of Benton. If Uncle Rod were a stumbling block to consummating the deal it would not make sense to bump him off *after* the talks were called off. Why bother? They would at least wait to see if we kept the account.

For that matter, so would Ben. Why go for three million instead of two when he might not get anything, anyway?

I got this hollow feeling at that moment. Why would Larry? Why would Mary? *Why would anybody?*

When had Ham Sheldrake said the talks were called off? About three the afternoon of the murder.

Hadn't the killer known? Who would kill because they *might* get more money?--*if* we kept the account and *if* Transpublic were still interested?

I had not looked at it that way before. We had learned Benton was going into review the morning of Uncle Rod's death, and that afternoon the talks with Transpublic were put on ice. The murder had happened between 7:30 and 8:00 that night. Greed did not seem as plausible a motive in light of the timing of those events.

Did all this bring me back to Paul? He was the only one of the partners I could see as having a motive if I took the Transpublic deal out of the picture. His job would still have been at stake--Transpublic or no Transpublic. And anyway, a few hours after we had heard Benton was going into review, Paul probably still thought the Transpublic deal would eventually happen--even if it was on the shelf. Everyone probably thought the snag was only temporary, and Paul's need to do something was surely immediate. Uncle Rod may have been in the middle of giving him the boot. Maybe Paul had lost his head. Perhaps it was a crime of passion and the suicide cover an afterthought.

But wait. What had Nickie said? She seriously doubted he would kill for money or a job. He'd bragged about an offer he'd recently received.

That could be a red herring, although he did seem to be a hot commodity. How could I forget the $25,000 signing bonus? Heck, speaking of his financial situation, if he got canned he'd get a $130,000 from the repurchase of his shares of stock in the agency.

Soho emerged from the water. I realized my adrenaline was pumping so I got up and started to jog. Soho fell in behind me. Occasionally, he would run off on a side trip to chase a few ducks back into the water or he would sprint ahead of me, but I became so absorbed I hardly noticed.

Could the timing of the murder and events with Benton and Transpublic be connected? It seemed as though dominoes had dropped one after the other--Benton in review, Transpublic's pull out, Uncle Rod's murder. Why would calling off the deal prompt someone to murder? And, if Nickie were right about Paul not being motivated by greed, who did that leave?

That left Ben, Mary and Larry. They were the only other shareholders, the only ones with anything to lose or gain. But what would any one of them lose or gain by killing Uncle Rod *after* the deal was called off? Nothing.

Now I was really stumped. Greed could not have been the motive. It was looking more and more like Sally did it.

Unless I was missing something. I had to be. I didn't want it to be Sally. Oh, Lord, I didn't want it to be her. But I had to find the truth. Maybe I wouldn't turn her in, but I wouldn't rest until I knew.

There was only one thing constructive I could do at that moment. Go home and go through those files again. I felt certain the answer was there. I'd simply missed it, that's all.

15

I worked well into the night, took out every manila folder and looked at every sheet of paper. I read whatever had anything to do with one of the partners or the ownership of stock in the agency, but I saw nothing in the files about Transpublic. The only thing on Benton of any interest was a copy of a letter from Ben Haley to Arthur Fletcher confirming a conversation which apologized for a cost overrun on a series of tv commercials and agreed to eat half the overage. Later on I found a copy of the letter Fletcher wrote agreeing to the proposal. It concluded with a blunt statement not to let anything like that happen again. Perhaps Paul was not my man, but he certainly caused his share of problems. The amount the agency was forced to swallow came to more than $50,000.

It was after midnight when I finally crawled in bed. Nickie came in after I was asleep. She didn't so much as blink when I got up the next morning, showered and dressed for work. I've no doubt she was still asleep when I arrived at the office at 6:30.

The alarm was off but the doors were locked when I got there. Assuming Paul had worked as late as Nickie, it seemed doubtful he would be here this early--even though we had agreed on the time.

I walked under the ficus trees and into the corridor to the conference room and thought about those doggone files. Maybe the killer only believed they contained incriminating evidence. I didn't want to face the conclusion I was coming to, that Sally had done it.

Or, could something be in those files I simply didn't see? I could picture them in my mind, two metal frames with green files hanging from them, stuffed with manila folders.

What if Uncle Rod knew someone might come looking for whatever it was?

I stopped in my tracks, snapped my fingers. Of course. Of course he knew someone would look. That's why he hadn't put it where someone easily could find it. It wasn't in one of the manila folders.

"Morning, Durston. Glad to see you're on time. Can't stand it when I'm up before the suits."

Paul stood at the end of the conference room table in front of a stack of poster boards. He picked one up, looked at it with his head tilted and his lips pursed, as if trying to decide whether it suited him.

I felt the urge to bolt to my apartment to check out the idea that had just come to me, but I walked into the room instead.

"Don't you ever sleep?" I said.

"Copped a few Zs on the sofa in Rod's old office, took a shower in the executive washroom. I will have to admit, however, your uncle's office is just a little bit creepy with the lights out."

"How late did you guys work?"

"It was after two. Oh, your girlfriend asked me to let you know she wouldn't make it into work. I gave her the day off--comp time."

"Nickie told you about us?"

"After two people move in together, it's hard to keep things secret long--telephone numbers, that sort of thing.

Don't worry, I can be discreet."

I came around the table to have a look at what he had in his hand. It was the two-page ad, except now the picture had been drawn so I could actually tell what it was and there was a slightly different headline.

"I like it," I said.

"Yeah, it came out pretty well, I guess. Your Nickie is talented." He nodded. "You know, I like this print ad, but I think I'm going to present the tv first."

"So you don't mind her being one of the Benton team, even though the two of us have become romantically involved?"

"What do you mean, the Benton team? We don't assign art directors and copy writers to specific accounts at Durston Negus."

"Oh no?" I said. "What about my memo?"

"What memo?"

"The one that spelled out the lineup of team members and the rationale for including each."

He looked at me and shook his head. "Let me give you a friendly piece of advice, Durston. If you want to keep a secret from me, put it in a memo. Fucking waste of paper."

"You didn't read the memo?"

"I already said, *what* memo?"

"So you didn't see the note I accidentally attached to the back of it?"

"Look Durston, if you want to present a team to Rita because you think it's the kind of bull she'll buy, then be my guest. Just don't force me to stick to it when the time comes for me to give out assignments. If I got a copy writer and art director who aren't busy, that's who gets it. All our people are good, and there isn't anything mystical about furniture. It's not like cyloid silica jell or some damn thing like that, that takes specialized knowledge."

"Sure," I said. But I was flabbergasted. He hadn't even seen the note. "Excuse me a second, will you, Paul? I have to take a leak before we get started."

I hurried down the hallway to the men's room, walked inside and looked at my face in the mirror. I looked as though I'd seen a ghost, and maybe I had--or at least maybe one had communicated with me. My intuition had been correct--Paul was not my man.

Why was I so unnerved?

Because intuition was just that--intuition--a feeling and nothing more. Now it was a fact.

Which meant?

Which meant Sally had done it. I'd already guessed it. I just hadn't admitted it to myself. Unless just possibly my idea was correct about where Uncle Rod might have hidden something practically in full view. If so, either Larry, Mary or Ben still could be the murderer. If only I could scoot home and have another quick look.

But I couldn't. I had to get back to the conference room and map out the presentation with Paul.

We had it all worked out within a couple of hours. I would go on first, lay out the background, cover the research and the rationale leading up to our strategy recommendation. Then Paul would come on and present the creative work. When he finished, I would return for the wrap up and closing argument. Other than that, Larry and the other partners would sit there, look pretty, and make nice noises if called upon.

With sequence and content decided, Paul and I each took seats and studied our notes. The others would not join us until just before nine when Rita was scheduled to arrive.

Mavis Alfonso brought in a pot of coffee, pastries and fruit at 8:30, and Jill Lathermill stopped by at 8:45.

"How do you feel?" She asked.

"Great. Paul and I seemed to have clicked. We're going to knock her dead."

She took my hand and squeezed it. "I know you will, Brian. We're counting on you."

She had no idea how much pressure that put on me. It

was going to take every ounce of will power to keep my mind glued on the presentation with the files at home screaming out to me, my own future hanging in the balance, and with Jill and her family counting on me for their salvation.

Larry walked in. "You guys ready?"

"No sweat," Paul said.

Mary arrived on his heels. "Do you think Rita would miss me if I wasn't here? I have to get the books closed--today is the end of the month."

So it was. It was Halloween.

"Mary, if you can spare the time, I wish you would stay," I said. "I don't want this to sound sexist, but I guess this will. You're a woman, the rest of us are men. Rita is a woman."

"I get the picture," Mary said.

The phone rang; Larry picked it up. "She's here."

I went to the lobby and escorted Rita back to the conference room. She looked as professional as ever--something about those tortoise shell rim glasses did it, and the way she dressed--only this time she wore a gray flannel skirt, a dark blue blazer and a white pinpoint cotton blouse, a much more traditional outfit that I ever would have pictured her in.

I poured her some coffee and there was the usual round of greetings and small talk. As before, I wished Mary would say more and that Larry would keep his trap shut. He came across as the huckster he was.

Eventually Rita took a seat, and I walked to the head of the table.

"We've been busy in the ten days since you were here, Rita. In that time we've visited and interviewed thirty seven of your dealers in three states, talked to financial analysts to get their views of the condition of the furniture industry and, without revealing your plans, we've gotten their views of your competitor's cedar chest business. We've also conducted twelve focus groups with a total of one hundred and twenty-one respondents who fit the profiles of cedar chest purchasers as well as those likely to receive cedar chests as gifts.

"So, what do we know now that we didn't know before? Let me share what we learned."

I picked up a wireless remote and punched a button. A slide appeared on a rear-projection screen behind me.

"We found that stock analysts are watching Benton closely. They're anticipating you will soon be making a dramatic move.

"And they view your competitor as a cash cow. Highly profitable, there's a wide margin of profit in chests, but they also see your competitor as over-the-hill with an aging management team, locked in a declining business. The company is also cash-rich and ripe for a takeover.

"Dealers, too, are looking to Benton for dramatic action. Word has gotten around that you are an innovator, and there is a buzz building in the business that you will take Benton to a whole new plateau. They hope you will take them along."

I punched the button and the next slide came up.

"That's a lot of pressure on you, but not without good reason. Your move into cedar chests could be the dramatic and successful stroke the industry and analysts are expecting. You may actually take over your competitor-- take his business without shelling out a cent. That's smart."

I punched the forward button and the screen went dark. Rita's eyes met mine.

"But it won't happen, Rita, you won't be able to pull it off, no one will, without some very smart marketing and communications, communications directed at the right people, saying the right things."

I punched, and up came the color-coded map.

"You may want us to follow up with a quantitative survey, but our qualitative research indicates you should concentrate your communications efforts where sales of cedar chest are already significant--as indicated by this map." I quickly explained how the map had been developed and the system of color-coding. "Ten million dollars is a lot of money, Rita, but the United States is a big place that can gobble up more advertising dollars than that in a hurry. Your budget should be spent wisely, and that means spending it in a targeted way." I gave her some examples, including spot tv in selected markets, dealer tie-ins and cooperative advertising, as well as the use of regional editions of magazines to concentrate coverage in the pink through red areas. "As my Uncle Rod used to say, Rita, fish where the fish are biting."

She nodded--I was getting through.

"At the top of the list of important things to do, however, we need to use the most compelling selling message possible. I cannot place enough emphasis on this. Our research tells us the idea of a trousseau chest is passé, even though this is the approach still being used by your competitor. We recommend you move out in front of the past, recognize that times have changed. Let me explain what I mean. To illustrate my points, I have taken more than twelve hours of video tape of focus group research and boiled it down to a few minutes. Let's take a look."

I motioned to the screen behind me.

"When asked about the idea of giving a young woman a chest for a trousseau, this is what one lady said."

The face of a grandmother appeared in stop action, then began to move:

It brings back the old hope chest idea, and I'm willing to bet you dollars to donuts they don't like that. They're thinking about going to college or getting a job. Lord help them, they want independence instead of a man.

The screen momentarily went dark and I said, "Another lady summed it up more succinctly . . . "

For goodness sake, what year is this anyway?

"Well put," I said. "So, it's logical to ask what new approach might we use to sell cedar chests? There is a certain amount of romance attached to them because of the hope chest, trousseau tradition. With that in mind, we tried suggesting that men buy one for their wives as a birthday or an anniversary gift. Let's see what our respondents said about that."

A middle-aged woman shook her head:

My husband better not go out and buy one of those things without me there to pick it out . . .

Another said:

. . . you could trust my husband to get something really gaudy--you know?

Rita chuckled.

"It is humorous, I agree. But think how much better off we are knowing how people will react to a message before we spend money to advertise it.

"We learned that grandmothers and many mothers know the meaning of a cedar chest, remember receiving one themselves as a rite of passage to young-adulthood. For them the tradition is important, but it is also dated. The trick will be to capitalize on latent goodwill and modernize it in such a way that giving a cedar chest becomes desirable. Listen to this."

The little gray-haired grandmother flashed onto the screen and said:

Hinton's Furniture Store used to give a miniature chest to every girl in our high school . . .

Followed by another:

That's the meaning of the hope chest--tradition.

And another:

I'd like to see young girls get back to the tradition.

"The question is, how can we bring them back in an age when lifestyles are so very different?" I paused for emphasis, then spoke slowly. "We believe we should begin by selling the practicality of a cedar chest."

Faces flashed on the big screen in rapid succession:

You know, a cedar chest is a practical place to store certain items. I still use mine for blankets and sweaters. . . .

My granddaughter told me, 'Grandma, if you're gonna give me something, for goodness sake make it something practical. . . .

Maybe this ad agency here could do some advertising to convince people it's an up-to-date idea. . . .

If you tell them it's a practical place to keep wool in the summer, they'd go for it. . . .

The screen went dark.

"We must reposition the cedar chest as practical storage furniture a young woman will value while simultaneously holding on to the undertone of tradition and sentiment that is meaningful to givers. One of the approaches we tried on focus group participants did just that. Let's see what they had to say."

I like that . . .

If my mother or grandmother saw that, she'd be inclined to go out and buy it for me. . . .

. . . that would do it. . . .

Of all the approaches you've shown us, this is the one that makes the most sense. . . .

I stopped the tape and put down the remote.

"Practical storage with a touch of tradition and sentiment, an approach that brings to mind the rite of passage inherent in the trousseau chest but makes the giving of it appropriate for today. We want to set the Benton cedar chest apart, to make it a special gift, one that transcends others, makes VCRs and microwaves look like what they are, VCRs and microwaves--equipment subject to wear and tear, which will eventually wear out and be cast out. Not so with a Benton chest. It will stand above the alternatives as a timeless family heirloom."

I had been studying Rita's face. She seemed to be taking in every word, nodding at all the right moments. It was time for me to get off the soapbox.

"Here now, to show you precisely how we intend to accomplish this, is our creative director, Paul Williams. Paul."

Paul stood and walked to the head of the table with his stack of mounted layouts and storyboards. It occurred to me that in deference to the importance of the occasion he had actually put on a tie today, although he still wore the usual flowered shirt and no jacket.

"That was great, Brian. You nailed it. This work I'm about to show does exactly what you said." He looked from me to Rita. "I understand you came to Benton out of fashion. Is that right, Rita? Tenth Avenue?"

She nodded.

"I used to be at Hubert Blatz," he said.

She smiled and pointed at him. "Manny Krystal."

"You got it." Paul sighed. "Imagine. From New York, New York, to Benton, Virginia. Your head must be spinning, still."

"Tell me about it," she said.

"Ever been to that off-brand gas station in Waynesboro? What's the name of it? Wilco?"

She nodded with a smile.

"Never seen anything like it. Doubles as a K-Mart. I bought a pair of sunglasses there once. Knock-offs of Ray Ban Aviators? $3.95. Do you believe it? I don't think you can buy a stick of gum for that in New York. And the Tastee-Freeze. Have you eaten at the Tastee-Freeze?"

She shook her head.

He showed her the palm of his hand. "Don't."

Rita chuckled.

"Okay, okay. Now, to what Brian was saying--practical storage with a touch of sentiment and tradition. What you're going to see will not be what you're used to seeing in the fashion business. In fashion, the dress, the gown, the handbag, the fur coat is *it*--all inclusive. The customer is buying what she sees, and that's all. That means we want her to see elegance and style, glamour. In the case of Benton cedar chests what we are selling goes a helluva lot deeper than the surface. Tradition, sentiment, the rite of passage-- as Brian said."

He turned a tv storyboard toward her and pointed at the first frame. "We shoot this commercial so the edges of everything are a little fuzzy, so it gives a kind of nostalgic feeling. The whole spot has a misty quality, like maybe it's happening in someone's mind or memory. In this first frame, a young woman is opening the door. You can tell she's just moved into a new apartment, packing boxes are scattered around, the rug is still rolled up, books are in stacks. She finds delivery men at the door and they are carrying a Benton cedar chest. It has a pretty ribbon and bow tied around it. The men pass by with the chest and the young woman pulls off the envelope that's attached. She opens it. Then, as the girl looks at it, we hear the note read in an older woman's voice:

Ever since your momma brought you home from the hospital people have said you were a lot like me. It's hard to believe that tiny baby girl is grown now and starting on her own. I wanted to give you something practical to mark this special day, since practicality is one of the qualities we share. This Benton cedar chest will hold your blankets and your sweaters and keep them safe in summer. It will also give you room to store your most precious memories and maybe even a place to put your feet up. But most important, it will give you something to remember me by and pass to your own granddaughter, someday. Because most people don't know the secret that we share. We're two of the most sentimental people in the world.

"Then there is a tight shot on the product and an announcer's voice comes on and says, *Benton Cedar Chests, give her the gift she'll be opening the rest of her life.*"

Did I detect a tear in the corner of Rita's eye?

"I like it," she said.

"What grandmother would buy a microwave after seeing that?" Paul said. "I hope that new plant of yours has the capacity to crank these things out fast enough."

He showed her another tv spot along the same lines, followed by an in-store display based around a frame blown up from the first tv spot, a sweepstakes idea to get furniture store salesmen excited about selling the product, and dealer merchandising aids and co-op advertising materials. Then he finished with the two-page magazine ad.

He held it turned toward himself so that she couldn't see it.

"This is a color spread that would run in regional editions of women's magazines, in *Southern Living*, and maybe in the *Mormon Tabernacle Times*." He chuckled.

As far as I knew there was no such thing as the *Mormon Tabernacle Times*, but except for that crack Paul was on his good behavior. I hadn't heard him use the f-word even once.

He turned the layout for her to see.

"The older woman is standing behind the younger one with her hands over her eyes, and the headline says, 'Try to Guess. It's Something You'll Be Opening Forever.' And the copy says, 'Your momma always said we were the practical ones in the family, which is why I'm giving you this Benton cedar chest. It will protect your woolen clothes from moths and it will give you a place to store your most prized possessions in that tiny, but attractive new apartment of yours. But what your mother doesn't know is, underneath the practical exterior of each of us, we are two of the most sentimental people in the world. That's why I'm giving you a gift you will open many times, and someday, pass on to your own granddaughter.'

"We've got a shot of the product in the lower right hand corner and the caption in boldface, 'Benton Cedar Chests, A Gift She'll Open the Rest of Her Life.' So what do you think?"

"I like it," Rita said. "I like it a lot."

"So do I," Mary said.

"Good work guys," Larry said.

I stood, took Paul's place at the head of the table, and looked Rita in the eye.

"This is the part when I'm supposed to summarize and go for the order," I said. "Let me do so as briefly as possible. We've looked at the situation from every angle, Rita. We've talked to dealers, we've talked to industry watchers, we've conducted extensive focus group research among consumers. We believe we've found the best possible selling message and a way to execute the message that will have people lining up to buy Benton Cedar Chests. That's what you want out of your advertising--the assignment you gave us ten days ago. I could go on and on. I could summarize in infinitely more detail. But another thing Uncle Rod used to tell me is, a good salesman knows when to stop selling.

"You must have questions on your mind, Rita. Are there any we can answer?"

Rita nodded. "A terrific presentation and a most compelling recommendation. You and your staff are to be congratulated. And you, too, Paul. It will be a hard act for Martin and Arnold to follow."

"Thank you," I said, and took a seat across from her.

"I don't really have any specific questions about the presentation. It was very clear." She leaned forward with a finger in the air. "But I do have one question, which has to do with dealings Durston Negus and Benton had in the past. As I mentioned to you, Brian, my predecessor's computer was missing when I arrived, and a lot of records vanished along with it. But after grilling my ad manager, Sam Trenton, about any problems there may have been, I find that production cost overruns were a rather large bugaboo. The question is, what assurances would we have that they won't be a problem in the future, assuming your agency keeps the account?"

I felt the blood drain from my face. That damn Sam Trenton, I thought he said he was on our side. I looked around for Ben to help out with this one.

Larry, Mary--no Ben.

Where was Ben? That was right, he hadn't been there the whole time, had he? Not since Wednesday.

Then it struck me. It entered my mind fully hatched like a great big screaming hawk in a power dive. Ben's ambition to be a millionaire, cost overruns, Arthur

Fletcher's computer, his threats about firing the agency, the master cylinder of his Jag--devoid of hydraulic fluid, Uncle Rod's files untouched since Wednesday--suddenly it all fit.

"I think I should answer that question," Paul said. "Frankly, many of those problems were caused by me."

I felt compelled to stand up and run from the room, to get home as quickly as possible, but I held myself back. Nickie was there, Ben might be there, too, trying to get in--

"It was my drive for perfection, I'll admit it," Paul said. "It's hard for me not to change something when it's not quite right, no matter how small or insignificant an imperfection may seem to be to others. But, I'm a perfectionist, and it hurts me to see something go out of here that is not as good as it can be. That means changes, of course, and unfortunately, in this business changes cost money."

I looked at my watch, it was almost ten o'clock, the time Rita was supposed to leave. Should I bolt, or stay? Nickie's life might be in danger.

"Rod Durston and I had several long, heart to heart talks about it," Paul said. "He even threatened to fire me once because of it. Anyway, the bottom line is, I've seen the error of my ways. Rest assured, Rita, it won't happen again. You can count on it."

"And if by some unforeseen chance it does happen," Larry said, "I can assure you no overages will be passed to you."

"Wait a minute," Mary said. "What about legitimate overruns? Sometimes clients ask for changes, too."

I saw Larry give her a kick under the table.

"I don't think that's going to happen," Larry said.

"Does that answer your question--and clear up your concern, Rita?" I said.

"I believe it does," Rita said. She stood; looked at her watch. "Good timing, it's just about ten o'clock."

"When will we hear from you, Rita?" Larry said.

"I see presentations from Martin and Arnold today, too. But I'd like to sleep on it. I find that's the best way for me to make a big decision. Let's say you will hear from me tomorrow. I may even stop by. Win or lose, I like to make the notifications in person. I appreciate how much time, effort and emotion you have invested this."

"Thank you, Rita," I said. It took every ounce of my willpower to remain calm and pleasant as I escorted her to the lobby and said good-bye.

As soon as she was out of sight, I bolted through the door and ran down the street to the parking garage.

It's a wonder I didn't get stopped by the cops on the way--I drove like Richard Petty in the Charlotte 500. I could hardly think I was so worried about Nickie, but as I ran the red light at Belvedere it occurred to me that maybe I should not go barging in. Suppose Ben had her at gunpoint?

What should I do?

I punched the numbers of my apartment into the car phone keypad and pressed the send button. It rang once. Twice. A muffled noise and some static came over the hands-free speaker, followed by the clatter of the handset at the other end as it bounced off of something and landed with what sounded like the thump of a hammer against an empty oil drum. Then I heard Nickie's voice, muted and frightened, call out, "No, stop!"

The hair stood on my neck.

The line went dead.

I punched the end button, and looked up just in time to avoid slamming into a slow-moving pickup truck.

My heart was palpitating. I punched 911.

"Emergency."

"There's an intruder in my apartment."

"Your name, sir."

I stood on the brake, turned the wheel, skidded onto Plum Street. Two blocks to go.

"B-Brian Durston." I gave my address--I almost couldn't speak from hyperventilation. "I, I just tried to call my girlfriend. Sh-she picked up--sc-screamed for help. He-he's after her. I-I'm almost there."

There was a short pause. "Don't go in, Mr. Durston. A squad car's on its way."

"For God's sake, make it fast."

I barely slowed down as I approached a stop sign, darted across Floyd, stepped on it as I shot down Plum, skidded sideways into the middle of Grove Avenue, missed a ramshackle Toyota by inches and skidded to a stop near the alley behind my apartment.

Don't go in, the dispatcher had said. *A squad car's on its way.*

Lord, I didn't even hear a siren.

I was out of the car, through the back gate into the walled garden, onto the back porch. The door had been forced. It was open three inches. Splinters stuck out around the lock.

Where was Soho?

I stood to the side, peered through the glass.

Oh God, there he was--in a heap on the floor. That bastard Ben must have shot him.

I pushed through the door, knelt down. There was blood beneath him and he wasn't breathing.

The rotten, filthy scum.

Then I heard the siren. Not just one siren, now. It was two, maybe three.

The dirty bastard had killed Soho.

What about Nickie?

I crept to the door of the kitchen that led into the rest of the apartment, turned my back flat against the wall. A strange composure settled over me, a sense of calm that descended in slow motion from my head all the way to my toes. It felt as though I were encased in an invisible bulletproof bubble--invincible, like Batman, and Ben was the Joker. The difference was, I was out for revenge and Batman would have been after justice. I wanted to strangle the bastard, crush his larynx with my bare hands. If he had harmed Nickie--I would also pluck his frigging eyes out. One at a time. Slowly.

I leaned into the doorway, could not see him. I left the safety of the kitchen and crept forward down the hall.

The sirens grew louder. One of the police cars screeched to a stop in front. Then another. The sirens died. Doors slammed.

Ben's voice called out and for once his baritone voice shrieked. "Don't come in. I have the girl and I have a gun."

I sprinted to the front of the house, into the living room as he whipped around, his arm around Nickie's neck. "Hold it, Durston, or I'll shoot." The announcer's pipes were back.

I pulled up. The gun was pointed at Nickie's head--her eyes went from extra wide to clamped shut--a grimace on her face.

From then on it was as though things happened in slow motion.

"If you want a hostage, Ben, take me. Let Nickie go."

"Put your hands up, Durston."

I raised them. "Let her go, Ben. I'll cooperate with you."

"You and your goddamn snooping. Why couldn't you leave well enough alone?"

He squeezed her neck, pressed the gun to her head. She began to whimper.

"I should blow her fucking brains out. If she hadn't been here this wouldn't have happened."

"Ben, the police have this place surrounded. You can't get away. Why don't you give up? Make it easy on yourself."

"I need time to think."

I had to reason with him, to try to get him to surrender, but I couldn't think of what to say. I just started talking. "This isn't going to work, Ben. Why don't you let Nickie go? She's never done anything to you. She was borrowing my computer, that's all. Lord, when did writing a novel become a dangerous occupation?"

He glanced out the front window then back at me, his eyes wide.

Keep talking, I told myself. "Did you find what you

were looking for in the files, Ben? A copy of a letter, wasn't it? My guess is, it's Uncle Rod's copy of a letter from Arthur Fletcher to you. Fletcher was firing the agency, wasn't he, Ben?"

Ben's nostrils flared. "That goddamn Paul Williams, and that goddamn Mary MacMann. He caused the cost overruns and she insisted we bill the fucking client."

"Pretty stupid of them, wasn't it, Ben?--right in the middle of negotiations with Transpublic International. You knew they would call off the talks if we lost our biggest account. I must hand it to you, Ben. They were dumb, but you were smart. Old Fletcher ran a one-man show, didn't he? Even his ad manager didn't know he was going to fire us. But you knew, didn't you? The two of you were tight, so he told you first, then made it official by putting it in writing. Wrote the letter himself on his computer. He also must have told you he was going to drive the Jag to work the next day. Hadn't been out in a while, had it? So you slipped into his garage and drained the master cylinder. Then you stole his computer so the letter wouldn't show up on the hard drive. You could have just deleted it, only you didn't know his filing system. That was a problem for you, wasn't it, Ben?"

"Got it all figured out, haven't you, Durston?"

"Another problem must have been the copy of the termination letter that went out to Uncle Rod in the mail. You must have tried to intercept it, but somehow it got through. Uncle Rod put two and two together mighty fast, I'll bet. I'm surprised he didn't turn you in right away."

"He acted so goddamn high and mighty all the time, but he was as greedy as they come. Shit, he was going to make almost ten million dollars off the deal, except he wanted to hold back some stock so he could give it to you, the dumb shit. He should have been willing to sell it all."

"Then Rita came on board and put the account into review, anyway," I said. "After all you had done, that must have been a blow. And Rod, his conscience must have gotten the better of him. He was going to blow the whistle, wasn't he? The deal was kaput, so why let a murderer go free?"

"The sonofabitch," Ben said. "He was even going to pretend he didn't know, that he had just figured it all out. Oops, I think one of our people accidentally murdered one of your people." Ben giggled hysterically, then regained control. His expression became serious. "Rod got what he deserved."

Suddenly, a masculine voice came over what sounded like a bullhorn: "This is the Richmond City Police. We have the building surrounded. You cannot escape. Come to the front door. Throw out the gun."

Ben edged closer to the window, his grip still tight around Nickie's neck, the gun still pointed at her head. He glanced out the window, then back at me.

"Why don't you do as he says, Ben? You aren't going to get away. You've seen enough of this kind of thing on tv to know that."

"There must be a way," he said.

"Think about it, Ben. Think about your wife, your kids. Think about those two great little boys of yours. What are they going to think?"

"Shut the fuck up."

"Give up, Ben. It will be easier on you. Let Nickie go. Walk to the front door, throw out the gun. If you give yourself up, they'll go easy on you, I'm sure of it."

"I told you to shut the fuck up, Durston. Do you know what the penalty is for first degree murder in this state? It's the fucking electric chair. If I give up they'll have me on two counts."

He had a point.

"At least let Nickie go, Ben. She's an innocent bystander, for heaven's sake. Take me instead. You said yourself my snooping got you into this. I'm the one you ought to have as a hostage. Look, Ben, let me talk to them. I'll call them on the phone. Just let Nickie go first. You let her go and I promise, I'll make them give us a jet plane and a full tank of fuel and a pilot. We can fly wherever you want to go. We can even make them give us money, Ben. How much you want? A couple million in cash? No sweat. We'll get a jet and a pilot and two million in twenties and hundreds. Old bills. What do you say?"

His brows furrowed. "Where would we go?"

That was a darn good question.

"We'll go to Libya, Ben. They'll give you asylum there. You'll be a hero. You know how they love to tweak the nose of the United States. Hell, they'll probably give you a ticker-tape parade down the main drag of Tripoli. What do you say, Ben? I hear it is beautiful in Libya this time of year. Blue sky, low humidity. Just let Nickie go."

"You're so full of shit, Durston. You think I'd go to Libya, for Chrissake?"

"Where else are you going to go, Ben--North Korea? I hear it gets awfully cold in North Korea." I thought for a second. "Hey, I've got it--how about Cuba? It's not that far to Cuba. We won't even need to refuel."

"The last people who hijacked a plane to Cuba were sent back," Ben said. "They're probably still in jail."

"Really? Darn, that's too bad. Okay, that brings us back to Libya. Or we could try Iraq or Iran. What do you say? Let Nickie go, and I'll get on the phone. You want more than two million? How about five? That should keep you in style in Libya."

I could tell from Ben's expression he was thinking about it.

The voice came over the bullhorn again: "Hello, in there. It's time to give yourself up. Come to the door and throw out the gun. We'll give you five minutes."

"It isn't going to work, Durston," Ben said.

"What do you mean?" I said. "Of course it will work. I'll get on the phone and call them, get all the details worked out. You know as well as I do, they're not going to shoot you if you have a gun pointed at me."

"You're the one who said that I've seen enough of this sort of thing on television to know it isn't going to work." He shook his head and let out a sigh.

"There's a first time for everything, Ben. Here's what we do. We send Nickie out there, see. And she tells them what you want. Five million in cash and a jet plane--full tank, pilot. It's got to be one with long-range capabilities--we'll demand that. Once she gets the ball rolling, I'll get on the phone with them and work out the details. How can we miss?"

"They'll pick me off with a sharp shooter on the tarmac. Poof, top of my head--gone." The way he said that, he was almost in tears.

"Look, Ben, I'm trying to help you, I'm doing my best, buddy. Let's think about this together. Come on. You said yourself, there must be a way out."

"Yeah. There's a way all right. There's only one way." Tears streamed down his cheeks. "I really fucked up, Durston. All I wanted was to make some money. To be comfortable financially, that's all. I came so goddamn close. Two million bucks practically in my hands. I could see it in my bank account already. Then that fucking Arthur Fletcher decided he was going to can our ass. After all the fucking sucking up I did--practically gave him a blow job every time I saw him." Ben wiped tears with the back of the hand that held the gun. "You should have seen how cool I was with him, Durston. You'd have been proud. We were up at his place at Wintergreen. He showed me his goddamn cars for the ten-thousandth time. Said he planned to drive the Jag the next day. It was going be a terrific day for a ride with the top down. Was, too, as it turned out. All I did was make a little detour on the way out of there that afternoon. He had it coming, Durston, believe me. The ungrateful bastard."

The voice came over the bullhorn again. "Hello in there. Three minutes. You are down to three minutes."

Ben took his arm from around Nickie's neck and shoved

her toward me. She fell into my arms, sobbing. Then he raised the gun to his temple, closed his eyes and pulled the trigger. The left side of his head exploded. I felt the spray.

16

As a guy whose father died when he was maybe a little younger than Ben's boys, I can testify it wasn't easy growing up without a dad. But my uncle filled some of the void, and at least my father died an honorable death, although senseless in retrospect, at the hands of the Viet Cong. Uncle Rod had been right, suicide doesn't solve anything--it makes matters worse.

Most people have read or heard accounts of people who've been clinically dead and later are resuscitated-- how they seem to pass through a dark tunnel and then arrive at the ceiling and look down at their bodies and maybe at people standing around talking about them. I could imagine Ben doing that. He'd thought he would escape, and he did escape two long trials, the appeals, and after approximately a ten-year ordeal, a hot seat compliments of the Commonwealth of Virginia. In a way it was sporting of him to spare taxpayers the expense of that. But now he could do absolutely nothing about the heartbreak and the shame his family would experience. He could only hover somewhere in the fourth dimension and watch, barred from participation, not even able to make comforting remarks or to give advice or explanations, or loving strokes to ease the pain. He had created a hell for the ones he loved, on top of which they had to endure the grief of the loss of a husband and father.

My grief was heavy as well, and made it impossible for me to feel sorry for Ben. I felt deep compassion for his family, but I hoped the little black gremlins from *Ghost* had come and whisked the S.O.B. away to wherever bad guys went. It was clear he had planned Soho's murder. He knew for certain I would be at the presentation. He had put a silencer on his gun, cracked open the back door with a crowbar and thwack--right through the head.

These thoughts ran through my mind late that evening as I parked under tall trees near the tennis courts west of the lake. Nickie and I got out and met at the rear of the car. I lifted Soho out of the trunk.

It's strange how attached one can get to an animal, a dog in particular. They become important to you. You know they have the same feelings as any human, and they certainly give you love. A close friend had died.

We carried Soho's body down the hill in a burlap sack. I thought of the times he'd climbed on the bed with that sheepish look, and snuggled close. Nickie and I knew the campus police would probably have carted us off if they knew what we were planning, but it was Halloween night, so we figured they had their hands full elsewhere.

We stopped in the middle of a wooded area on the Westhampton College side above the lake, in the long dark shadows of birch trees. That's where we laid him to rest. No one saw us in the darkness, digging.

I had a feeling Soho would be happy with the spot. Dogs, like people, no doubt leave their mortal remains behind, but I figured both hung around for a while to see where they ended up. From here he would see the ducks and the water and the path we had run on together so many happy times.

I picked up a tennis ball that lay nearby, threw it as far

as I could and stood for a moment, watching. I could almost see him go after it--hurl himself into the water. Nickie touched my hand, and I put my arm around her, pulled her close. It was dusk and the lights of the commons shone warm and inviting, reflected off the black, mirror-like surface of the lake. Ducks quacked softly. There was the occasional honk of a goose. I inhaled the smell of water and algae and decayed leaves. Then my ears perked up. Across, on the other side, the chimes in the brick and stone bell tower began to play Edelweiss.

Finally, as the last chord lingered in the cool fall air, we turned and walked up the hill to the car.

The next morning, I sat in silence at my desk. It seemed to me I should be in better spirits. I felt grief, of course. That was to be expected. Soho's death was horrible. It would take days, weeks, maybe more to get over it. But there was something else I couldn't explain, an uneasy feeling. I was fidgety, as though something lurked in my mind just below the conscious level, trying in vain to break through.

What was it?

The pain would recede with time. I knew it would, and there was so much else to be thankful for. Uncle Rod's death would be reclassified. Nickie and I were both witnesses to what Ben had said, and the clincher was that I had found the letter from Arthur Fletcher. He indeed had fired the agency. The letter had been taped to the outside of one of the green hanging files, on the back where no one would look under normal circumstances. Uncle Rod had hidden it there. He'd known Ben might try to find it.

Henry Valence, Uncle Rod's lawyer, had assured me Sally would now receive the insurance money, which meant I would receive my share as well.

I drew the number five on a scratch pad, followed by five zeros, then made the comma.

Why didn't that bolster my mood? My dream was now

in reach. Tomorrow was the deadline to buy the stock, and although I did not have the money yet, my friend at the bank had told me they would give me a bridge loan if the partners would not allow a grace period.

I ripped off the sheet and crumpled it.

Maybe that was what bothered me. Did I really want to plop down all that money to be in business with Larry Negus? What a huckster. And Mary? She was nice enough and competent, but was she ever blinded by the cash. Ben was the only guy in the bunch I had respected and admired. He had fooled me, big time.

The mind-blower of all, of course, was Paul.

At least I had learned how very easy it is to misread people. Paul was rough around the edges, he had an ego the size of Godzilla and a mouth that ran like a gutter, but he'd been terrific in the presentation and had shown remarkable marketing savvy on top of considerable creative talent. The guy I'd once been gunning for turned out to be the jewel in the crowd.

My telephone rang.

"Miss Maloney is here to see you, Mr. Durston."

An invisible hand clutched my throat. "I'll be right out."

Paul and I reached the lobby at the same moment. We raised eyebrows at each other.

Rita stood as the two of us approached. "Good. You're both here. Where we can talk?"

We made our way along the oriental runner to Uncle Rod's old office, took seats around the coffee table--Rita on a high wing back, Paul and myself on the sofa.

Rita crossed her legs and adjusted her glasses.

"Can we speak in confidence?" she said.

"Sure," Paul and I said at the same time.

"I know a lot of your staff must have been involved in putting together the presentation, yesterday, but I wanted to talk privately to the two of you because from my vantage point it seemed to be your show.

"First, I want you both to know how very talented and

articulate you are. I thought your recommendations made perfect sense." She turned to me. "The research was illuminating, Brian, and the strategy unassailable." Then to Paul, "And the creative approach--my congratulations--it almost brought tears to my eyes. I figure if you can come close to doing that to me, you have something special."

Paul's eyes darted at me and we both nodded and smiled.

"Unfortunately, however, I'm not going to award you the account."

The bottom of my stomach dropped away.

"I'm sure you understand," she said. "My God. I can't--not after yesterday's revelations. It's all over the front page of the papers--even the *Wall Street Journal*. My stockholders would think I had lost my mind if I awarded the account to Durston Negus."

I could not believe she was saying this. "But the person responsible, Ben Haley, obviously, he's no longer a partner."

"I'm afraid your uncle was not without blame," Rita said.

"Yes, but he checked out some time ago," Paul said.

"Please try to put yourself in my shoes," she said. "Think about what happened. To prevent getting fired, the director of client services of Durston Negus murdered the president of Benton, and the agency's president helped cover it up. But even after all that, the account went into review. Now, after the truth has come out, suppose Durston Negus ends up keeping the Benton account? I'm sorry, but I'm not going to be put in the position of trying to explain that to anybody, much less to my board of directors." She shook her head. "And the public. After the media got finished with it, they'd be certain I was in on the conspiracy."

"What about unassailable marketing strategy, and creative work that almost brought you to tears?" I said.

"The presentations by Martin and Arnold both had a lot

of good in them as well," she said. "There really are some very fine agencies in this town."

For a moment we were all silent. I was speechless.

"Which one is going to get your business?" Paul finally said.

Her brow furrowed. "I haven't decided. It really was too close to call. I'm thinking of giving them each another assignment--let them shoot it out. I may even open it up to other agencies. Barber Martin is one we overlooked. They've been after me."

It was clear her mind was made up, but I said what I was thinking, anyway.

"You know, Rita, this doesn't seem fair at all to the people here at the agency who had nothing to do with Arthur Fletcher or his death."

She nodded. "I realize that, and believe me, I thought long and hard about how to handle this. I could have called and said you guys were eliminated, that I had decided it would be a runoff between Martin and Arnold. But frankly, I came to the conclusion that wouldn't be fair--you should know what a good job you did. That's why we're having this little chat, fellows. I hope you'll keep what I've said under your hats."

"Hey, this business is too small to go blabbing stuff around," Paul said.

I nodded.

Rita stood. "I was sure you'd understand. You guys are good, really good. I'm sorry we won't be working together." She gave each of us that sincere through-the-tortoise-shells look as she shook our hands. "You don't need to show me out. I know the way."

I watched her leave, then sat in the wing chair. Paul flopped on the sofa.

"What a fucking kick in the teeth," he said.

I stared at him. I'd been on the losing end of new business presentations before, thrown my heart and my soul into them as I had this time. When word came we'd lost, I'd felt as though the baby I'd been carrying for nine months had arrived stillborn. But for some reason I didn't feel that way this time, and it wasn't because of Rita's kind words. I felt a sense of relief instead--as though a 400 pound gorilla had just climbed off my back.

Paul cupped his hand around his ear. "Hark, can you hear it, Durston? The sound of a buzz saw warming up. Rum, rum, rum. Heads will roll. The blood bath is about to begin."

"Tell me something, Paul. Have you ever thought about starting your own agency?"

He cut his eyes toward me and tilted his head as if to let the thought in.

"Have something specific in mind, Durston, or is that question hypothetical?"

"You know, if you were to leave the agency, they would have to repurchase your stock. You'd get $130,000--if my calculation is correct. A nice hunk of change to get one started, especially if you had a partner who put up a like amount."

"I'm listening, Durston. Keep talking."

"They're going to have to eliminate a bunch of salaries around here, as you just mentioned. Now, if yours and mine were taken out, along with another few people we might want to have in the new agency with us, there'd be a sizable dent in what they'd have to cut. Quite a few lower-level employees who would otherwise be laid off would keep their jobs."

"My mother always said I'd turn philanthropic some day."

"How does this sound?" I said. "Durston Williams. Has a nice ring, don't you think?"

He rolled his eyes. "You fucking suits are all alike. Get real, will you? Let's recognize what's important in an ad agency, which as we both know is creative. Why else would a client have one? The name should be Williams Durston."

"What about the alphabet?" I said.

"What about the alphabet?" he said.

"The letter D comes before W," I said.

"Here, let me throw you a straw, Durston, since you're grasping for them. Or better still, a three word example that ain't alphabetical--Doyle Dane Bernbach."

"Uh-huh," I said. "Bernbach was the creative guy and he's last. Is that your point?

"Okay, so they fucked up. Let's see--Foote Cone Belding. They put the account guy last in that one."

"Have it your way," I said. "Williams Durston. Or maybe we could just call it, The Partners. I kind of like the idea of not using names. It would set us apart. But the fact is, I really don't care."

"Good, then we'll decide later. You know, we'll need a copy writer. Think Nickie will want to come along for the ride?"

"I'm sure she will, at least until her novel hits the best seller list. Jill Lathermill would also be nice to have on board. What do you say?"

"Jill Lathermill? Yeah. She'll do, for a suit." Paul stood and stuck out his hand. "50-50. Is it a deal, Durston?"

I got up and shook it. "Feels right to me."

Paul snapped his fingers. "I know an account we can pitch. They're looking at agencies now. A company that makes furniture."

"Yes, good thinking. In fact I know someone there, Rita Maloney. Think I'll give her a call."

We hooked arms, danced the little step from *The Wizard of Oz*, and skipped out of Uncle Rod's office.